The Terrain
of Paradise

The Terrain of Paradise

Barbara Haynie

Five Star • Waterville, Maine

Published in 2003 in conjunction with
Barbara Haynie.

Set in 11 pt. Plantin by Myrna S. Raven.

Printed in the United States on permanent paper.

Library of Congress Cataloging-in-Publication Data

Haynie, Barbara, 1947–
 The terrain of paradise / Barbara Haynie.
  p. cm.—(Five Star expresions)
  ISBN 0-7862-4474-7 (hc : alk. paper)
  ISBN 1-4104-0127-8 (sc : alk. paper)
  I. Title. II. Series.
 PS3608.A97 T47 2002
  813'.6—dc21   2002026622

Dedication

Thanks to my husband for making me mad enough to try my hand at writing, to Professor James Work for encouraging me and pointing the way, and to my brother Brian and his fishing buddy, Vance, for letting me share their fishing camps. And in memory of my Siamese cat, Mink, and my horse, Slinger.

Acknowledgement

I have used verbatim excerpts from Vance Herring's E-mails to my brother because they're so much better than anything I might have concocted. Thanks, Vance, and you really ought to try taking the plunge yourself.

Acknowledgments

One

Déjà vu all over again. The return trip was an unreeling of her leaving, a steady slow-motion rerun of that vintage movie, in reverse. The Utah desert flew by yet seemed a mirage of stasis, the unchanging glaring earth and the sparseness of pale scratchy foliage along the roadway defying advancement. The Beamer seemed to be the only passenger car on the highway, rocked by shock waves from swift cone-headed semis sweeping past like giant ships sucking some lone windsurfer into their wakes. Her own speed seemed to make no dent in the stationary Utah atmosphere.

"Who was it that came up with that line, eh Gus?" Maggie hated that she couldn't remember details, considered it a near handicap. "I have a memory like a sieve," she'd apologized to her friends over the years. Maybe she could put that frustrating trait to some good, though. Maybe searching it for trivia would keep her mood from freefalling in the desert's monotony.

Forget asking Gus. He's still out like a light. Too bad for her and too bad for him. She'd have welcomed any kind of companionship in this landscape, but Maggie had been forced to sedate Gus for both their sakes. Previous car trips had unleashed a surprising characteristic in him, a temper of extraordinary dimension for an animal as small and benign as her Siamese cat. Small, maybe, but hardly benign. In spite of a knockout cocktail he slept fitfully and woke frequently to howl, bite the cage, and turn somersaults in frustration. The hangover he'd suffer tonight would make her feel so guilty that she'd find it almost impossible to force herself to knock him out again in the morning. *Nothing like traveling for days in a car with an agoraphobic cat to strengthen your resolve.*

What am I doing out here alone headed toward God knows what anyway? Hadn't she asked herself that very question when she'd left so long ago? It could've been at this very same milepost, halfway between either end of her journey, that she'd first felt the absolute misery of it all, the impossibility of restitution through any means, especially flight. But she'd gone on, *and had never stopped running until now.* Well, no misery this time. This time her actions had seemed perfectly clear when she left, but then, she'd left pretty fast, without giving herself time to think it all through, hadn't she?

So unlike me. In the years since that first departure, she'd developed the need to plan everything meticulously. After all, spontaneity had proven awfully costly in her case. *This new me* is *good, though, I mean, that's the whole point, after all, isn't it? This is all about changing.* But the western desert landscape stretching to all horizons magnified the rift she was re-creating in her life. The desert was too empty after years of replete streets, too big after more than a decade in a two bedroom apartment, too quiet, too bright, too open to any and all directions after the tightly-structured life in which she had so carefully insulated herself.

She turned on a CD, James Taylor philosophizing about being specks in a vast universe. *Great, just what I need.* Gus awakened, yowled pitiably twice, dug furiously at the bottom of the cage beneath the padding, and curled back up, paws over his eyes. *Wish I could do the same.* Why did she feel so unnerved? She and Jilly had traveled together for years through the west. And before that, any pretext for travel had sent her and Hale overland. They would make

10

any kind of delivery for anyone to anywhere just to get out and go. They had hauled livestock and equipment, or driven relatives halfway across the country and back for holidays, crossing the west in every direction several times over before Jill was born, hitting the road in a shuffled pack of used cars she'd labeled "Hale's heaps," a sleek silver Camaro, an old rolling hulk of a Caddy with some kind of huge engine, a Ranchero that dragged a black oil cloud train. And God forbid they should hit snow or ice in any of them. How many times Hale had laid out chains in the snow, bare-handed as if immune to the cold, while she sat behind the wheel, waiting to ease the car into them as carefully and smoothly as sliding her leg into a nylon. Those were wild trips of youth; wild scenery seen for the first time, wild weather challenged and survived, wild speed down the long straight stretches, wild lovemaking at night in low-rent motel rooms or shabby canvas tent when they camped. Or in broad daylight in the back seats of "heaps" pulled just off the highway when they couldn't wait.

Together being the operative word. *A pissed cat is just insufficient company.* The brightness, if not the loneliness, could be resolved. She rummaged around in her daypack for the pair of dark shades she wore at the beach. *Jaysus, I look like Tom Cruise in these. I've got to let my hair grow.* Gus's tranquilizer was beginning to wear off. They'd been traveling for over eight hours. He opened his eyes, pupils dilated. "Gus, what's up? You've never been cross-eyed before." How come no one ever found her brand of "Déjà vu all over again" humor amusing, anyway? Jilly and Hale did. Must be some kind of genetic trait. *Wishful thinking.* None of her current friends seemed amused by her, which left her to laugh quietly at her own remarks into the bathroom mirror or the open refrigerator door at night. She'd been

11

keeping almost exclusively female company these days, whose brand of humor ran to jokes about men and sexual innuendo. *Well, let's face it,* beyond *innuendo.* They seemed to find her puns and comic outtakes annoying or pointless rather than funny. *Really, there are some things that only men can supply in life.*

Maggie checked the temperature on the Beamer's instrument panel. For all that Utah desert brightness it was only forty-five degrees outdoors. *Heated car seats are a modern fucking marvel. Now if they only made humidifiers an option.* She could feel the dry air shrinking her sinuses, shriveling her skin, and straightening her hair. *Imagine what it would be like in January.* She was going to miss the soft climate, the smell of eucalyptus trees.

Mid-April had seemed a safe departure date, but only after cautious scrutiny. Even minor storms could create havoc on the roads she'd be traveling, and she hadn't the courage for dealing with *that.* The most frightening drive of her life had been a whiteout, also in April, between Cheyenne and Fort Collins. It was insignificant in size, just a spit from the heavens. It had been snowing lightly when they left Cheyenne, like settling ash, but within five miles the snow had become a furious wall of exploding white that had erased the roadway and all trace of surrounding traffic. Maggie had been clenching her fists in fear by the time she'd asked Hale if they should pull over, knowing it was impossible even as she'd asked, since they could barely see the taillights of the semi-trailer crawling at fifteen miles an hour a few feet in front of them. Stopping meant risking a crash from any direction, or worse, triggering a chain reaction of collisions. Too dangerous to go on and too dangerous to stop, an insoluble conundrum. She had never known how Hale had driven on, navigating blindly, but he

12

had out of sheer desperation, when she had given up, impotently wringing her hands. And something had miraculously guided them through. At the end of twenty terrifying miles, a gentle rain barely wet the pavement, and by the time the lights of Fort Collins appeared, the weather was dead calm. It was as if the storm had never happened. All in a distance of twenty-some miles.

So when Maggie saw a weather report of calm across the entire map of the central western states, she had decided to go, impetuous but careful. Maybe she'd drop the careful once she arrived, but please, no storms for the next few days. She'd have enough to weather once there. Not to mention the turbulence she'd left behind. God, she'd barely given notice. They must want to murder her at work. But she'd seized the opportunity, *carpe diem,* when she'd seen that weather report. She had needed the smoothest sailing possible to set sail at all. *And I used to think I was so gutsy.* "Well, okay, so neither of us are brazen travelers, are we Gus?"

The desert glare reflected in the dark ellipses of her shades. The Beamer was a capsule, immune to outside forces, but an incubator of interior forces, causing instant replays of the past to fast forward and rewind through her mind.

She hadn't suspected that her mother's death would be so pivotal. It was an anticipated event, after all, a certainty, a release from long-term, malignant pain. Jilly was still living nearby, thank God, and often dropped in to bolster Maggie's mood during the illness' difficult last weeks and in the long days following the funeral. It seemed the next generation filled the gap of the previous to some degree. Maggie had braced herself for loss, but she'd never expected a total unraveling of her life.

Jilly's acceptance of a job in Boulder so soon after December graduation had compounded her distress. *Closer to her dad; farther from me, as soon as she could possibly go.* She knew it was stupid and shallow to feel jealous of Jill's love for Hale. She knew in her heart, if she were completely honest, that he was not mean enough to intentionally try to take their daughter's love from her. He wasn't like that. After all, she'd had her way laying out all the rules they'd adhered to through these years. He had never fought that, not once. Jill had belonged to her three-quarters of every year for fourteen of them now (actually, that was a lie, too. She belonged to no one, and hadn't from the first breath she drew. Jilly chose to love unabashedly according to her own inner gyroscope and nothing else). But Maggie had suffered bittersweet pangs every fall when Jill's love for her dad and his ranch had come home with her from her summers in Wyoming. *Why should I have felt so jealous of something I didn't want for myself? But, really, how could Jilly not succumb?*

Then her mother's estate had been settled, an amount larger than expected, which her accountant recommended she reinvest without delay, and she'd taken a plunge. She had first thought of investing in tech stocks, as absolutely everyone had advised, but the word *tangible* kept resurfacing in her mind, until she'd finally called a real estate agent friend, attracted to the idea of the *real* in real estate. She fully intended to buy a property in Palo Alto, maybe something she could live in herself and rent to a roommate to alleviate loneliness. But at a certain point in her search for the right property, envisioning the details of the future she was laying out, it had seemed absurd that she should have a roommate. One had roommates in college, for chrissake.

This revolution of her mind had spread contagiously.

The target of her discontent had become larger. Palo Alto had changed anyway. Not only had it become dizzyingly congested, but prices had soared beyond her scope. After all, she'd gone there fourteen years ago for *more:* to experience life more fully, to expose Jill to more, more than the ranch, more educational opportunity, and, frankly, to make more money than either she or Hale or both of them would ever make on that rinky-dink property outside Saratoga. But now, regardless of her upwardly-mobile job, the cost of living was making a moot point of her earnings. *Okay, okay, there were other major reasons I left. Let's be honest, Gus. Yeah. No more dishonesty. That's also the whole point, huh?*

"Hey, Gus, puss, puss," she said aloud, wriggling a finger through the wire front of his carrier to wake him, "I'm going to make a pit stop before we hit Salt Lake City, little buddy. We need a peaceful spot for an outdoor kitty stroll. Besides," she was talking to herself now, "we need gas, and I don't want to stop again until we get to Evanston." Maggie pulled on a sweatshirt, steering with her knees while she pulled it over her head. She'd brought only one change of clothes. She had kept her clothing needs as simple as possible when she'd left, enjoying the thought that power dressing in macho suits would now be a thing of the past, overkill where she was headed, and a discard she wouldn't regret. *Good riddance. I'm dying to be a slob again. Now there's some honesty for you.* Seems like honesty could be a prickly thing. *Yeah, I know, don't I know.* Though too big for her, she'd grabbed two discarded pairs of Jill's blue jeans for herself because she had none of her own, hadn't owned a pair for at least a decade. *Did that mean anything? If we are what we eat, are we also what we wear?*

Trying to walk a stoned cat in a harness behind a gas station just off I-80 and convince him to relieve himself is not something

15

I want to repeat. This move has got to work out! Poor Gus. So stressed out. And the indignity of it all! *Cats hate to look silly,* she thought as Gus staggered a few steps and sat down to get his bearings. *Yeah. Me too.* He pulled against the unaccustomed harness she'd bought for the trip, sniffing tentatively as she guided him toward sandy spots on the bare ground behind the building. The air, cool and motionless, was shot through by the wracking wail of passing trucks.

With Gus relieved and safely restowed and the Beamer's tank topped off, Maggie pushed through the plate glass door covered with stickers advertising motor oil, hot dogs, Camel cigarettes, and at least four types of credit cards, trying but failing to ignore their messages. She was the only customer in the place. The matronly woman at the checkout had a kind face, soft and doughy, seemingly unscathed by desert living, and not at all what Maggie had expected. *Good.* Anything but the hard, weather-beaten, chain-smoking types or the could-care-less, body-pierced losers of the urban gas station-minimart-junkfoodshop-video rental-carwash joints. *Just being totally honest.*

"Pretty cat you had out there."

"Well, pretty is as pretty does, and he's mad as hell right now. I hate putting him through a long car trip like this, poor old Gus."

The lady chuckled as she ran Maggie's credit card through the machine. "I don't mean to criticize or anything, but there's nothing very Siamese in that name."

"No, I know. But we just couldn't find an elegant name that fit him. We went on and on calling him 'kitty.' Then my daughter, who was about twelve at the time, started calling him 'silly kitty,' because her dad called her 'silly Jilly,' and then she'd change it to 'silly pussy,' 'soupy poopy,' you know, all kinds of crazy spin-offs. One day when she tried some gazpacho soup I'd made for the first time . . . well, you know how kids hate anything different . . . she decided it was a 'silly kind of soup,' 'silly soup,' she called it, 'like our "Silly Soupy." ' It was 'disGUSting GUZpacho' to her and Gus's name is what stuck out of that." Maggie realized she'd rambled. "Sorry, I know it's a long story, but it proves there's a logic in that name, for all the ethnic mix-up . . . there is a logic . . . I think."

The cashier's chuckle went with her face and doubtless came naturally to her. "Well, at least he'll never feel he has to live up to a name like that."

Ah, thought Maggie, *what luck! Nice and smart, both.*

"Does he have much farther to go?"

Curiosity killed the kitty cat. "Just another half day or so."

"You need some water for him, or anything?"

"No, no. I'm okay. But thanks."

"Sure. You and Gus have a nice trip. We don't see too many Siamese cats traveling through."

"Yeah, I suppose not. I just wish he were better company." Maggie turned back to the cashier before opening the door to leave. "Speaking of company, you must live near here. Don't you find it awfully lonely?"

The cashier smiled patiently. "You know, you're about the millionth person to ask me that, so I've had to think about it, and I'll tell you, it's not lonely for me at all. It's more peaceful. I've got lots of family near here, and these small desert towns develop a strong feeling of community. We all help each other. People think the desert is for escapists or hermits, I guess, but I don't think that's how it is, at least not in this state."

"Well good. Now I won't be feeling so badly about these sad little treeless windswept-looking places I've been

17

passing." Maggie pushed the door open. "Well, thanks. Bye."

The cashier watched through the glass door as Maggie walked to her car. *Nice,* she thought. *Very pretty, too. But she's way too thin. Tsk. Why do women think they need to starve themselves these days?*

I'm letting the isolation of this drive spook me, all right, or I wouldn't be giving long drawn out explanations to total strangers, Maggie thought as she stepped into the car. The Beamer's door whumped closed. *Back in my cocoon.* "C'mon, Gus. Let's be on our way."

"I should be on my way right now," she sang, "with a lump in my throat . . ." Her voice escalated with their speed as they merged back onto the freeway. "Home," she twanged, switching songs and styles, "where my thoughts are waiting, home, where my true love's waiting, silently for me. You never did like my singing, did you Gussus Pussus?" She stroked the dark paw he pressed against the cage door. His lovely ermine paw. "Bad choice of song, anyway." *It's not our home (yet), and my true love is long gone—well, I mean, Hale is still there, but the love is just a memory from a bygone era, like the song.*

Don't let this desert get to you. "I guess I'm just not a desert rat, Gus." That wasn't really true, though. Maggie loved the Sonoran deserts of Tucson and Baja California. And Monument Valley was one of her favorite places, and Canyon de Chelly, and Santa Fe, and the high sage desert she was headed toward. *It must just be flat deserts I don't like. Especially salt pans, like the Mojave, Joshua trees notwithstanding. What weird prejudices we develop.*

"My trouble is boundaries, Gus."

Maggie had always struggled to stay centered. The slightest confrontation caused her days of soul searching to determine if she had been in the wrong. Nearly anyone or anything could cause her mood to fluctuate from one end of the spectrum to the other. She couldn't stand sad music or depressing environs of any kind, visual, audio, even the imagery in books, without withering. So the day's drive had been an elongated, greatly-decelerated roller coaster on every level, literally and figuratively, physically and emotionally.

The raucous California central valley traffic at the beginning of the day, its dour, hazy flatness snarled with a tangle of power lines, billboards, and highway signs, had given way to lovely rolling oak-covered hills. Those spreading oaks had become dark vertical slashes of firs and spruce as they had climbed into the Sierras, where Maggie had made her first stop for coffee at Donner Pass in Truckee. She had always found the Sierras more somber than the Rockies. Maybe the drier Rockies allowed for more space and light, a paler green, she wasn't quite sure. But it had struck her that the Sierra forest's melancholic density and darkness made an apt setting for the Donner party incident. The argument she and Hale had had the first time they'd crossed the pass together was always resurrected there, or at any mention of Donner Pass. The doomed group's culpability and stupidity, or at least poor judgment, and their blindness to possible remedies at hand was Hale's unbudging argument, while she saw, and would always see, the tragedy as inescapable natural calamity. *He was such a revisionist.*

As the Beamer had hurtled down into the Nevada desert at midday, her mood had dropped with it. If she were having a hard time facing a half day's insulated drive through this unending void at eighty miles per hour, how had those pioneers withstood weeks of crawling at oxen or mule pace; exposed to a land barren of all community and comfort, their only hope lying beyond the dark mountains before them, the mountains that would starve them to death and result in cannibalism?

Speaking of starving to death . . . She'd pulled a roll of Life Savers from a bag between the seats. Maggie wasn't stopping for any meals because she hated leaving Gus alone in the car and because she wanted to travel as far as possible that day. Besides, she always brought rolls and rolls of Life Savers on long drives because a friend had once told her that eating would prevent sleepiness from highway hypnosis. *She was right, too. Works like a charm.* She'd allowed each tube to dissolve slowly, not using her teeth until they were wafer-thin. The rolls shed snake coils of double-layered skins of foil and wrapper, which she'd stuffed back into the paper bag so the interior of the Beamer would stay tidy, a habit that permeated Maggie's life. The bag of supplies, a small red and white Igloo cooler, Gus's litter box and feed dish, and a daypack stuffed with a few clothes and toiletries were the only variances from the interior's customary Spartan neatness.

The Beamer sped along effortlessly as if on autopilot, a sleek bronzed manifestation of her urgency. But the desert seemed interminable to her. Its neutral tint gave the earth a spectral appearance, made it seem more a vague outline than a finished picture. The only signs of life, aside from the broken chains of eighteen-wheeled robots traveling east and west, were infrequent bird sightings, smudged silhouettes as large as eagles that instead proved to be enormous roc-like ravens as her distance from them closed, or black and white magpies reluctantly peeling upward from the asphalt at the last instant off gray fur balls of road-killed jackrabbits.

Impervious to state lines, the desert had crossed obliviously into Utah. Gus had had a nightmare (a daymare in this case?), woofing like a dog while his eyes blinked rhythmically with his galloping paws. *Chasing the magpies in his dreams, no doubt. Free from his frigging cage, at least.*

Signs of the lake finally crept into the desert's sphere. Maggie's mood lifted, flying aloft with the shifting flocks of airborne birds that filled the vacuum of invisible desert life she'd passed unnoticed. She drove through pastureland grazed by placid livestock and damp-smelling hay meadows. Signs of life!

Rimming a dead lake, however. The lake came into view, an impressive vastness undiminished by the scope of the hundreds of miles of desert just crossed. *And to think that it was ten times larger once upon a time.* A remnant of immense prehistoric Lake Bonneville, Great Salt Lake was a mere ghost, really. The ancient Lake Bonneville had filled from surrounding mountain drainage, overflowing into the Snake River, on through the Columbia Gorge, and emptying out into the Pacific. But over eons, evaporation had caused the lowering water level's outlet to be blocked and the lake had begun shrinking, had become saline, and had been reduced to one-tenth its size. Still a mighty oasis in this desert, in Maggie's opinion, Great Salt seemed worthy of its claim to greatness. It was the largest inland salt lake in the world, according to the tourist signs she and Jill had read on past trips together, though surprisingly shallow, averaging a depth of less than fifteen feet.

There's probably a veritable ocean of water below the lake floor, like so many rivers in lower California whose beds are dry until a week or two of rain turns them into raging floods overnight. A lake with a whole secret self, maybe. What a strange, exotic place this really is. Do the locals feel the eeriness of it, or has familiarity bred contempt? "And, see, Gus, I *can* remember details when they really make an impression on me."

The clambering energy of Salt Lake City demanded attention after the calm of the desert, its urban body laid open from top to bottom by road surgeons performing monumental plastic surgery, a face lift for the Olympic games, not yet neatly sutured, but still a gaping mess.

Finally, beyond the wild race through the city, swathed in the peace of the landscape's emptiness, the beauty of the Wasatch Range dissolved into a darkness that she regretted. She wouldn't see the great finned foothills that connected to the giant reefs farther south, or the jilting clash of color she'd given her own name to, "western sky blue," against the red tilted edges of ancient shores. The reefs down south were massive landslides that had subsided here, or eroded, or might even be lurking, sharp and jagged as ever, just below the surface, for all she knew. *Or is the whole thing a thrust fault or something else?* Ah, her confounding confusion of details. The drama of the distinctive geology of this pass through the Wasatch foothill formations seemed married to the Capital Reef and to Zion Park and to the big elevation drop at distant St. George beyond Zion. *They must all be connected.* Maggie had always tried to see the big picture, navigating by major landmarks rather than thin lines drawn on a map.

Ahead of her, a gleaming thin curve of moon hung on one edge of a paler full circle suspended above the rolling horizon. Once they cleared the foothills, Maggie pulled the car over and stepped out into the crisp air and silky silence to stare open-mouthed into the black dome of night, washed opaque by the Milky Way. *As can be seen only here, in the middle of God's real country, miles and miles from everything I've left behind.*

Back on the road, the Beamer droned on through the day's final miles, the green glow of its instrument panel shining along the edge of her jaw. The dim light just caught the curl of her ear, then spread above the deep set of her eyes across her brow. In spite of fatigue, her face was flushed with energy from the stars.

She chose a motel in Evanston far from the highway with a parking lot too small for the Big Dawg truckers. They'd have filled all the motels of their choice by this time of the night. Though it was off-season for tourists (*ha! sounds like we hunt them*), rooms weren't all that numerous out here. And there was no question of her traveling on. A firm believer in delayed gratification, Maggie had counted on a grueling first day's drive for the sake of an easy day two. Although she had steeled herself for a late arrival in Evanston, she had reached the limit of her endurance. So she didn't mention the cat to the rumpled, sagging man who dragged himself away from Dan Rather's commanding voice to check her in, stubbing out his cigarette in a glass ashtray on the counter top right beneath her nose. She couldn't risk being turned away. She requested a room in the rear, where she could sneak Gus in unseen.

With a relief equal to Gus's, she immediately released him. *I think this cat is bipolar.* Freed from the carrier, Gus recovered from his angst, and joyfully, if somewhat manically, investigated the room, working his dark nose and tail equally, then proved everything was still functioning by making use of the litter box and food and water dish Maggie had set up. She ate a quick meal from her stash of supplies while the lobotomizing blue rays of the TV broadcast that calming universal phenomenon, the news. Exhausted, she showered and fell asleep with Gus curled up by her face as always, the sounds of I-80 drowned out by his loud purring.

Maybe I'm bipolar too. Maggie attributed her brightened mood the next morning to a good night's sleep, the proximity of her destination, the fact that she was back in southern Wyoming after such a long absence, and her decision to not sedate Gus and leave him free in the car. "You're much better company today, my love," she said to him as he squatted serenely on the passenger seat. He seemed fully-recovered from his Beamer blues. *Maybe it's a good omen.*

Maggie enjoyed the grand scenery at Green River, knowing it was the last she'd enjoy until she turned south off I-80 past Rawlins. She liked the dominance of both the sheltering cliffs and the railroad's presence in Green River. There was a colorful history here too, because of the importance of the river junction in bygone days. But beyond lay hours of unappealing terrain. The tires rolled monotonously over the cool gray pavement. *Somebody must love Rock Springs and Rawlins. Maybe not. Maybe people settled there because they were made offers they couldn't refuse, extorted into selling their souls, or something. I mean, there's an entire planet to choose from, so why here? No offense to Rock Springs and Rawlins, of course. I just want to be honest again after that little deception with Gus last night.*

She passed Rock Springs without seeing much of it. All she really knew about the city was what she'd read during a brief flame of fame in the press concerning shady gambling and prostitution. *In the seventies, wasn't it? And tied to oil shale exploration money, I think. Oh, for a memory!*

Rawlins was about oil, judging from the refinery at nearby Sinclair. She could see the whole town spread out below the roadway's north rim, and was surprised to find its appearance pleasant and benign. *Okay, so things can change. Or maybe it's my perception that's so different now.*

The desert was less daunting than yesterday's. High plateau rather than low extinct ocean beds, life appeared more plentiful here. The ground was dark gray, not white, dotted with gray green sage, and there were hills, garishly colored, that approached and receded in waves along the highway. Antelope stood in the distance like statues, tiny porcelain crèche figurines, gazing or grazing in small groups, never seeming to move, which was a pity. She'd like to see them run, showing off their encyclopedic claim to fame as North America's speediest animal, but they were unobliging. There were more ravens and magpies perusing the road-kill smorgasbord today, and every so often she ducked to peer out her windshield for scavenging eagles.

Rounding one of a series of great sweeping curves, Elk Mountain came into view. Standing alone on the west edge of the plain that held Laramie, the lurking hulk played sleight of hand with scale, feigning ordinary stature while one drove on and on, interminably overshadowed by its bulk, hardly realizing that it still loomed just in front of you, then to the right of you, just over your shoulder, filling the corner of your rearview mirror until you reached the West Laramie Fly Store not knowing it had finally disappeared at some unknown point. She'd be paralleling the length of its west side today, rather than following the flow of I-80 traffic, the gleaming streaming flotilla of commerce and pilgrims circumnavigating the mountain's north end, sailing with the constant westerly wind.

Maggie eased onto Highway 130 at Wolcott Junction with relief, alone now, heading directly into the warmth of the sun and the leisurely frame of mind that seeped in as the freeway's roar receded to a whine, then a moan, then a mere whisper behind her. Unaccustomed to the peace, Gus stood, stretching his back while pulling his head against his chest, forming the narrow, asymmetrical parabolic arch programmed into all cats. Then he stood on his hind legs, front paws pressed against the passenger window, watching the scenery flow quietly past for a few seconds before resuming his disgruntled crouch in the center of the seat beside her. "Do you finally begin to approve, my much-maligned mouse muncher? My munchkin? My monster?" *Why do cats bring out the ridiculous in me?*

Praying no one would recognize her, she made her way through Saratoga's few intersections. *I should've brought a disguise.* The last thing she wanted was to make an entrance here not of her own choosing. *I want to be my own director in this little docudrama.*

As she resumed speed at the south edge of town, she jerked violently in her seat at the crack of a stone flying into her windshield. "Shit," she swore aloud involuntarily. *I came all this way through that purgatory of semis unscathed and now I'm sideswiped by some dually pickup a few miles from where I'm going!* "Just our rotten luck, Gus." *Luck can be such a bitch sometimes! Now comes the BMW factor, Bring My Wallet. Hey, forget expensive. Your insurance will cover this. But Beamer parts are going to be hard to come by way out here! I just hope the hole it left doesn't start running across the glass, right across my eyesight . . . Murphy's law, of course!* "It's okay, Gus, you can chill out, puss. Just look at your tail!"

How she hated that kind of adrenal reaction! She hated that part of her nature. She recalled a description in a book she'd read during college of a sensitive, high-strung female character, "nervous as a rat," and of having been shocked by an unpleasant recognition of herself. *That's me!* she'd thought. During their early years of marriage she had joked with Hale about it, suggesting that a slight twelve-hour-a-day marijuana buzz was what she needed, though she had never actually been into drugs. *I never inhaled,* she laughed to herself. *Maybe I should have.* How she had envied the laid-back! Hale's calm had been part of his attraction.

Both their hackles had settled by the time Highway 130 veered east ten miles south of Saratoga, heading for the Medicine Bow National Forest, or the Snowy Range, as everyone here called it. The Beamer began navigating curves, climbing from the open valley of sage and grass into denser alpine flora, chokecherry, serviceberry, and snowberry shrubs clumped beneath white trunks of aspen and narrow-leafed cottonwoods randomly scattered with spindly pines.

"Look, Gus, there's the Paradise Ranch entrance." Slowing the car, she craned her neck, straining to see down the curving graveled lane as far as possible, twisting in her seat to keep it in view, glancing again and again into her rearview mirror even after its image had disappeared, until she made an acute turnoff at the next lane into her own property, the property she had finally decided to buy with her inheritance.

Gravel pinged tires as the car came to rest. She peered through the windshield. Though no longer in motion, vibrations of the journey still resonated through her; the sound of the engine echoed inside her head. There was a certain reluctance to leave the car. She opened the door slowly, rubbing stiffness from her legs, and tentatively stepped out. Her foot alighted onto the solid, unmoving, still and waiting *land.*

Two

You have to like the idea of never being caught up to love a place like this. But then, Hale did. He thrived on long-term projects and staying busy, especially when it involved physical work.

"Hey, ole Limbo. How are you buddy?" The big brown horse, dark as burnt sugar, nuzzled Hale's extended palm. "Sure, sure, but is it really me you want, or the grain? As if I didn't know." He gave Limbo a rub along the bumpy ridge of his neck as the horse buried his nose in the bucket, blowing a few oats over its edge with his heavy breathing. The horse jerked his head up after a few bites, slobbering and spilling grain back into the bucket and onto the ground as he chewed. Two Belgians stomped in their stalls, impatient for their own feed. The fine dust they stirred curled slowly upward into the golden shafts of the waning sun, transparent tendrils that unfurled and disappeared like a time-lapse film of growing and fading flowers. Stacks of baled hay filled two of the five wooden stalls, thrown down from an opening in the floor of the loft overhead. Oddly-shaped leather tack and tools covered the wall on both sides of a big wooden sliding door like abstract pictographs. On the front of one of the empty stalls hung a battered sign that read "Sparky." A twelve-foot dory, newly-painted green with red trim, rested on a trailer pushed against the back wall.

Hale performed the feeding chores with economic effort in the concise, automatic choreography of an oft-repeated dance. When he had finished, he inhaled the damp odor of shavings and hay and earth and horses, dusting off hay particles clinging to the snowsuit he used as overalls and stomping crud from his boots while listening to the sound of the muffled munching and blowing of the horses. As always, he was aware of the satisfaction that settled over him from caring for creatures so dependent on him for physical and mental well-being. These responsibilities were no weight on him at all. They were buoyed by him like the flex in boughs that support winter snow.

He left the barn and followed a worn path that led through two ancient blue spruce trees grown together so solidly through the decades that an arch had been pruned through them to access the back door of the weathered house. He shed the snowsuit once inside the large bright mud porch, adding it to a row of clothing hung on pegs, a motley population of mismatched pieces for all seasons and uses. Gortex waders and other fishing gear hung in one corner above a tackle box. A long oak bench straddled a pile of worn footwear. There he sat to pull off his Wellingtons, which he casually tossed backward between his legs. When he walked through the glass-paned door into the kitchen, he saw a young woman sitting at the square table, holding her long hair back from her face as she slowly turned the pages of a newspaper.

"Jill the Pill! When did you get in?"

"Hey, Bad Dad!" The top of her head was level with his eyes when she stood up for a hug. "Oh, I haven't been here long. Didn't you hear me from the barn when I drove in? I knew you'd be down there with your pets." It was a tradition that she would tease him about spoiling the horses. "Your horses are a disgrace to Buck Branaman," she'd scold, Buck being a horse trainer famous around the West for his clinics promoting "gentling" rather than "breaking" untrained and spoiled horses. "He'd tell you they're not broke. Or, more likely, he'd kick the incorrigible beasts right out of his clinics."

"To hell with all that ground work shit," Hale would growl. "My horses are good guys, and you know it," he'd insist.

"That'll be the day, Mad Dad," Jill would come back.

"So, how's the new job going, Jilly girl?" he asked, sitting down at the table. Jill stepped to the stove to turn a flame on under the teakettle. The stove top was crowded with a washed skillet, a box of matches, a spatula and slotted spoon in an old metal Folgers coffee can, and a pair of faded green potholders with frayed edges.

"It's great, Dad. I like the people I'm working with, the lab is wonderful, and I think I'm going to enjoy the research we're doing." She fiddled with spooning sugar into a cup, and took some cream from the refrigerator.

The early gloom of dusk swathed the room. "Flip on the lights, would you Jill?" The room seemed warmer with the lights on and the teapot vibrating on the burner and Jill standing by the stove, looking so at home.

"So just exactly what will you be 'bio-researching,' if you don't mind my asking?"

"Oh, you know, Dad, the usual. Human cloning, vivisection, and cryogenics. See, the vivisection is in case the cloning fails, and the cryogenics . . ."

"Sometimes you're more funny than other times, Shill."

She laughed at their badinage. "Okay, okay. Seriously, they'll have me working on developing some equine vaccines. It's related to my masters research, so I feel pretty comfortable about it."

"And how do you like life in Boulder so far?"

"Well, I think the setting is gorgeous and the town itself

is great; it's stimulating in a kind of provocative way."

"And just what does that mean?"

"Well . . . it's got more flavors of new age alternative life-styles than the west coast ever dreamed of; the granola-heads make me feel ashamed every time I bite into a burger; the mountain bikers and runners make me feel guilty when I sit down to eat the burger; and it's so PC that I'm afraid to open my mouth." She paused. "No, Dad, I really like it, especially when the wind doesn't blow."

"Oh yeah. I saw on the weather report that the town nearly blew away last month."

"That I can get used to, but I'm not so sure about the cost of living."

"High, huh?"

"I thought I'd be money ahead compared to Palo Alto, but I'm going to have to think about roommates to cover my rent. That'll be real environmentally PC, though, when you think about it." She held the cup with both hands to sip her tea, then set it down on the opened newspaper. "I think it's a great town, Dad." Jill switched subjects without a pause. "Oh, while I think of it, something kinda weird, though. I've left a couple of messages for Mom and haven't heard back from her. Maybe she had business out of town for a few days or something, but that's not really like her. She hates leaving her cat alone."

"Isn't there someone you could call to find out?"

"Yeah, sure, but I keep thinking I'm worrying about nothing."

"Well, call someone, if it'll ease your mind. No sense in worrying needlessly."

"Yea, you're right. Maybe I'll call Jane, one of the ladies she works with, a little later when she'll be home from work." She turned a page of the newspaper idly. "By the way, where are the dogs?"

"They're over at the lodge with Rob. I swear they like him better than me. As a matter of fact, I was headed over there to help him start dinner, if you want to come over."

"You don't have any clients this early yet, do you?"

"No, it'll just be you and me and Rob tonight."

"Yeah, okay. I'll come over as soon as I finish my tea and read the paper, okay?"

"Everything you do is okay with me, Jilly my Lily."

"Gee, Dad, you finally hit on one I like. I actually like that one."

"I'll remember that." He stood up to leave and stroked the top of her head, a habit with him since she was a kid.

"It's great to have you close enough now that you can come up on weekends, Jill. It's just great," he said, pulling the door open to the porch.

"I'll be over in a little while, Dad." Jill watched him walk away with his awkward laconic gait, slightly-stooped and leaning forward, as if in deference to the space he occupied, as if he wanted to leave no mark on the earth. *He's like the long lean herons you see fishing along the banks of the river, so awkwardly graceful, treading lightly through the water without a ripple,* she thought as he disappeared through the opening in the spruce trees. She loved him utterly, unreservedly.

Rob was a year-round boarder who cooked, gardened, and ran errands for Hale, so even in the off-season Hale rarely ate alone. Because Rob was a damned good cook and Hale a shaky amateur, Hale played the role of *sous* chef each evening. He'd become pretty decent at chopping vegetables, as long as they weren't julienned.

The walk to the lodge meandered for several minutes through tall clumps of shrub willows bordering a stony creek, then crossed a short wooden bridge and swerved right at the rim of a shallow beaver pond that extended to a raised deck running the length of the rear of the building. Because the recent stretch of unseasonably warm weather had melted the ice, Hale could look for trout in the pond's clear depths, an involuntary reflex he performed each time he passed. Today he could see several thin darting shadows seeking refuge in the darkness beneath overhanging willows.

The dogs stood up, wagging and stretching as he tromped up the wooden stairs of the deck, Sheila hanging back shyly while Zeke pushed his nose aggressively against Hale's pants leg. Hale kneeled, holding Zeke against his chest to make room for Sheila to approach. "Hey, Shy Sheila girl. You can come over here for a pet. Give her some room, now, Zeke." Zeke tried to lick Hale's face jealously as he rubbed Sheila's ears. He rose and gave a final pat to the dogs before stepping inside.

They had created the lodge from the original ranch house, a long single-story frame building with a wing added at each end, forming an open-armed U with an increased capacity of fifteen rooms. The entire back wall had been replaced by full-length windows that seemed to bring the pond right into the room, which had been made into a dining area, darkened now as Hale crossed it to reach the kitchen.

Unlike his own, this kitchen was a model of order and efficiency, filled with gleaming equipment and utensils and emanating a rich aroma. In the center stood its chief operator, a large stub of a grizzled man wearing an apron over a plaid polyester shirt and camouflage pants that had slid below his belly in the front and the top of the crack in his ass in the back.

"Hale, me boy!" he bellowed at the sound of the other

man's step. "Come ta halp, hav ye? Eer-r-r, tayke a knayfe, laddy."

"I take it we're having lamb tonight, Rob."

"God, you're sharp, Hale. Yeer-r-re a shayrrrp 'un, awr-r-ite."

The identity of any dish that deviated from the typical western menu was revealed to Hale by Rob's crude imitation of the accent of its country of origin. Because the summer season's guests were served food that never strayed farther from all American fare than Tex-Mex, Rob relished the opportunity to unleash his imagination through the off season, running amok with exotic concoctions from Creole cooking to Teriyaki to Moussaka, and he had a mock accent to accompany them all. He occasionally threw in the most stereotyped mannerisms as a bonus, like a series of shallow bows introducing a Chinese entree.

"Your accents are criminal, you know that, Rob?"

"Stup yer whaynin an' git gawin with thet knayfe, ye slaycker yew."

"Now you're starting to sound like a pirate, not a Scot, you idiot. But then, that's probably closer to your actual heritage, come to think of it." Hale began dicing. "Will there be enough for three tonight? Jill's made it up from Boulder."

"Why didn't you say so, instead of letting me go on and on like a maniac. There's always enough for our Jilly. I'll give her the food off me own plate if I have to." Loathe to abandon the absurdity, Rob's accent died a slow death.

The two men had everything nearly ready by the time Jill made her way to the kitchen. "Oh, to have a woman around here again! You're a sight for sore eyes, Jill," Rob gushed as she gave him a hug. "She's becoming a real beauty, don't you think, Hale? How'd such an ugly cuss as you beget such a beauty?"

Rob considered himself a bit of a lady's man in spite of three failed marriages in his distant past and a low success rate in dating ever since. Jill played along convincingly; she wouldn't disenchant him for the world. The people who worked for Hale had a low turnover rate, often returning after even prolonged absences because other jobs were found wanting by comparison. Certain employees like Rob had been there long enough to have watched Jill grow up. They were her surrogate family and constituted a family of choice amongst themselves.

The three of them ate dinner in the kitchen, still warm and humming from the cooking, rather than the large dining room, which echoed months of emptiness. "Hmm, this is really good, Rob. Lemme guess . . . otter, is it?" Jill goaded, certain in the knowledge that Rob's ego was impregnable when it concerned his cooking. They caught up on personal events, local gossip, and future plans, sharing more than just food.

And they shared the cleanup. As they cleared the table, Hale asked, "Say, Jilly, would you like to ride over to Herb's place with me tomorrow? The horses need the exercise and, besides, I want to check up on the old codger. I've hardly seen him all winter and I want to find out what kind of trouble he's planning for me this year so I can outflank him."

"Sure, Dad."

Herb Miller was a crotchety character who caused Hale considerable irritation because of his poor judgment in just about everything, particularly in the maintenance of his own place, which abutted Paradise Ranch. Pathetic as well as irritating, he tottered around, whiling away his life tinkering on worthless objects or dreaming up hair-brained projects so he could complain about their results.

He was not the norm, though, as far as local neighbors were concerned. With Herb, Hale seemed singled out by fate for punishment. Contrary to this abrasive neighbor, Hale had discovered most of the local old-timers to be gracious, sturdy, generous types with almost elegant Old World manners. This made sense, since they were barely removed from the first settlers whose ties to European customs had hardly been affected by the world outside the isolated valley. The second and third generation local ranchers had the kind of Old West character that made them welcome members of Old Baldy, the exclusive private club established in Saratoga by a multimillionaire industrial supplies merchandiser. This strange addition to the valley's cloistered society had occurred long before Hale's dad had signed over Paradise Ranch to him. It had hardly made a ripple in the way of things, though. The millionaires stayed aloof from Saratoga. The old established ranchers of the Saratoga valley were Old Baldy's only exception to its "millionaires only" membership policy. Those icons alone straddled the two worlds, personifying the unique dichotomy of the community's social structure. The millionaires who came sought grand scenery, open spaces, and premiere hunting and fishing, but not friendship with locals. Because they wanted the region's setting and atmosphere to remain unchanged, they maintained low profiles.

And for the most part, their efforts had succeeded. Aside from the rows of Lear jets on Shively Field tarmac, the incongruous roars of their comings and goings that periodically shattered the peace, broke a few halters, and choked a few veal calves; and the clubhouse on top of a mesa barely visible from the highway, the town itself had remained a fairly normal Wyoming community of about 2,000 people. It had never suffered the growing pains of boomtowns like

Aspen, Steamboat Springs, or Jackson Hole. Those communities had lost their identities, swallowed by local ski areas. But Medicine Bow ski area, on the other side of the Snowy Range, was inaccessible from this side in the winter months, and had never developed into a glitzy resort in any case. So Saratoga retained its authentic laid-back, small-town, western character, notwithstanding ski areas, millionaires, Lear jets, and Old Baldy.

Herb Miller, on the other hand, would never have been welcomed as local color to the inner sanctums of Old Baldy. He was instead the type certain to be a thorn in the side of anyone in his path, and had played exactly that role with Hale for the nineteen years of their relationship. His small neighboring place was such a forlorn wreck that Hale had given it the moniker "malfunction junction." It had been divided off from Paradise Ranch generations ago for some aberrant reason, landing in the hands of Herb's ancestors, and the Adamsons had never succeeded in bringing it back into their fold. They liked to jokingly refer to the place as "The Paradise Lost Ranch." The fragmentation of their ranch was a tolerable sore point, but Herb's "stewardship" of the place made the situation an open wound. In spite of Herb's nature, however, Hale tried to keep an eye out for the old man, helping him out whenever he could get Herb to grudgingly accept it. "We'll go at midafternoon, then, if that works for you, Jilly. I've got to run some chores in town in the morning."

They spent the evening slumped in overstuffed chairs in Hale's living room, ignoring the drone of the television whenever an interesting topic surfaced. The house's largest room included a bay window that gave character to the front facade, an entire wall of built-in bookshelves crammed to overflowing, and a computer with all accoutrements and surrounding snarl of wires occupying one corner. On the wall above the computer hung a pair of jacket covers from old jazz record albums. These images Jill had studied until she knew their details by heart. One featured Dave Brubeck's "Take Five" recording, the other a jazz group she'd never encountered outside this room called the Don Scaletta Trio. "Any Time . . . Any Groove," it was titled, and was illustrated by a photo of nostalgically clean cut, and therefore presumably pre-postmodern, young men, captured playing mid-tune, isolated against an impenetrable background. She'd guessed it to be from the late sixties.

Jill had spent every summer since she could remember in this house, mostly in the kitchen and this room. Photos of her and her dad, or of her alone in every stage of growth, were lined up on a rough-cut log mantle over an open hearth fireplace. There were no photos of her mother among them, no real evidence, other than her own existence, of Maggie at all in the room. And any memories Jill had of her mother's ever having been here were from such an early period of her childhood that they were beyond her grasp. When she first became conscious of the oddity of her mother's complete absence at the ranch, she had asked Hale for an explanation. His gruff reply was only, "She hated the ranch."

The fireplace, built of large smooth river boulders, was kept blazing through all but four months of the year, but Jill had never seen those flames. Dreamy memories of the room's details and mood would steal unawares into her consciousness on cloudy days in Palo Alto. Now that she had left California permanently, would she find herself drifting off into mist-shrouded redwood trees from in front of this hearth?

Jill left the room to telephone Jane from the kitchen,

leaving a message when an answering machine was the only response. Before the sportscaster had read the last score, she turned off all but one lamp and tiptoed to her room, leaving Hale asleep in his chair.

The horses were fresh as they headed out the following afternoon, blowing and snorting and fretting in their bridles. Though the sweet-natured dude horse Hale rode soon settled, Limbo couldn't bear it, couldn't restrain the joy and the terror of being out, couldn't stop his wild antics until Jill allowed him to let off steam with a long stretch of trot that left Hale cantering far behind.

"He hasn't been ridden enough, wild thing that he is," Hale explained as he caught up to her, excusing his favorite.

"I don't mind, Dad. I think he's a blast when he's like this!" She stroked his neck to calm him, and he began to manage to stand himself.

They emerged from willow scrub as tall as themselves into a large hay meadow, a place special to Jill. Open to the sun, its plush surface was a favorite hunting ground for coyotes, especially just after mowing, when meadow mice and voles were evicted from their grassy homes by the swather's destruction. Red-tailed hawks and bald eagles competed for the same game as the coyotes, waiting and watching through all seasons from craggy perches high in the tallest trees bordering the meadow. Deer and elk cautiously grazed their way into the meadow's interior as evening air stilled and rivulets of shadow slowly flooded its gleaming floor. Circular glyphs of their deep sleeping nests looked still warm in morning's cool light.

Beyond the meadow rose a hillock of scattered pine and low sage where Hale's small buffalo herd usually grazed. Because the ranch was only 640 acres, Hale ran no cattle.

He hadn't acreage enough to be a working cattle ranch like the 4,000 acre dude ranch in the valley southwest of Saratoga, plus it wasn't his nature to provide a pseudo-cowboy experience at Paradise Ranch. When he first acquired the ranch, he tried to formulate a long-range vision for it based on concerns for overgrazing and with keeping the operation simple, employing a minimum of hands. So he made a decision during the winter of 1997, when Yellowstone bison were being slaughtered that January for wandering out of the park onto ranch land, to rescue a small number of them. He hoped he could make some money and keep the herd small by selling some off as breeding stock to an increasing group of people who either wanted to see the once-endangered species make a comeback, or who wanted to return lands such as tallgrass prairies to their natural state, complete with indigenous buffalo. It was no far-fetched plan, since an actual bison movement of sorts was awakening, including a radical fringe of diehards who thought the entire massive Great Plains should be returned to the buffalo because the settling and farming there had failed, resulting in a vast landscape of dying towns and wasted land.

Rescuing Yellowstone bison was a feat that many of Hale's ranching neighbors, and perhaps even the men he hired to help, thought utter folly. They thought he was an idiot, he knew that. It took a crazy man to do what he did, or at the least a foolhardy or sentimental man. A few who didn't speak out thought maybe he was a brave, big-hearted man. But he didn't care what any of them thought. It was all just about money for the others anyway. So, with great difficulty, he and a few men had baited the Yellowstone bison into large corrals. It was a terrible winter harshness they'd had to deal with, the same bitter weather that had driven the bison out of the park onto the rangeland to begin with. But they had made the treacherous journey south, hauling the wild bison in cattle trucks from that northern region to the ranch. Then there was the testing for brucellosis, which had to be done to deflate the fears of his neighboring cattlemen, who believed the bison might be contagious to their cattle, the same fear that had caused the Yellowstone slaughter. Out of all those tested, he had been forced to slaughter one pregnant female that tested positive. And it had also meant a winter spent reinforcing and heightening all his fences to hold the buffalo. But his strategy had paid off. The small herd had been profitable so far, the guests were mesmerized by the Old West symbols, these Yellowstone survivors, and Hale had a sense of satisfaction he was certain he'd never have felt with a cattle operation.

Jill spotted their humpbacked shapes in the distance, prairie whales in a grassy ocean; reincarnations of the red ochre totems that galloped through Neolithic caves. A few wobbly-legged calves clung to the sides of unconcerned females, or climbed beneath bellies to butt udders for a meal, or chased each other in games of tag, while a massive bull stood apart from the herd, as if made of stone. She saw mythic minotaurs in their shaggy forms.

Although no visible sign of spring's greening had reached the surface, she could smell moist growth around her. The horses spooked and jumped when they flushed a long-eared, leggy jackrabbit that zigzagged erratically, low to the ground with ears laid flat until it had reached a safe distance. Then it became upright, bounding across the field in high slow-motion arcs with black tipped ears now erect and front paws hanging, laughing backwards, Brer Rabbit style, at the foiled enemy while it skirted bunches of yucca cactus. Black and white chickadees and a lone downy wood-pecker coiled around aspen trunks, and a gray jay led the horses with short swoopings for awhile, boldly half-tamed. *All black and white,* she mused, *but of course, colorful birds are camouflaged in tropical flowering forests, not dormant wintry lands.* Summer would bring color, iridescent broad-tailed hummingbirds, green- and blue-backed swallows and lemony warblers. There would be gaudy ducks and bright mergansers on the ponds and the Platter River then. She was hoping to see the flashes of mountain bluebirds flying from post to post along the path of wooden fences, but there were none today. *It's still too early.* Announcing him-self noisily, a Steller's Jay made an appearance in his ele-gant dress blues as compensation. Wyoming was just awakening in April, yawning and stretching, still relaxing before the swarm of migrating and birthing descended, that frantic busyness of the animal world which paralleled but remained independent of man's dealings.

The horses grew bored and began playing with each other, shaking their heads and nipping with bared teeth. Their hearts were set on gamboling like colts, but training repressed them to a sensible display of bad behavior. Jill scolded them, singing; "Shame, shame, shame," she sang, "Bad boys, bad boys. Watcha gonna do? Whatcha gonna do when they come for you? Bad boys, bad boys."

"Knock that off, you two," Hale commanded the horses, laughing. "That goes for you too, Bilious Jillius."

She burst out laughing. "Oh, Crawdad, how do you come up with this stuff? I'll never top you."

They had picked up a trot in a piney area when Limbo leapt sideways from another flushed jackrabbit. He slipped and nearly fell to his knees, hobbled a few steps and walked on gingerly.

"Wait, Dad," Jill called. "I think he's off. Watch him a minute and see if I'm right." She rode ahead a few strides.

"Yeah, you're right. He is a little gimpy, Jill. I guess that's what he gets for behaving like a knucklehead."

"Can't really blame him for having so much untapped energy. But if he doesn't come out of it, I'll have to go back, Dad."

Jill pulled up and reversed direction when it became clear the lameness was more than momentary. "You go on, Dad. I'll lead him home and put a wrap on this when I get back. I bet it's nothing a little stall rest won't fix." She dismounted and started back, saying, "Have a good ride, Dad. And don't worry about Limbo. I'll see you later." She stroked Limbo's lowered neck as she walked slowly alongside. "Poor guy," she crooned. "Now you've got an owie, you poor silly thing, you."

"Don't get chilly, Jilly," Hale called as she led Limbo away. Both horses were miserable about the decision. Hale coerced his vigorously, but the horse had no heart for the ride now that he was alone, and dawdled reluctantly onward, dragging his feet and casting longing glances behind him.

As Herb's place came into view, Hale could see movement through the stand of river birch, mountain maples, and alders that grew along the low-lying area between him and the cabin. *He must be out taking inventory of his junk pile. Or maybe tinkering with some piece of equipment that hasn't budged in twenty years. Or, more likely, doing something that will bother me. Maybe figuring out a new way to let my bison out again or setting a trap that will injure my dogs, or digging up the phone line, or . . . God only knows what he'll come up with next.*

By the time he'd cleared the thicket and could see the

human figure moving away from him along the fence line more clearly, he was less certain it was Herb. *Who the hell else could it be? I can't remember ever seeing another human being at Herb's place.* The figure seemed to be walking the fence length, then stooped to examine something on the ground. *I guarantee that's not the backside of Herb Miller I'm looking at.* His horse chose that instant to fully appreciate the extent of his loneliness, whinnying brokenheartedly. The person at the fence jerked around and raised a hand to block out the sun at Hale's back, searching for details of his outline which had disappeared into the solid form of the mountains behind him.

"Boris, dollink!" Maggie exclaimed when she recognized him.

Well, I'll be damned. "Natasha!"

Three

What have I done to myself this time? was her first thought as she stood on the threshold, peering into the interior of Herb's cabin. Her heart clunked like a stone. Fortunately her decorating taste kicked in, dictating her second thought, "Oh my god, this carpet has got to go." Released from his carrier, Gus jumped onto the lowest windowsill, craning his neck to peek around the side of the house. He chattered at a jay that flew past. "I can see how much help you're going to be," Maggie said scathingly.

The main room was a square, symmetrically divided on one side by two square windows. And the logs were squared. The oldest, sturdiest cabins were sometimes constructed of hand-planed logs made into flat-sided timbers that fit together more snugly than typical round-peeled logs. The mortar filled in and held better between the flat surfaces, and there was a more solid and permanent aspect to them. Maggie and Hale had always thought the old cabin had potential beneath the layers of Herb's follies.

Emptied of furniture, the thin rug covering the floor was a map of Herb's movements and furniture layout. A gritty trail had been gouged that led to the center of the room where it forked right and left into the kitchen and bedroom respectively. *When I'm gone, someone will be looking at my traces just as I'm seeing Herb's now.* A bathroom, painted coral pink, had been added beyond the kitchen rather than the bedroom, unfortunately, sometime after the onset of indoor plumbing. And most recently a rickety enclosed back porch had been tacked on and connected to a slatternly out-

45

building Herb called his "annex" via a raised walk constructed of deck planking. Everything Herb had ever done to the cabin had been an affront to the original structure, which was in fact a fine sturdy frame.

The heart of the cabin was a masterpiece of a fireplace. Pieces of large angular granite and quartz rock had been selected to fit together so perfectly that no mortar was visible, melded as beautifully as the monumental dry-stack construction of the Incas, but reduced here to a credible scale. Contrasting colored stones had been used to form an arch over the hearth, further evidence of the builder's patient work and concern for quality and design.

Maggie spent early afternoon pulling up edges of the carpet with a prying tool she fashioned from a piece of metal scrounged from junk in the back yard. She rolled the carpet into a long tube and struggled to drag it through the back porch and out of the house where she stowed it alongside the cabin's wall. A floor of neatly-joined wide dark oak planks was now exposed. *My god, it's perfect! To have covered something so beautiful with something so ugly! What a man of superlatives was Herb. "No accounting for taste" just doesn't do him justice.*

Next she stripped to the bones and scrubbed clean the entire cabin in anticipation of the impending arrival of her furnishings, using the bucket of basic cleaning supplies she'd packed into the Beamer's trunk. Maggie the Reformer, cleansing the house of all dirt, stains, impurities, blemishes, imperfections, and encumbrances; purifying, unsullying, unadultering, unsoiling, wiping blank. She swept the floors bare. Dusty rotted curtains were pulled down and discarded. Crusted oilcloth linings were peeled from kitchen shelves. Maggie the Penitent. Kneeling in the light, she methodically wiped the flyblown windows and sills clean as slates, mumbling to herself repetitively and chanting a few tuneless songs. She bowed over the bathroom tub, scraping and scouring until it gleamed. She washed the walls in sweeping motions like deep salaams. Maggie the Trinity: Joan of Arc, Hester Prynne, and the Merry Maid in one. Finally, exhausted, filthy, and disheveled, she stood, hands clasped in front of her, surveying the fruits of her labor. A sleek empty quarters, polished and wiped clean of every imprint of Herb's residency, now lay expectantly fallow, pregnant with potential, a receptacle for her will and identity.

Gus draped himself casually across the bathroom counter as she stood under the wide soft spray from an old metal shower head sprouting vertically from a claw footed cast-iron tub, washing away the day's grime which clung to her. *There's nothing I can't survive so long as I can have a hot shower,* she thought. She felt nearly reborn. She lit a small fire in the fireplace afterward, then she and Gus sat together on the hearth, eating from her diminishing supplies by the light of a pair of candles she had found in a cupboard and listening to soft classical music on her small portable short-wave radio while she sipped red wine she'd bought just for this purpose.

When they were finished, she rolled out a futon pad fetched from the Beamer's trunk, laid down onto it, arms crossed over her chest, and stared at the darkening ceiling with pounding heart until she finally slept. Maggie, cleansed, saved, and nearly reborn. Gus stretched out full length beneath her right arm, watching the dying flames in the fireplace. Long after she slept, he stared with eyes gleaming and tail gently thumping into the harsh shadows of the deep recesses of the bare room, watching for movement.

★ ★ ★ ★ ★

Her furniture did not arrive as early as promised the next day. She might have driven into Saratoga to reinforce her supplies, but she had resolved to wait a few days before venturing into town where she'd likely be faced with explaining her presence to old acquaintances. So she strapped the harness onto Gus and took him outdoors to reconnoiter the grounds around the cabin. "We don't want you to attempt an incredible journey back to Palo Alto, do we, Gussy? And we don't want you to end up as some coyote's entree either."

As she followed the cat's wanderings she picked up a jar half-filled with pine needles and dried leaves by the swirling winter winds. She broke off some golden stems of faded rabbit brush blooms and stuck them in the jar, surrounding them with pieces of draping native clematis that wound through the junk piles, their swirling cottony seed heads a symbol of the yard's seamy neglect, like tufts of stuffing poking through worn ticking.

The front yard was dappled with shade from a sparse pine grove. Dark stains seeped from shrunken clumps of dirty snow amidst the anchorage of the trunks. Twisted narrow-leafed cottonwoods wore messy hairdos of magpie nests. *I'll have some of this cleared out, she thought, but I don't want to make the cabin too visible to the road.* A tall arched Woods Rose bearing large orange hips growing beside the front door cheered her. *I like this rose, she mused. I really like that this rose is growing right here. I'm surprised the robins didn't steal all the fruit last fall.*

Only one man arrived with the furniture, so it was up to her to support one end of everything larger than a wooden chair during the moving. She shut Gus into the bedroom

48

while the truck was offloaded. The feat was only manageable because she had regarded this move as a further reduction of her already lean life. She had sold or given away all articles she considered even remotely extraneous during her last days in Palo Alto, reminding herself, *I mustn't reduce my life to nothing.*

The two worked silently but for the few words needed to decide who should walk backwards (mostly Maggie) and the grunts and groans of heavy lifting. She could sense the thinly-veiled surprise in the trucker's expression as he gazed around the cabin's interior while she signed the bill of lading.

"So, you're going to be living here all alone?" he asked with genuine disbelief.

"Not totally alone," she answered. "I've got my cat for company, and some neighbors that I know from years ago who aren't too far away, so I'll be all right."

He turned to look back at her after stepping into his truck. "You take care, now," he called with false heartiness. *I'll be fine. I'll be great. I'll be happy here,* she thought as he pulled away leaving her standing alone in the threshold.

The supper she shared with Gus that evening was much improved from the first night's. Gus had a chair to sit on. The largest pieces of furniture were all around her, residing in their permanent locations. Throughout the evening she began to divide her efforts randomly among the maze of half-emptied boxes, wandering slowly as on some long-forgotten path viewed anew through memories elicited by objects she pulled from boxes. Gus rummaged noisily from one box to another.

I'll have to remember where I put this flashlight. She had become so dependent on the uniformity, the continuity of her previous existence that she was caught in the sway of confusion, in spite of the reemergence of these familiar details of her life. Everything would now be in a different place. An untried pattern would emerge to shape her comings and goings. She would no longer be able to coast automatically on the comfortable track she had so taken for granted. The loss of a sense of intimacy with her surroundings destabilized her more than she had expected. *This is how I will be as an old lady.* Her inability to remember details, though passed off as mere nuisance, actually fueled a deep fear of loss of independence, evoking images of herself as aimless and white-haired, ambling about vacuously, alone and unloved.

A warm band of rose-colored light painted the tops of the trees and the ridges of the surrounding hills when Maggie awoke the next morning. *Things always seem so much better in the daylight,* she thought with relief.

She riveted her eyes to the vista while sipping her coffee, as if the permanence of the mountain stillness could be appropriated. The rooms of her cabin, though still a work in progress, lent some comfort through the homey touches now evident, the jar containing the dried sprigs on her table, the quiet ticking of her clock, the warm nest of her bed. Gus lay washing himself in the sun, pausing to raise his head, tongue protruding, to glance her way for approval.

She spent an hour resetting all digital clocks on the appliances, hooking up the computer, and checking for the phone connection she had prearranged. Telling Gus to be a good boy and to stand guard, she left the cabin somewhat reluctantly to drive into Saratoga for groceries.

Shadowed by the Snowy Range, the valley was still gray as sheet metal. The only thing astir was a lone pheasant cock walking sedately across the highway in front of her.

Must be an escapee from someone's fowl menagerie, she thought, fairly certain there were no wild pheasant at this elevation. *It's funny. Nearly every exotic that's been imported into this country has set the environmentalists raving about how they crowd out native species, but who doesn't love the pheasant, though he's a Chinese import? I've never heard an unkind word about a pheasant. And no wonder,* she thought as she slowed down to admire him. "Don't get run over," she called as she passed him.

It was early enough that the market was still slow. *Try to be philosophical,* she thought, making an effort to tolerate something she detested so much. *Grocery shopping is the crux of life,* she told herself as she walked the aisles. *We work mainly to come here. The food we choose illustrates who we are; it sustains us and determines to some degree whether we are healthy or not. And the absolutely boring and trivial nature of an action so necessary for survival is a perfect symbol for the paradox of the human condition.* But grocery philosophy couldn't last, and soon fell apart. She filled the shopping cart with household items from her list. When she passed the cosmetics shelf, she backed up the cart and slipped a tube of lipstick into her pocket when she thought no one could see her. *It's criminally overpriced,* she rationalized. *Plus, these big box stores make way too much money . . . and they pull all that phony part-time employee layoff stuff so they don't have to pay benefits.* She kept justifying her action until she had almost reached the checkout counter, but finally felt so guilty that she slipped the lipstick into her cart at the last instant. She couldn't do it, not even as a liberal protest.

The girl who tabulated her purchase smiled noncommittally at Maggie, oblivious of the drama that almost was. "Plastic or paper?" she asked. *Ignorance is bliss.* She dragged each item across the scanner. "$47.73 is your

51

total," she said, staring beyond Maggie to the next counter. "Have a nice day." *The universal language of retail.* Passing through the automatic doors, Maggie had a fleeting image of herself being led away in handcuffs wearing no lipstick. *Don't be ludicrous.* She closed herself into her car. *One thing for sure, there are no grocery stores in heaven.* As she pulled out of the parking lot, she watched in her rearview mirror as the whole building blew sky high. *I wish.* Maggie felt a slight disappointment at having escaped notice. It had been a lonely two nights at the cabin. In a town of just 2,000, it was uncanny that she remained anonymous.

The morning sun had reached the valley by the time she headed back. Slowly traversing its flat surface from west to east, the light was a counterpoint to the clouds sweeping through from the opposite direction, dappling the brilliant land with nervous shadows. Upstretched fingers of trees dipped into the gold that poured from the bowl of the sky as the sun tilted over the edge of the earth. All the valley shone like a hushed golden promise. As Maggie passed through, her fingers relaxed their grip on the steering wheel.

There was a dial tone when she returned to the cabin. She was connected! Logging onto the Internet, she began to type:

Hey, Jane. Long live the technocrats! I'm here in my cabin with Gus at my side. He says "hello, and pass the sardines." I miss you already. Do you know you are the only person on earth I have fully confided in? Now I am here speaking to no one but myself and Gussus. Beyond the two of us, there is no one within fifteen hundred miles with whom I can be as completely honest as I've been with you. No wonder I miss you so much. You asked me what

52

the hell I expected to gain by returning to Saratoga. I have an answer for you now. I am looking for some peace. Don't think I'm crazy. Long E-mails are like long good-byes; everyone hates them, so more later. Love, Mag.

She watched the screen as the envelope twirled and disappeared.

When she finally came across her bird feeder amidst her "garage stuff" stowed in the annex, she took it out to the line of lodge pole fence behind the junk pile to hang it. She wanted to center it in the view from the kitchen window, so after hanging it from the top of the teepeed fence, confirmed the location with a sighting from inside the kitchen. She grabbed the bag of birdseed she'd just bought and returned to fill the feeder when she heard a loud plaintive whinny. Looking up, she could barely make out the figure of a horse and rider for the halo of brilliant sunlight surrounding them.

Before Hale could even finish dismounting, Maggie began explaining herself. Wrapping her arms across her non-existent chest, she pulled on her shirt-sleeves until they covered her hands, twisting the ends in balled-up fingers. "Look, Hale, I want you to know it's not like, 'Maggie the Cat is back,' or anything. I'm not here to cause trouble or interfere with you or your life in any way, I swear."

"Whoa, whoa, there, Maggie," Hale laughed as he wrapped the reins around the fence rail a few times. "Jesus, Maggie, give a man a chance. All I was going to say is that you're looking wonderful. You're just looking great! And *then* I was going to say what in the hell are you doing here?"

She could laugh then. "You've still got that million-dollar smile, Maggie."

"Well, come in for a cup of coffee. I need some reassuring. I've been getting cold feet ever since the furniture truck pulled out. So, come in, and I'll tell you all about everything."

"Okay, but let me put my horse in Herb's corral. I'll lead him around through the front." He put the gelding into a small corral Herb had built for fattening a calf every year. The horse started picking at a few grassy tufts before Hale had even finished pulling off the bridle and loosening the girth.

"What a difference already!" he exclaimed when he stepped into the house. "Who would even guess it's the same house?" She was pleased that her efforts counted for so much, though she'd barely begun.

"Just wait until I tell you what I intend to do with the place."

"Well, yeah, sure, but first tell me how you got here."

She poured coffee into his cup. "You still drink it black?"

"No, I use a little sugar now, like a half teaspoon, please."

They sat at the small table in the kitchen before a large picture window. The trunk of an old lodgepole pine stood close to the cabin here, its dark gash splitting their view, dividing their figures. Gus jumped up onto the table, sliding a few inches on landing.

"I hope you aren't one of those people revolted by cats on tables," Maggie said. "You didn't used to be."

Hale stroked Gus, who arched his back in pleasure. "Nah. You have to learn to roll with the punches in the guest ranch business, after all, so a little furball like what's his name here . . ."

"Gus is his name. Don't look at me like that. Jill named him."

". . . like ole Gus here . . ." The cat threw himself down on his side, flipping his tail while Hale tickled his flank.

"Careful! He'll scratch you! He hates being touched there."

But Gus rolled onto his back as if hypnotized.

"I never knew you were a cat person, Hale."

"I'm sure there were lots of things you never knew about me, Maggie."

She looked down into her coffee cup, dodging the accusation by total avoidance, shifting the subject. "How I got here . . . Well, I'm sure Jill told you that Mom died."

"She did. Yes, I'm awfully sorry."

"Yea. Me too." She glanced out the window at some tattered pieces of plastic hanging along a section of fence at the back of the yard as they lifted and danced gently in the breeze. She sighed into the pane. "My biggest regret is that we just couldn't get close, even right at the end. I think we both wanted it, but it just didn't happen. And now it's too late."

"I'm awfully sorry," Hale said again, not really knowing anything else to say.

There was a world more to say about her mother's death, but no words for it. Her mother had been a woman who did her duty by everyone and loved no one, so Maggie had missed her mother her whole life. She took a drink of coffee as if to fortify herself. "When her estate was settled I had to make some decisions. Where exactly did I really want to be? How was I going to use the estate? And Jill was leaving. Could I and should I do anything about that? I decided to invest in some property with part of the estate. I really thought I would find a place in Palo Alto, but something kept nagging at me." She looked straight at Hale. "You know, Jill hardly ever talked to me about you and the ranch when she'd come home at summers' ends. I don't know why, exactly; she just never did. But the one thing she did mention several times was that Herb was the fly in your ointment." Maggie lowered her eyes to sip her coffee.

She's still beautiful, Hale thought, watching her lean against the window, *though paler and thinner than before. And she has a more patient look than before, like she's been slightly frayed by life. But there's no cynicism in those eyes.*

"I guess I did vent about Herb in front of Jilly more than once, but he wasn't anything I couldn't cope with. Hey, if my place didn't surround his on three sides, it might not have seemed so 'in my face.' "

"Well, anyway, I was missing Jill so much after she had moved, and knowing she'd be up here every weekend possible, I thought I might kill two birds with one stone. So I had a real estate friend contact Herb about selling the place. I knew he must be about a hundred years old now and figured he'd either be hunkering down in his cabin until he died or darned well ready to clear out. Turns out he was ready to go."

"God, I can't believe it. I thought the old buzzard would die here and I'd have to be the one to find the body." He ran his palm down the length of Gus's tail, the gentleness of his touch belying the harshness of his words. "But where did he go? As far as I know he didn't have any family."

"You'll never believe it. He moved to the gulf coast of Florida. It turns out he did have a long lost brother there. They'd never gotten along, but the brother wanted to patch things up in their old age, you know, before it was too late."

Hale gave a final pat to Gus's flank as he laughed and stood up to set his emptied cup in the sink. "Imagine Herb in a tropical shirt! I guess he got the last laugh on all of us."

He pulled his jean jacket off the back of his chair. "I hate to leave so soon, Maggie, but I've got to start back or I'll be bucked off in the dark. You should come over and have dinner with us. Jill's here, you know, but she'll be leaving tomorrow to get back to work."

"No, no, Hale. I really am serious about not horning in. Besides, I bit the bullet and went to the store this morning, and bought some stuff to make corn chowder. I'm dying to try out the kitchen in my new home, you know, make it homey with the smell of my own cooking."

"Gee, maybe I should get that recipe from you for our cook, Rob. He'd love to try out a Boston accent." He explained Rob's routine.

Maggie laughed. "Well, this chowder is a long way from Boston. It's Mexican style with jalapenos. *Por eso, puede practicar Espanol.*"

"He's already done that with his paella Valencia. Let's not add fuel to the fire." He walked to the door. "Thanks for the coffee, Maggie. I can't believe you're back . . . Maggie the Cat is back. Wait until Jill finds out."

"Tell her to come see me tomorrow morning before she leaves, if she's got time. Believe it or not, I've already got phone service, so let me give you my phone number. Then she can call me if she can't make it." He watched her lips as she scribbled a number on a note pad, mouthing the numbers silently. She frowned slightly, concentrating. Sitting in the sun had brought some color into her face. She raised her eyes back to him and handed him the note. *Don't look at me with those eyes, Maggie.*

"G'bye, Hale," she said softly.

"Adios, Maggie."

As he stepped through the door she called, "Hale!"

"Yeah?"

"You're looking good yourself."

"Thanks, Maggie. Good-bye."

She walked into the bedroom to look in the mirror when he had gone. *God! And I wanted to look so perfect when I ran into him for the first time!* She was wearing the same sweatshirt she'd worn on the trip, even grubbier now. It was yellow, a color she thought made her look pale. Jill's jeans were oversized on her, and there was a rooster tail in the back of her hair from last night's sleep that hadn't tamed down through the day. *I have got to grow my hair out!* she came close to crying out loud.

Jill was there first thing the next morning. "Oh, Mom, you're the wildest!" She stood inside the threshold staring in disbelief and alternately hugging Maggie and looking into her bemused face. Then she shook Maggie by the shoulders. "I can't believe you made the trip out here all alone without telling anybody, especially me, who could've helped you and kept you company, for heaven's sake . . ." she couldn't resist scolding. "And the timing was so funny! When Dad walked in last night I was just starting to tell him the wild news that Jane had just told me on the phone. And he said, cool as a cucumber, 'Yeah, she's over at Herb's place and she wants you to come by tomorrow morning if you have time.' 'If I had time.' I'm sure, Mom!" Maggie had led her into the center of the room, and still held her hand. Jill looked around her and shook her head. "I don't understand at all, Mom. I just can't believe you're here. He always told me you hated the ranch."

Maggie laughed. "I just missed you too much, Jilly. I had to come, love. But I promise," she began, reassuring Jill with the same earnest disclaimer she'd given Hale, "I *promise,* cross my heart," which she did as she spoke, "I'm not here to horn in on your life or your dad's life, and *especially* not the life you two have together. I promise, Jill. I really do." She looked at Jill seriously, expectantly.

"Oh, Mom. How could you think . . . Mom, I'm *happy* . . . I'll *love* having you here. You don't know how often I've wished you were up here with me, never mind with Dad, I mean with me. I've imagined how it would be to have both of you near me in one place, and especially here. Now it really will be Paradise. The real thing!"

Maggie smiled her beautiful broad smile, a smile that a girl on a swing smiles on the first day of spring because she can finally go out to play again after the long winter indoors. She slipped her arm around Jill's waist and twirled her, sweeping the room with her other arm. "But, hey! Look around! Whatdya think, so far?"

Jill strolled through the house with Maggie. "How wonderful the walls and the fireplace are. Somebody loved this place, didn't they? They built it with care, you can see that. And here it's been all covered by Herb's 'malfunction,' as Dad calls it, all this time!" She shook her head without even knowing it. "And your things, Mom! Who'd have thought your wonderful Palo Alto artsy fartsy things would look so great in a log cabin?"

"Oh, please, Jill. 'Artsy fartsy?' That's not very pretty. That's maybe even downright ugly," she laughed at Jill's mild slur against her finicky taste, then led Jill into the kitchen. "Have you had breakfast? Well, sit here anyway and keep me company while I feed Gus and get a bite for myself."

"Oh, Gus, you big galoot!" cried Jill. "How are you, puss?" She fussed over the cat, picking him up and stroking him as she held him against her chest. "Was he a terror on the trip?"

59

As they chatted, Jill studied the kitchen and living room more carefully. "I never realized it, Mom, but nearly all your furnishings and art works are primitive. I guess it should have struck me before, but they seemed so modernist in our Palo Alto apartment. They actually suit this rustic cabin, though. I mean, I wasn't just teasing." Maggie had collected folk art through the years, mostly from countries she had visited, but also from other sources, from flea markets and garage sales, import shops and museums. It was the only type of shopping she really enjoyed, unlike, for example, grocery shopping. There was a beaded mask from Baja California, a Panamanian mola, an Australian bark painting. A piece of tapa cloth hung on her bedroom wall and a Kilim rug covered the floor beside her bed. In the kitchen hung an abstract expressionist drawing she was convinced no one else liked, no matter how ardently her friends protested that they did. She had haunted student shows in art departments, adding to her collection a piece of avant-garde pottery and a small sculpture. The wooden furnishings she had chosen over the years were all simple unadorned forms, gleaming with a patina from years of obsessive touching and polishing, each piece a votive to repression. All had come from a variety of sources so that nothing matched. Their arrangement resembled a museum setting, the space around each item adding undeserved stature to some of the pieces. She wanted few but interesting items, detesting clutter. "Everything needs room to breathe," she would say. "The house is a sculptural piece, too, so why cover it up with too much *stuff?*" Objects from nature were among the few embellishments, a smooth black stone, a white shell, a patterned feather.

"I remember having read that Georgia O'Keefe's house was so spare and minimal that visitors were shocked at the severity of her life, especially knowing she was plenty loaded and it was self-imposed," Jill said. "So I wonder what else you have in common with Georgia, Mom?"

Maggie laughed. "I'll give that some thought and let you know."

"I hate to, but I gotta go, Mom. I've got a long drive back, and the weather is supposed to turn pretty bad. And my little Honda may be good in the snow, but I'm not."

Maggie walked Jill to her car. "It's so wonderful, but so strange seeing you here, Mom. And, don't think I haven't noticed, by the way, that you never answered me. I thought you were supposed to hate the ranch. I mean, you and Dad both led me to believe that. So, where did that truism come from and go to?"

"Oh, Jilly. It's such a long story. Really. I'm not being evasive. But let's save it for when we have some time to talk. Next time, okay?"

"Okay, Mom." She pecked her on the cheek. "Don't be too lonely, all right?"

A high wind wrenched the landscape by mid-afternoon. Trees moaned in pain as they twisted beneath it, recouped during lulls, then bowed from the next blows. The first few fragile flakes of snow strained against the velocity but could not hold a grip. But by dusk, when the wind waned, a dusting of white clung tentatively to the surface of things, and by nightfall its thick layer covered all. Objects were equalized and prejudices obliterated by the neutrality of its blankness. The junk pile became one with the lovely landscape.

It would be cruel to take my poor little Californian native out into this, Maggie thought, picturing the Beamer shivering but sheltered within the annex. *Besides, it wouldn't make ten feet in this stuff. It's not even front wheel drive.* "Let's face it, Gus, we're stranded. At least we've got all the modern conveniences to keep us comfy and connected."

The phone and electricity disappeared about the time the snow reached the top of the cabin's foundation. *Don't panic,* she told herself as she lit candles and placed extra logs on the fire from the pile Herb had left in the annex. She pulled on an extra sweater. When she put Gus in her lap, his purring comforted her. She had dozed off when the muffled sound of an engine wakened her. When she opened the door, Hale stood stomping snow from his feet.

"That fool Rob has made way too much beef Bourguignon tonight. Frankly, I think he poured more burgundy into himself than over the beef. So you've got to help us out, Maggie. Come eat with us tonight."

She had never been so happy to see another human being. "Can I bring Gus?" she asked.

"Here, kitty, kitty, kitty!" Hale called absurdly.

The emergency generator played bass to the quiet jazz accompanying their meal. "I must get one for myself," she said, referring to its muffled whirring and gesturing at the lights and the running appliances.

"They're expensive to run, but we do a pretty lively Christmas business these days and can't afford to be caught with our pants down by a little rough weather."

Rob had outdone both himself and the French language for the occasion, then had disappeared from sight with some vague excuse and a loud *"Bon soir!"* in parting. They sat alone in the dining room over emptied plates. From an old recording, a vocalist she didn't recognize crooned lazily, *Gonna take a sentimental journey.* Gus crouched in his carrier on the floor beside her.

"So, how is the guest ranch business these days, Hale?" Maggie asked politely.

"It's good, Maggie," Hale answered like a salesman pitching his product. "You should see the rates dot com millionaires are willing to pay these days for a chance to live like a land-poor, down-in-the-mouth, in-debt-up-to-the-eyebrows rancher. I'm guessing that dude ranches are benefiting from movies like 'The Horse Whisperer' and 'All the Pretty Horses.' Most of them are booked up a season in advance." He delivered the words with a flourish. "Now, as for Paradise Ranch . . ." He stirred the remnants of food on his plate.

"What, aren't you sharing in the bounty?" she asked, leaning her elbows on the table to look more directly at him.

"Well, you know, my real love is the fishing. I'd fill the place with nothing but fishermen, if I had my way. I'm no cowboy and I'm not a rancher either, but I guess I've learned a little about fishing the North Platte after all these years. The fellows who run the tackle shops around here keep recommending me as a fishing guide. So I'm keeping busy enough, if not exactly making a killing." He sounded somewhat defensive.

"You don't have to sell me on it, you know," she said delicately. "I'm on your side." She smiled sweetly, but Hale didn't respond to either the smile or the words.

"I did notice that the stuffed fish outnumber elk antlers and cow horns around here," Maggie teased, twisting in her chair to take in the room's walls.

"Oh, you noticed my minnows, did you?" He laughed at the foolishness of them.

Each room in the lodge and all of the six detached cabins sported a giant taxidermied trout over its door, and one wall of the dining room was crowned by the grand daddy of them all, a twenty-eight inch German brown leaping off his mounting plaque with a gaping mouth that looked like a sneering laugh.

"He's thumbing his nose at us, isn't he?" she asked.

"Yeah. Like Herb, he thinks he got the last laugh, but look who's stuck up on the wall. If you think he looks arrogant, you should see the home page of our web site. There's a trout that swims across the top of it over and over in jerky little leaps." They both laughed, and Hale's defenses seemed to disappear. "The truth is, Maggie, we're doing quite well here in Paradise. I have to turn away some fishing clients. And, aside from the fishing, I've got a small string of horses, the restaurant, and a few mountain bikes to entertain the non-fishers. We do a chuck wagon dinner gig with my team of Belgians in the summer and hayrack or sleigh rides in the winter. People can cross-country ski into a couple of yurts set up on the BLM land that surrounds us. There's even a musher from Riverside who can bring her dogs and sled up here on short notice." He swung his legs out from under the table around the side of his chair to cross them, speaking with real enthusiasm now, warming to his subject. "I've made a bit of money on the bison, and we cater to hunters in the fall. And believe it or not, I still do some consulting for the local engineering firm, you remember the one that started up in 1985, the year before you left?"

"C'mon, Hale, no way! I can't believe you're still working as an engineer. How on earth have you kept abreast of things?"

"I've got a lot of free time in the winter months, you know, and it's not like I'm completely out of touch here, not in today's world," he said, nodding toward the computer in the foyer. "Yeah, I help Wyoming businesses and organizations set up and maintain computer networks. You'd be surprised how aggressively local businesses have gone online." Hale recrossed his legs. "I'm also on the substitute math teacher list at Saratoga high school during the winter months," he nodded in affirmation. "Yeah, I like that a lot, actually, even though a few boys who know me too well cut up in class when I sub. That's okay. The truth is, I get a kick out of them." He grinned.

As she leaned over to check on Gus, the drone of the generator ceased abruptly. Hale stood up to check switches and picked up the phone.

"It looks like everything is working again, Maggie. We're lucky tonight. It can be out for eight hours sometimes, if you recall."

"Oh yes, I remember," the words firm, but spoken quietly. "One of my fears about coming back was whether or not I could face the snow. It takes a certain grit to live in snow country, you know?"

"I've never thought you lacked grit, Maggie. I never thought that was why you left."

She looked away from him, toward the center of the room. "I'm sorry I never exactly explained that, did I, Hale?"

"No, you didn't."

An awkward silence descended that neither could break.

"I think I'll be okay about the snow," she finally said, rallying. "It's really sort of unbearably beautiful. When you live away from it, you can have a longing for the way a new snow seems to cover the sins of the world."

"You should stay here tonight, Maggie. I've got plenty of room to spare, after all."

"No, Hale. Thanks for the offer, but if you don't mind driving me back, I'd appreciate it."

* * * * *

They might have been the only surviving souls on a silent arctic sea as the 4x4 pickup swam through waves of drifted snow. Maggie could see Hale's large hands wrapped loosely around the steering wheel, rocking left and right with the play of the wheels as they ploughed through resisting drifts.

"I'm glad to hear you're still making use of your engineering education. You know that was a huge issue with me when you decided to move up here permanently. I hated that you weren't going to stick with your good engineering job. I'm sure I made that crystal clear to you at the time."

"Crystal clear."

Maggie felt chastised, as he'd intended. "I'm a lot less bossy these days, Hale. I've learned a few things over the years, I think you'll find." She let her contriteness settle, filling out all the space, but then grew taller and added, "That doesn't mean I'm trying to prove anything to you, Hale. What I do mean to do is right some wrongs in the time I'm here."

"Aren't you staying for good, then, Maggie?" He'd focused on her last few words.

"I don't know. I haven't decided. I have enough money to take some time to figure out what I want to do over the long term. For now, I've got big plans for converting Herb's mess into something valuable. Crass of me, isn't it?"

"I didn't know you'd become such a capitalist, Maggie. As I remember, you and Kennie used to have some kick ass debates with him aligned at the Ayn Rand end and you siding with Che Guevera or someone."

Maggie had to laugh. "What a hypocrite I was." Her laughter faded to sobriety. "Speaking of Ken," she ventured slowly, "How is he?"

"I don't really know myself, Maggie. That summer after he graduated is the last time we were ever close. I'll bet I haven't seen him and Diana more than half dozen times since you left. I'm sure I wouldn't recognize his kids if they walked up to me. For one thing, they all took after Diana, not him."

"I hate to think you two haven't stayed close. You were so funny together in those days before Jill was born. All those feats of oneupsmanship. He was always complaining that you were your dad's favorite, you know. The lengths he would go in order to outshine you in front of your father! And he always had to catch the first, the most, or the biggest fish, too, remember?"

They pulled up to her cabin, and Maggie collected Gus from the floor where he'd been pretending he was not in a vehicle. She had left some switches turned on as a show of good faith, so lights shown out from the cabin into the calmed night, like a lighthouse in the dark.

"Thanks, Hale. And tell Rob that the food was 'magnifique'."

Returning through the waning storm, the animation of Hale's expression gradually slipped from his face. The blackness of the night seemed to absorb the effort he'd made to fortify himself through the evening. By the time he reached his own door, his visage was almost grim.

Dear Jane: Yes, I'm looking for peace here. But I don't mean an escape from frantic city life or job stress. I mean peace of mind. I've got to begin to forgive myself. I think the first step will be leveling with Hale, but I don't know how I'm going to find the courage. I'm exhausted from the weight of twelve inches of snow, among other things. Adios. Maggie.

Four

Spring snow can't last. Cold gave way to the sun's momentum. Snow reduced to mush, then to watery film over saturated soil, freezing nightly into crusty solid. Precise edges of animal tracks disintegrated and sank slowly below the snow's surface. Mushroom-shaped cornices collapsed into shapeless heaps, and branches sprang upward as globs of white dropped from them. Meadowlarks sang, staking their claims, and horses stretched out to nap with bellies facing the sun. Spring would have its way.

Hale wakened after the storm as if from hibernation.

"You seem kinda cranky this morning, boss. Long night?" Rob fished slyly.

"Knock it off, Rob. It's too early in the day for me to have to scrape crap off my boots."

"She's a mighty fine-looking woman, Hale."

"Don't you have toast to burn or something?"

He went out to the barn after breakfast to check on Limbo's leg. An icy stubble covered the horse's muzzle. Hale leaned over to pick up the left front, waving away friendly nibbles at the back of his belt. He flexed the ankle joint gently backward, monitoring Limbo for flinching, then replaced the foot and stood to pat the fuzzy neck. "You're just a faker, aren't you? You were never really hurt at all, huh? Just wanted to get back to your cushy stall to avoid the snow." He slipped a halter over Limbo's head and led him from the barn. Limbo sprayed sloppy snorts through the air as Hale shooed him into a trot on a small circle. The horse tossed his head and arched his neck to play with the halter rope as he sprang expressively, lifting his legs high to clear the snow.

"Okay, you handsome dude. You can go out with your buddies today. There are no kinks that I can see. Have fun!" he called, releasing the horse into the pasture. The Belgians had lifted their heads at the sight of Limbo, snow drizzling from long-haired chins. The reunited trio exchanged greetings like long lost war buddies, but broke it short to get back to the business of grazing.

What a life! Hale stood still, gripping the top of the fence, his big hands spread wide, a foot propped on the bottom rail, watching vacantly, then returned to the lodge with measured steps.

Maggie sat silently at her sunny table, staring through the window at the receding snow. From the direction of Paradise Ranch, a thin white plume rose from the lodge's fireplace, barely discernible from Maggie's window, concealed by a band of trees between the two properties. She could see her reflection in the glass and idly smoothed down the back of her unruly hair.

Carrying her cup into the bedroom, she changed into some warm work clothes and slipped on a pair of shallow rubber boots. *These will never do! I've got to pick up some better gear, and soon. I mean, even the Beamer is all wrong. God, did I really think I could just stroll back into a life here?*

She stroked Gus before stepping out the back door and walked to a tangle of barbed wire at the outer edge of Herb's dump. *Where do I even begin to start?* She yanked at a strand of wire that seemed to reach out like a hand from a huddled metal body drowning in the soil. Frustrated, she jerked against the resisting mass. A coiled end flew out of

69

the ground and whipped her wrist. *Wounded already and barely into battle.* She turned her attention to wooden pieces of the jumbled puzzle. *At least I can burn these, until I can hire someone with a truck to haul off the rest.* She piled together a collection of rotted fencing, crooked window frames, peeling doors, plywood sheets, posts, planks, poles, pillars, and even the seat of a two holed outhouse, most of it buried in the pile and therefore dry. When the mound reached her own height, she doused it with lighter fluid and set it afire, then watched it burn until all that remained was a black sore on the earth.

She was recognized on her second trip into Saratoga. When she walked into the sporting goods shop to buy some sturdy work clothes, the lone salesperson happened to be Jo Sifford.

"Oh my god! Maggie Adamson! Or is it Everhardt again?"

"Well, hello Jo! Give me a hug! I know, I know. Divorces can be so confusing. It's Everhardt. I took back Everhardt when I moved to California."

"Well, what are you doing back here, girl? As far as I know, and I know just about everything that goes on here, you have never once been back since you left."

"Believe it or not, I bought Herb Miller's place."

"Oh my god! I must be slipping. How did Herb sell out without me knowing about it?"

"Don't beat up on yourself, Jo. It just happened four days ago, and neither Herb nor I bothered to take out an ad about it."

"Well, what in the hell are you going to do with that old run down POS property?

"Oh, I've got plans."

"Weren't things working out for you in California?"

"Yeah, sure. I had a wonderful life there. But I guess you know Jill got a job recently in Boulder."

"Yes, I knew about that. But why move back to Saratoga and not closer to Boulder, then?"

"Oh, Jo. It's a long boring story."

The bell on the door rang as a woman towing a toddler came in and sat down in the shoe department.

Maggie started flipping through a rack of jackets. "Go ahead and help them, Jo. I'm in no hurry and I need quite a few things. I can just look until you've finished with them."

"Listen, Maggie, I'll tell you what. If you've got a few other errands to run, you could come back just before my lunch break and we'll get you all fixed up and then I'll take you to lunch at the Beef Palace. It'll be my treat."

Maggie laughed. "All right. I'll be back in about thirty minutes then."

The Beef Palace had been in Saratoga longer than anyone could remember. It had gone through a series of remodelings, each one creating more confusion in the building's architecture. *Please Seat Yourself* was hand scrawled in chalk on a small blackboard at the entrance. There was a no smoking section that made no difference whatsoever in the amount of ambient smoke. The mounted trophies of local game animals ringed the room, staring blankly at each other, a ubiquitous jackalope in the center. Yellowed Charles Russell prints with burnt parchment edges mounted on blackened particleboard hung on the walls above booths upholstered in patched red vinyl. Hundreds of names were scratched into the peeling resin of the table tops: "Reyanne sucks. Bill Severs was here. Class of '87. Go Lobos." *Plebian pictographs,* crossed Maggie's mind as she slid into a booth by a window.

The place served fabulous coffee, prime rib, burgers, shakes and pie. Specialties of the house included venison, elk stew, and Rocky Mountain oysters. Near the end of the list was buffalo stroganoff.

"So, c'mon Maggie. What does Saratoga have that California doesn't? You can tell Jo."

"Jo, you know I'd confide in you in a heartbeat . . ."

"Ha!" Jo cackled. "Maggie, you always were a riot."

"You must be the only person on earth who thinks so. Seriously, Jo," Maggie continued, "I know what you're driving at, and no, I'm not here because I'm after Hale."

The waitress was a teenaged girl wearing abundant eye makeup skillfully applied. She greeted Jo and took their order while eyeing Maggie circumspectly.

"I think she's envious of your hairdo, Maggie," Jo cooed when the girl had walked away.

"Oh, this hair! I've got to let it grow out! I wish it would hurry and grow!"

"I like it. It's cute. Boyish. Makes you look like that other gorgeous Maggie on 'Northern Exposure.' "

"Right. Boyish. So women like it. Great."

Their coffee was set onto the table. "Look, Jo. I mean, I *am* here in one way because of Hale. I'm cleaning up an eyesore and getting rid of a pain of a neighbor, both of which drove him crazy. That's the one thing I know about his life at Paradise Ranch."

Jo looked into Maggie's eyes. "I don't mean to be blunt or anything, but, why should you care, after all these years?"

"Don't hate me, Jo. I counted on running into a lot of resentment for the way I left Hale. I'm sure the people here love him and figure I'm a flaming bitch."

"You've got me wrong, Maggie. I figure when a marriage

breaks up there was probably blame enough to go around. Things aren't always as they appear. Maybe Hale wasn't such a great husband. I don't know. I'm sure you had your reasons for leaving. What I mean is, why help out a man you don't even know anymore, after fourteen years of not lifting a finger?"

"Actually, Jo, let me set one thing straight. Hale was a damned good husband. He didn't deserve what I did to him. I might have explained that to a few souls here before I left, for his sake. There's a lot of things I should've done differently. That's one reason I'm here, to set a few of them right. But I didn't come back here angling for some ridiculous rekindled romance. Like I even believe in romance anymore."

"Maggie, Maggie. You sound like life has kicked you in the teeth."

"Well, don't feel too sorry for me either. I've had plenty of good relationships since I left Hale. It's just that I finally came to the conclusion that love is just a word, after all."

"You mean, as in something society made up? Like a social construct."

"For heaven's sake, Jo!" Maggie laughed. "Have you been taking a semiotics course at UW or something?"

"Ha! I just love throwing stuff like that out to prove we're not all a bunch of hicks up here," laughed Jo.

"Don't laugh. You know that's one of the reasons I left. I thought life here was so fucking provincial. I was sure I was missing out while the whole wide world rolled past. And I'm still not sure I'm ready to bury myself in the kind of obscurity you feel living in a state with less than half a million people in it . . . the only state in the union that loses population every year."

"Low blow, Maggie. Besides, we gained a few last year."

"It's the truth and you know it. The only thing I've heard about Wyoming in these fourteen years was the Matthew Shepard murder."

"Oh, Maggie. That's not fair! The vast majority of people in this state were appalled by that crime, and you know it. You can't label all the people of Wyoming a bunch of rednecks, you know. I hate it when outsiders do that. It's shallow and elitist. Besides, it's a crock. Just look how people around here have reacted to those ten wild horses someone shot to death on the BLM lands between Rock Springs and Rawlins. People are livid. And I don't mean just animal rights activists. I mean even people who think there are too many wild horses on grazing lands, like the ranchers and the BLM personnel. Though you wouldn't expect it of them, they've condemned the shootings right along with everyone else."

"Yeah, but were they as concerned about a gay man?"

"You just might be surprised."

Maggie sighed and looked out the window. "I know, Jo. I know you're right. I'm just not sure I can fit in any better now than I could when I left."

Their food came. The conversation lulled as they passed the salt back and forth and turned their attentions to the plates before them.

"You're right about one thing, though, Maggie," Jo said between bites.

"What's that?"

"People around here do think the world of Hale. And there were a lot of accusations against you after you left, especially when he fell off the deep end."

"Was it so bad for him, then?"

"It was pretty bad. He drank pretty heavily for awhile there and kind of let the ranch go all to hell. And a few unscrupulous women took advantage of the situation and moved in on him."

"I never knew," Maggie had stopped eating. She shook her head slowly. "I don't know if I want to know now."

"Well, it took him awhile, but he pulled himself back together. I think as soon he saw that Jill was old enough to really start noticing how things were with him, he cleaned up his act. By the third summer after you left, when Jill must have been about eight, he made some major changes in his life and has never looked back."

Maggie stirred the food around on her plate. "Never looked back? You think that's really the case? I wonder, Jo. If that's true, I envy him."

As they parted after lunch, Jo grabbed Maggie's arm, giving it a strong squeeze. "I feel so privileged to be the one to start the rumor about Maggie Everhardt being back!"

Yeah. Maggie the Cat is back!

Hey, Jane. I'm missing you tonight. You and a few million other Californians. And the soft air. And the ocean. And the elegance. Did I make another HUGE mistake, Janey? Please be a good friend and tell me I didn't. Go ahead, LIE. Gus misses you too, especially that black skirt you wear that he sheds all over. I'm going to let him outdoors starting tomorrow, but only during the days. Don't want some owl getting him, let alone a coyote or some kinda wildcat or other things that go BOO in the night. Kiss your husband for me. Tell me again, there are marriages that turn out, right?? You two, you really ARE happy? I've barely made a dent in things here, but I've got no choice but to plug on. Happy Trails. Mag

Five

A rhythmic clanging shattered the morning's calm. With a flip of a switch the roaring orange innards of the forge flamed to life like a heart in the body of the deluxe burgundy pickup's camper shell, pumping heat into air already unseasonably warm for late May. A horse sighed nervously, shifting his weight away from the farrier who lifted a front leg, pinioning the cannon bone between his own shins. A sizzling plume of smoke rose as the piece of red-hot iron pinched in the caliper's vise was pressed against the sole of the hoof, filling the air with gray stench. A bucket spewed and hissed as the shoe was dipped into water to cool, and with the tap-tapping of driven nails and the scrape of a rasp the song ceased with no fanfare but the stomping of the horse's feet.

"That's one down and seven to go," the farrier said to Hale. Glen's stout compact shape was as perfectly suited to shoeing as if he'd been genetically engineered for the job. A tree stump of a man, he wore a pair of heavy work boots ("I found out real quick you don't want steel-toed boots if you want to keep all your toes"), blue jeans wrapped in scarred leather chaps (a shoeing apron, to be precise) like chorizo in a tortilla, a long-sleeved shirt over a T-shirt, a copper bracelet on his wrist, a baseball cap that read COOP in red letters, and a carefully-coifed handlebar mustache. Clear blue eyes glittered in his ruddy face as he flashed a wide, perfect smile. "Dontcha just love this time of year?"

The dude string had to be readied for its fast-approaching debut, the first trail ride of the season. Hale released the horse into the paddock and led out the next in line.

"Hey, Lucky old buddy. Ready for a set of new high-heeled sneakers?" Glen asked, rubbing the horse's shoulder. He lifted a foot and picked out the sole, then pulled his hoof knife from the apron's thigh pocket.

It was a motley crew of horses. Several paints, a palomino, a leopard appaloosa, a liver chestnut, a gray, and a pair of bays. All were disgruntled about the end of their vacation, the hot weather, their itching shaggy shedding hides, and the feel of shoes again after months of going barefoot. The farrier felt every bit as disgruntled as the horses, and for many of the same reasons.

In his own way Glen Stoner was a renaissance man. He wrangled at Paradise Ranch, started green colts for everyone in the valley, shod horses for more than twenty clients, and sold real estate, and was equally ambitious in all of these endeavors. He was a popular character in the Saratoga area, especially with horse owners, and most especially with female horse owners, who often had designs on him.

Hale's only designs on Glen were in keeping him happy while he worked. He'd noticed the shoes always fit better when Glen was happy. Glen's company was a lot more palatable under those circumstances too, and since Glen refused to work on a tied horse (too dangerous), their companionship was not exactly voluntary. Blarney, gossip, and cowboy philosophy were Glen's repertoire.

"You know, Hale, western riding isn't all that different from English, in a lot of ways. I mean, we try to get the horse's hind end up under him and our goal is to get a horse to carry himself, just like they do. We just go about it in different ways."

Hale's feet were sodden from bringing the horses in across the creek. He needed to spend time with Rob discussing some kitchen equipment maintenance, and was in the midst of organizing gear for the season's fishing floats.

"I wouldn't know, Glen. All I've ever done is hop on well-broke horses for nothing more complicated than an easy trail ride."

"Oh hell, Hale. Don't be so damned modest. You're a good hand on a horse."

"Nah. Nope. Jilly is the rider in the family. Well, and Maggie was wonderful on a horse. That's where Jill must have picked it up. Not from me. I guess you didn't start working here until after Maggie left, though, so you never saw her ride, did you?"

Lucky took a half step forward, leaning heavily on Glen.

"Here, here! Back him up a little bit, could you Hale? He's gonna break my back."

"C'mon, Lucky." Hale clucked at him twice, pushing him backward a step. "His name was 'Papoose' when I got him, you know. Well, hey, that name had to go, so I changed it, and now he's not sure *who* the hell he is!"

"One thing for sure, he doesn't think he's lucky today," Glen joked.

I know just how he feels.

Maggie's cabin was transformed. She had scraped and painted all the trim a sage green, in the National Park Service style. The clapboard walls of the add-ons had been stripped and recovered with cedar shakes. Tufts of the scattered remains of mice nests connected by a network of miniature trails like freshly healed scars were the only lingering signs that the back yard had been knee deep in trash. And those telltale remains would blow away in the first windstorm.

Maggie had found a salvage company in Laramie willing to make the lengthy drive for a large load of scrap iron. And Hale had taken a few items that could be made useable—a harrow missing a few tines, an old disc. "When did Herb ever use a single implement on his place? What in the hell did he have any of this stuff for?" he grumbled. "Most of it is too rusted to ever be used again." The pieces of shredded plastic that had hung like ragged paper dolls from the wire fence had been cut down from their scaffolds. A strand of chili pepper lights shone round the outline of the kitchen window. A pale tan cat with large dark ears sat on the back stoop sunning himself and surveying his territory. He leapt off the porch and bounded toward the annex as Maggie stepped forth with a shovel in hand.

"Hey, Gussus Pussus. Come help me dig."

A stack of peat moss bales and cottonseed mulch had been pulled to the end of the tailgate of the used blue and white GMC 4x4 pickup she'd recently purchased. She pulled a peat bale onto the ground, stabbed it open with her spade, and shoveled the brown powder over the ground until the bale became light enough to lift. Then she picked it up and poured the remainder over the 20'x20' area she had demarcated for a garden, an area already devoid of grass from years of sunless burial beneath mounds of debris.

When she had spread all the mulch and peat, she dug into a large cone of steer manure dumped nearby, first carrying shovelful after shovelful, then standing and throwing it across the ground in big arcs. When she'd finished, a four-inch layer of mixed organic meringue covered the bare dirt.

"Now comes the hard part, Gus." The shovel did not slide easily into the soil. Though all frost had melted away, the ground was packed and rocky. When she jumped with all her weight onto the shovel, a single discouraging clod of dirt was unearthed. But once a hole had been punched, there was an exposed edge to work against, and digging came easier.

She double dug more than she should have, until her shoulders ached and a dull throb pulsed at the point of her hips from jumping onto the shovel. Maggie the Masochist. "It's time for a break, Gus," she said and began walking to the house, turning to see if he was following her. Gus was digging furiously, ears pinned against his head. When he stopped digging, he sat atop the hole, tail up. "Oh, Gus. Not in the garden! C'mere, you rascal." Picking him up before he had finished burying the hole, she carried him into the house. "I want to have things look perfect when Jill comes, you silly puss." She turned him upside down in her arms where he lay passively, purring and staring slightly cross-eyed into her face, one fang exposed beyond his jaw. "Only a mother could love a face like that."

Bad weather had prevented Jill's visits for several weeks, so Maggie was especially looking forward to her coming. She'd missed Jill's youthful energy and enthusiasm, the family connection, the love. Jill still bunked in her own room at her father's house, but spent long hours with Maggie, helping with the cabin's cleanup whenever she could. From her summers at the ranch, Jill was used to hard labor. She had grown tall and strong, long of limb, and could swing a pick like a man.

She helped her mother finish digging the garden that weekend. Working side by side and butt to butt, they took breaks to laugh and pant and lean on their shovels when lungs and legs begged for mercy.

"What are you going to do with so many vegetables,

anyway, Mom? You can't possibly eat four hundred square feet of veggies by yourself, you know."

"Now you tell me!" Maggie fussed, feigning ignorance. "Don't be a killjoy, Jilljoy." She wiped her brow and looked around the area they'd dug.

"Anyway, I have it all figured out. I'm going to sell or trade out fresh produce to a bunch of people. Rob wants fresh lettuce and spinach and peas. He wants some snow peas in particular to freeze for the Asian dishes he cooks in the winter. If the season is long enough, I'll have tomatoes. I've told the garden center to save me some large Early Girls. I love those tomatoes anyway, early or not. And besides, I'll be planting a part of this in flowers too," she said, sweeping her hand around, envisioning what would be.

Maggie picked up Gus, who had sauntered over for attention. "I was so amazed to find a garden center in Saratoga! A nice one, too."

"There are some advantages to having your tiny little town discovered by a group of millionaires," Jill reflected.

Maggie traded Gus for her shovel. "Besides, don't you think the Beef Palace could do better with their salads?"

They laughed and talked about trivial things as they worked when sufficient breath allowed. The digging finished, Maggie took Jill into the house to show her the collection of seeds she would be planting, then poured themselves coffee before walking back out to the garden to admire their work.

"You love this, don't you Mom?" Jill asked. "How you must have missed gardening all those years we lived in our Palo Alto apartment. And you didn't even have a houseplant!"

"Yeah, but I had plenty of other things I loved in Palo Alto, Jill. I mean, don't be feeling sorry about my life in

California, for heaven's sake. There were compensations there that are big heart pangs now that I'm here. I loved walking along the ocean at Half Moon Bay. I loved going with Jane to San Francisco to see what craziness the galleries were foisting on the public. I loved our drives through the wine country."

"Yeah, I miss the sourdough bread and the moist air and the Cypress trees and the great seafood," Jill agreed. "I miss Jane, too."

"Oh, Jilly," Maggie nearly wailed, "don't even mention Jane. I don't know what I'm going to do without her. I really don't know." She bent over to pick up a rock that had been unearthed and threw it beyond the fence. "How I miss the easy access to everything under the sun that I had in Palo Alto, especially the books I could get at the university, you know? We're a long way from anywhere here, don't you think, Jill?"

"That's one way of looking at it, Mom. We're either a long way from anywhere or we're right in the middle of being where it counts. One or the other."

"Or maybe both, huh?" Maggie turned her head to look as far as possible around her, then turned a full circle on one spot. "It is so empty here, and so big. So still, like it's silently watching us. Sometimes I feel blotted out."

"You're getting cabin fever, Mom."

Maggie laughed. "Oh, I get to town plenty. I go over to the lodge, too, when I feel too lonely. I can always lend a hand, if not my ear, to Rob, or go out and run Hale down somewhere on the place. He drops by here too, once a week or so, but he's starting into his busy season, so I imagine I'll see less and less of him in the next several months. We had been going in to town for dinner every once in awhile, you know, just to keep everyone guessing."

"Really. Reeeally. No, I didn't know. So are you two dating again, or what, Mom?"

"Don't be silly, Jill."

"Well, I mean, you are looking good these days, Mom. All this work you've been doing agrees with you. You're looking very fit."

"You talk like I'm a race horse or something."

"And your hair is growing out. It looks good, Mom." She ruffled the hair that had finally begun to lengthen down the back of Maggie's neck. "How come you haven't got any gray hair, Mom? I must've been the perfect child."

"Right, Jill. My life has been a plush pillow wafting on a spring breeze and you were just a little putto angel asleep on it." They laughed together at the ridiculous image. "Wrong gender, though, Mom," Jill couldn't resist pointing out.

"I have an idea, Mom. You come see me in Boulder. You'll cure your cabin fever, kick up your heels, we'll have some cappuccino, and I'll take you to the CU library. I've got a card there, and if you want to borrow some books, I'll check them out for you. You can even help me choose a roommate. I've been advertising and have had a ton of responses."

"Gee, Jill. Hmmm. I just might take you up on that." She smiled thinking of it. "There's Gus to take care of. But Rob told me he'd be happy to spend the night at my place babysitting if I ever wanted to take off for a few days. It turns out he's a cat lover. He takes all the dinner leftovers and gives them to the barn cats."

Hey, Janey! I'm happy you think I'm sounding healthier these days. Certainly, my living quarters have improved. My view is now a garden plot laid out in neat rows with colored seed packets optimistically waving above the dormant rows, like flags at a track meet starting line before the events. Even Gus is looking sleek and glossy these days (good mousing here). I'm getting to know Hale again, if slowly. Very slowly. Okay, a snail's pace. The fact is we've had no consequential conversations to date. E-mail me some of your nerve. Take care. Will you ever come see me? Love, Mag

A silver BMW merged into the midday Friday south-bound traffic of U.S. Highway 287 out of Laramie, heading past Tie Siding's giant yellow fireworks billboards, up over an open grassy hill wearing its customary small herd of antelope. Tall Ponderosa pines at Virginia Dale reflected in psychedelic green waves in the gleaming side panels as the Beamer swept past the old stage stop. Huge boulders loomed over the roadway, concealing the new Benedictine abbey. Ship Rock still laid anchor just off the starboard side as the car swept past Owl Canyon, then past a giant rock splatted in a solitary heap onto the grassy valley between the cliffs in some unfathomably distant past, now made postmodern by garish ever changing graffiti: "Go Rams" in green and gold, "Cowboys" in silver and blue, "Amy, will you go to the prom with me, check one: Yes. No." The silver bullet sailed along the asphalt strand, paralleling the northernmost piñon grove in the continent, past the Forks Café at the Livermore turnoff and Ted's Place at the Poudre Canyon turnoff, whipping over the highway as if the globe were rotating beneath it like a flipping Rolodex. It detoured around the traffic of the front range cities of Fort Collins, Loveland and Longmont, climbing to Horsetooth Reservoir, then heading through the beautiful Masonville valley with its stone quarries, cherry orchards, and llama ranches; paralleling a stony Stegosaurus, the jagged ridge called The Devils' Backbone, traveled along the red rim rocks east of Carter Lake, through the tiny village with the peculiar name of Hygiene, veered west on St. Vrain toward the foothills, and south to the slanted Flatirons of Boulder.

Slowing its pace through the city, it stopped impatiently at the lights of the Pearl Street Mall, then wound up the hill of Arapaho Street, climbing the tree-lined lane westward, finally coming to rest in front of a small Victorian house facing south through a tiny flowered yard, where Jill's smiling face appeared through a lace curtain in the window.

Jill came out to the BMW and swung open its door. "So you finally get to see the place! Come on in. I've got some coffee on for you. How was the drive down?"

"Bbbrrrrer" purred the Beamer as it dieseled before dying. "I swear, Mom, that car of yours seems almost human sometimes."

As Jill showed Maggie into the house a clatter stomped down the stairs heralded by a shout, "Hey, Jill! Have you seen my helmet?" Clad in nothing but a pair of shorts, an earring, and a tattoo, a male figure nearly ran into Maggie, falling back onto the stairs to avoid collision.

"What a wonderful entrance, Ryan. Great timing, too," Jill said sarcastically. *A chip off the old cat.* "Meet my new roommate, Mom. Ryan Kilkelly, this is my mother, Maggie Everhardt."

Ryan stood up, brushed his right hand on the back of his shorts and extended it to Maggie. "Wow! So you're Jill's mother. Wow!" His short hair was vertical and very yellow, contrasting with two days' dark stubble on his pointed chin. Gray eyes grinned sheepishly from dark brows.

"He may not be Mr. Articulate, but he's a great roommate," Jill blurted when Maggie raised her eyebrows after

Ryan and his helmet had departed through the door with a bang. "For one thing, he's almost never here, so I basically still have the whole place to myself. Don't look at me like that, Mom."

"I just hadn't pictured your roommate as quite so . . . *male,* Jill."

"Oh, Mom. C'mon, join the twenty-first century, already. It's great having a male roommate. He doesn't want to use my razor or wear my clothes. At least, I don't *think* he wants to wear my clothes . . . I mean, we *are* about the same size . . . Just kidding, Mom! He can fix the toilet when it won't stop running. And, I have to say, I feel safer with a man here. Boulder has had a few freaky things happening in the last couple of years, after all."

"It's all right, Jill. You don't have to explain to me. I mean, you're an adult with excellent judgment. I'm sure you know what you're doing. I love your yard, by the way . . ."

They lunched at The Healthy Harvest Café, sitting outdoors to watch the passing parade. The view through rows of street trees to the west ran abruptly into sea blue foothills. Cool mountain air tempered the sun's warmth. Maggie surrendered to a luxurious sense of well-being as they dined, gazing around her at the bustle that had been such a part of her west coast life. When they had finished, they drove through dense traffic to the red stone buildings of the university where Jill guided Maggie through the campus arm in arm.

Jill sat down at a computer in the library while Maggie browsed the stacks. She found fiction in the remotest wing of the basement. *It's a university library, after all, not a public library.* She was currently reading contemporary works by authors from developing nations, a system she had come to accidentally when she fell in love with a Jamaican novel, stumbling across it in a travel magazine review, then seduced by its spiciness. Now she was hooked. She pulled paperbacks from the stacks in order to cut to the chase for most recent publications and also for a foolish, pragmatic reason she abashedly conceded to—she wanted a whole stack of reading material, and the paperbacks were lightweight. Many of the newest paperbacks were by female authors. *Affirmative action?* That was fine with Maggie. *It's about time.*

She might as well have thrown darts as use this system, but it had worked; it had led her to wonderful works by Samoan, Australian, Indian, and African authors who made her dream of exotic places. With her lack of boundaries, she felt like she'd actually walked through the authors' terrains, lived in their times and inhabited their skins. Pulling bright colors from shelves, Maggie read jackets or a few paragraphs of text, and slipped them back in place. A shallow pile of books grew slowly in the crook of her arm. In the end, she chose six new novels that seemed promising, then returned to the computer where Jill still sat clicking away. Her daughter looked up and smiled. "Find what you wanted?" She brought the computer back to its home page, then checked out the books Maggie handed her. Maggie collected them and hugged them against her body as they walked to the car.

Jill drove east. "Now I'm going to take you to the quintessential Boulderite happening, Mom."

"So, just where are you taking me?"

"You'll see."

They traversed the city in a stutter of stoplight unsynchronicity. *Hurry and wait,* Maggie thought. *A person could die from waiting. And, of course, we all do.* "I think

Beamer feels more at home here, Jill."

"You mean, *you* feel more at home here, right Mom? Don't be in denial, now."

"I wouldn't deny it for an instant, Jill. Why would you think I'm the 'in denial' type, anyway? No, really, I'm curious. I'm as up front as the next person, aren't I? I freely admit, for example, that I miss the stimulation of a wonderful town like this. I miss it terribly, as a matter of fact. I miss architecture; I miss the prosperity, though I hate to admit it, liberal that I am; but it's true, I feel low if I'm not around prosperity. Without it, the meanness really gets to me. But here, it's like I feel I'm among other believers. Kindred spirits. I miss this kind of variety in people, their clothing, their cars, their hairdos—yes, even Ryan's—their hobbies, their houses, their gardens. God! I miss their quirky genius. I really do. I wish you hadn't even brought it up, Jill."

"And yet, Mom, I will tell you something. You're blossoming at Paradise Ranch. You've gained some weight, which you really needed to do. You seem stronger, healthier, more assured and positive than I've ever seen you. More assertive."

"Assertive? When have I been lacking in 'assertive'? What about the fact that I was quite successful in my job in Palo Alto? They loved me there. They still miss me, so I've been told. How about the fact that I created a life for you and me on my own? That I bought and paid for an apartment that appreciated ten times over in a decade. I learned Tae Kwon Do, for Chrissake." *Howl!*

"I agree, Mom. You did great. I recognize all of that. But you were never good to yourself, Mom. You always put everyone else first and yourself last. You did everything you had to and nothing you loved to do. Your job . . . you brought it up . . . it's a perfect example. You had big plans for your degree in journalism, but you became a technical writer so you could earn good money. I know, I know, don't have a conniption over there. I can see your expression, Mom, you know, out of the corner of my eye. I have excellent peripheral vision, you know; I probably got it from you. What I'm saying is, I understand that you had to do it partly for my sake, but squandering your creativity on subjects you cared absolutely nothing about couldn't have been the road you wanted to take. It seems to me that, for the first time in your life, you're doing something that is your choice and seems to be good for you. And, believe me, from what I understood, I would never have guessed in a million years that the ranch would be good for you."

She looked over at the side of Maggie's face and grinned wolfishly. "And you were never that good at Tae Kwon Do, you know."

The thread of their discourse snapped as they reached Valmont and 28th and pulled into the parking lot of Wholesome Foods. When Jill opened the door to the store, they stepped onto a magic-carpeted entry that led into an Epicurean never-never land. Maggie stood to look in awe but was swept along in a school of shoppers to the spacious gleaming deli bar, where smooth young men in white aprons slapped huge slabs of crusty bread over fist-sized portabella mushrooms and six choices of cheese. Vegetarian dishes prevailed, prepared with the flavors of thirty different international cuisines. Countless flavors of espresso and cappuccino flowed in rivulets from glowing canisters. Macaroni, potato, mixed green, tofu, vegetable, fruit, and chicken salads beckoned healthily from wide gleaming bowls. Maggie dared not walk through the galorious calorious dessert section. Beyond the delicatessen lay a sea of kitchen paraphernalia and health foods for sale, the endless waves of which tossed with the motion of swarms of people looking, handling, roving, talking, comparing—shopping! There were six checkout counters for the delicatessen alone, trailing long lines of antsy customers. The whole place revolved in busyness, reveled in exotica, radiated political correctness, and reeked of hipness and health; the spending a paroxysm of prolific profligacy and profit. Maggie jostled about in the pandemonium, overwhelmed and slightly rattled by the frenzied excess after the quiet sparseness of her Wyoming world. As she and Jill wandered through this health food epicenter, she had a funny feeling of slight alienation, as if she were a detached, involuntary voyeur made to witness through accidental circumstances a minor obscenity. She was in wonderment by the time they left, departing the same way they had come, but swimming now against the onrushing flow.

"Whew!" she said, settling back into the car seat. "Wow, Jill, whew! So that's Boulder! I'm dazzled!" Maggie the Perky, the Utterly Cheery.

Jill gave Maggie a sly glance. "Yea, I find it kind of appallingly perfect in its slick utopian smugness too, Mom."

The Beamer bore them back to earth. In the quiet of its sequestered pod, they eased into intimacy. Maggie turned to look at Jill. Choosing her words carefully, she asked gingerly, treading ever so lightly, "So Jill. I'm curious. I understand that coed roommates are common in the current era. But, could I be so bold as to ask, what does one do about sexual temptation when cohabiting with a really cute guy like Ryan? That is, if and when one is trying to keep the relationship platonic or businesslike, or whatever?"

Jill laughed. "I'm surprised you have to ask, Mom. I haven't noticed either you or Dad having much trouble with abstinence all these long years, at least so far as I can tell."

"I *could* say that's none of your business, Jill, but I'd be a terrible hypocrite considering the question I just asked you," she laughed easily at herself.

"I'll tell you how we manage, Mom. We just act like an old married couple, you know. I leave hair in the bathroom sink, he leaves the toilet seat up, we argue over what to watch on TV, he walks around rumpled and unshaven, stuff like that, and lo and behold, just like an old married couple, who wants sex?"

"I'm sorry I asked."

"No problem, Mom."

The next morning a silver Beamer streamed north on I-25, past Johnson's Corner's old-fashioned truck stop, beyond the gesturing dinosaur assemblages of a Timnath farmer, crossing the St. Vrain, the Big Thompson, and the Cache La Poudre rivers, straddling the Wyo-Colo state line, turning left at Cheyenne, that capitol city held in the open palms of the plains, climbing the ridges to the goblin hoodoos of Vedavoo and the pristine piney forest and wildflowers of Happy Jack, dropping like a stone down the slope into Laramie. It turned onto Snowy Range Road, traveling the ironic line between abandoned MX missile silos on one side and the Oregon Trail on the other, climbing through the hillside hamlet of Centennial at the base of the Medicine Bow Mountains with its phony, permanently-stationary, black and white junker police car, skirting the user-friendly ski area, breezing along the quartzite mountains of the Snowy Range rising like the Cheops pyramid behind icy aqua glacial ponds, cresting the ten thousand foot pass, sliding down the western slope of the Medicine Bows towards the Saratoga valley until it finally pulled into a hidden drive where stood a square-logged cabin with sage green windows ringed with chili pepper lights illuminating a Siamese cat who sat on the window sill, waiting and waiting . . .

Dear J, It was painful leaving the lively streets of Boulder. I felt a million miles and a thousand years from civilization by the time I reached Saratoga. How can a canary like me live among these two thousand rugged mavericks? Then while I watched the moon rise from my window, I could hear a Great Horned owl that's been calling outside my cabin night after night. A light came on and went off in the Lodge over at Paradise Ranch and I heard a horse whinny from far off. All at once I thought, "mine!" and I stopped cowering.

What does it all mean, Janey, my friend? Love, Mag

Six

Hi Maggie, it's Hale. How are you? If you can tear yourself away from that garden of yours, come over to the lodge for a few minutes. I'll give you a piece of the rhubarb pie Rob just pulled from the oven . . . Yeah, I knew that would get your attention. Thank God we're back to home cooking. He's speaking normal English again at last. Well, sort of, anyway . . . Yeah. I think you're right, that Russian accent for the Chicken Kiev was the worst yet. I hate it when he calls me 'bossinski.' Oh, and, hey! I think I've found a good carpenter for you . . . Yeah. I'll tell you all about him when you come over. Okay, see you in a few minutes.

Hale looked critically into the bathroom mirror, combing his fingers through his hair. His was the kind that would be a wavy silver mane in old age, but for now he kept it short and combed straight up. He ran a razor over his chin, though he had shaved five hours earlier, and swallowed a swig of mouthwash.

When Maggie walked into the lodge there was a piece of pie on a table in the dining room. Behind the plate, a large vase of red iris and purple lilac blooms filled the room with color and scent. Centered in the pie wedge burned a single candle. Triggered by her entrance, a plinking strumming of a ukulele began in the kitchen, an entrance cue for Rob and Hale singing "Happy Birthday," Rob ending with a jazzy little flourish of corny chords while Hale cracked up at his brash exhibitionism.

"You sneaky angels," she laughed, intentionally flubbing the phrase. They looked so ridiculously pleased with themselves. "I don't deserve this. Really I don't." Hale pulled a chair out for her, "Nobody deserves this," waved her into it, and sat down across from her to watch her eat the pie, while Rob retreated to the kitchen. "Mmmm. This is fantastic!" she called out for Rob to hear as she took her first bite. "Aren't either of you going to have any with me?" she asked Hale.

"Sorry. I've already nearly foundered on the stuff, and *Rob's watching his weight!*"

"I heard that!" came from out of sight.

When she had finished her pie, Hale led her to the barn under some pretext. There, waiting in his stall, stood Limbo, his coat gleaming, hooves oiled, mane braided, and sporting an English jumping saddle and a snaffle bridle. It was a sight from Lexington or Madison Garden, not Paradise Ranch. "What in the world is all this? Did you do all of this, Hale?" She gave a little shouting laugh at something that she hadn't considered. "Oh, come on, now. Don't tell me you braided his mane yourself?"

Hale laughed at her disbelief. "Well, *sure* I did, Maggie. See, you just . . ." He took a braid in his fingers. "Okay, busted. Nope, I had a friend's daughter do it this morning."

"Oh, Hale, he looks beautiful! Where did you get this saddle?"

"I figured the place could use some diversity. Actually, it was too good a deal to pass up. The braider just recently talked her mom into a fancier brand."

"Oh, I get it." She opened the stall door and walked up to the horse to stroke his neck. As she reached toward him, Limbo arched his neck, curling his head backward prettily to sniff her hand. *Just who are you?* "Limbo, what an upscale yuppie you are! Oh, Hale, he's beautiful! His coat is gleaming! And look at his color! He looks like he's made of chocolate, or maybe licorice." Then she had to laugh at her own words. "Listen to me! I guess I must think he looks good enough to eat."

Hale launched into a spiel that spun off his tongue as if memorized. "Look, Maggie. I wanted you to see him like this because I've got something to ask you . . . a proposition, I guess. I thought you could do me a real favor, kind of a reverse birthday present. Limbo here is just too much horse for the guests. They're not able to sit his big gaits and he can't tolerate amateurs either. But if I take him out of the guest string, I can't ride often enough to keep him in shape. So I thought you might be willing to start riding again to help me out with Limbo. I'm sure he'd thank you for it. He's smart, believe me, and needs a challenge, not to mention the attention. So, what do you think?"

"Oh, Hale. It's a wonderful thought." Imagining it put a shine into her eyes, but reality snuffed it out. "But you know I haven't touched a horse in a decade, Hale."

"I know, Maggie. I know all that. But you were awfully good once upon a time. C'mon, hop on for a few minutes and see what you think of him. C'mon. What can it hurt?"

She rolled her eyes at that remark.

"Okay, so that was the wrong thing to say. I think you should try it, though. I really do Mags."

That was the right thing to say. He hadn't called her that name since the early years of their marriage, and it pulled at her powerfully. She began to waver. "I don't know, Hale. I'm just wearing blue jeans and loafers."

"Here, I also just happen to have a pair of boots that ought to fit you . . ." He stepped out of the stall and produced some boots from behind a grain barrel, magically, like a white rabbit from a hat.

"Oh, come on! Are you telling me you've still got my old boots?"

"I know, I know, it's a little crazy. But I found these after you took off, and hung on to them for Jilly. When she outgrew them, I just never got around to throwing them out." The boots were polished and soft, like they'd been oiled regularly, the insides stuffed with newspaper so they wouldn't collapse. Maggie hesitated, then reached for them.

Pulling and stomping, boots on, she stepped up to the big horse. "You need a leg up?" he asked.

"I guess I'll have to. He's too tall, and I'm too out of practice." It was awkward, her needing this kind of help. It placed them beyond their comfort zone with each other. There was so much need for caution still between them that even the slightest intimacy seemed all wrong. Tentatively they circled each other, as if they had never danced before. So much had to be avoided; it was like trying to embrace without touching, this dance of theirs.

She gathered the reins in her left hand and faced the horse, bending her left leg at the knee. When Hale wrapped his right hand around her thin ankle, sliding it along the boot midway up her shin, she was acutely conscious that it was the first time he had touched her since her return. She remembered he used to like to run his hand down the smooth contours of her legs.

"Are you ready?" he asked. She nodded. "On three, then. One, two, . . ." He lifted as she sprang off the ground with her right foot. She was aloft effortlessly and settled lightly into the seat of the saddle.

"I can't tell what that look on your face means, Maggie."

Her face had reddened and she seemed flustered. "Nothing, Hale. It's nothing. It's just . . . oh, I don't know . . . it's nothing, really," she said evasively, avoiding his eyes.

The pleasure in Hale's face was the best part of this

birthday gift. "Well, why don't you take him out for a spin? I rode him pretty hard yesterday so he wouldn't be feeling too cocky today for you."

She turned and rode into the hay meadow as Hale followed on foot. The sway of his walk felt as familiar as her own. Her weight relaxed down into the stirrups, settling, sinking, sliding her back to a time of hazy happiness, like the dreams she used to force into her mind to escape the pain of the dentist chair, dreams of galloping bareback across endless plowed fields, galloping and galloping on a horse she loved, a big horse with a sense of humor and sturdy legs with white sox full of black holes.

"Don't expect too much from him. He's never been ridden English before," Hale called ahead to her as Limbo's big stride put distance between them.

Maggie rode the meadow in a large oval, swaying with his swinging walk, bending Limbo's neck gently left and right a few times in big arcs as gently as a bird preening its wings. He stood quietly, patiently, with bowed head as she stopped to shorten the stirrups a few holes, just champing the bit gently as she leaned to pat his neck when she finished. She asked him to step into a trot, then urged him forward out of his customary western shuffle with a thrust of her own trunk and a thump in his ribs. Limbo flicked his ears her way, then stepped out big and free, happy to follow his natural inclination for a change. They flew around an imaginary ring with bounding strides, flowing together on a course through the swishing grass. Then she pushed one hip forward and felt the three beat waltz of the canter lifting them like a rocking chair, traveling through space like a flying carpet, until she asked him to slow down, whoa, good boy, pat, pat, what a good boy, whoa, down, down, down to the trot, trot, trot, to the walk, walk, gooood boy, and a halt right in front of Hale. Breath came out of her with a shout, and joy with a radiant smile.

Ah, Maggie, don't smile that smile in my direction. It makes my heart hurt. "You looked great out there, Maggie. You looked like you'd never missed a day. You looked like champs . . . both of you."

"Oh, Hale! I'm so rusty!" she gulped breathlessly. "But even so, I can tell he's a natural for dressage, and I'll bet he can jump too. He wants to go!"

"That's just what I've always thought about him. I've seen him jump on his own, Maggie. And I don't think I've ever seen another horse do that, but I swear I've seen him jump on his own just for fun."

She stroked his neck, bending forward to look into his eye. "What's his breeding, Hale? He certainly isn't the typical Quarter Horse ranch horse." She dropped the stirrups from her feet and, swinging her right leg over his back, hopped to the ground with a dancer's grace.

He moved as if to catch her, but retreated a step instead. *Oh, how we used to meld and blend together.* "We don't have a clue, Maggie." *Stick to the subject. Just the facts, and nothing but the facts.* "He's a BLM horse, believe it or not, that Glen picked up as a four-year-old. Yeah, you know, the wild horses the Bureau of Land Management rounds up off federal land so the herds don't overgraze it. The prisoners at Canyon City start them, then they auction them off. Well, Glen bought a few for our dude string. That's where his name comes from. We called him 'Limbo Land' because he was from some rough god-awful scrub desert. A tough rangy leggy four-year-old when we got him, barely broke. A wily desert rat he was. So, I guess he's a mustang, well, a wild horse, technically. We think he's got some draft in him because he's so big and bulky, and, from the looks of his head and neck, we think he must be part Thoroughbred too." Hale chuckled. "Let's face it, he's a Heinz 57. We call him our American tepid blood."

"Well, you're a blue blood at heart, that's what you are, you old Limbo," she said, hugging his big head. " 'Limbo Land,' " she whispered into his ear. Never knowing she'd missed a pressing dance cue. The rhythm, the timing, still all wrong.

Hale led him to the barn where he pulled off the tack, while Maggie gave Limbo handfuls of grain. "You were a good boy today, Limbo," Hale praised, brushing the saddle marks from Limbo's back. "And don't you worry about looking prissy, Bud. Jenny will be coming back in awhile to pull those braids out." Focusing on the horse.

As the last gulp of grain disappeared from her hand, Maggie said, "I can see I'll have to plant an extra row of carrots in my garden." Avoiding Hale's nearness.

They turned Limbo out with his buddies, where he looked quite elite in his braids. "So, what do you think, Maggie? Will you ride him and make something out of him for me?"

The inevitability of her answer made them both smile. "You always did know just what to get me for my birthday, Hale."

As they walked to the lodge Maggie dusted off her seat and shirt front with her hands, leaving one hand across her chest where she could feel her heart beating. She looked at Hale happily, then broke into a little exhilarated laugh, like a schoolgirl.

Hale brushed some hay from her short hair, gone wild from the ride. *Another touch,* she thought. "Happy birthday, Maggie," he said. "Happy birthday." One step closer in their dance. One moment of grace.

Then he suddenly remembered, "Oh, I almost forgot! I wasn't lying just to get you over here, you know. I really did locate a carpenter for you."

"Another birthday surprise? You can't do wrong today, as far as I can see," she grinned. *Don't flirt!* "So, who'd you find?"

"Well, he's an interesting young guy who lives over in Baggs. I'm not going to tell you too much about him. I'll let you find out for yourself. But I will tell you that I heard his work is top quality. I've got his number for you up at the lodge."

When she left, she was still astride, riding on the sweet fragrance of lilacs and iris that filled the cab of her pickup.

The carpenter pulled in punctually the next morning and extended a hand before she had the door all the way open. "Hello, Mrs. Everhardt, I'm David Heerman."

His hands were long and thin. *A pianist's hands, not a carpenter's,* she thought. Tall, but so thin that he did not look strong, except for a pair of extremely square shoulders. He gave an impression of luminosity. His eyes were pale, watery, and red-rimmed, surrounded by blond lashes. He was a sketch of a man, a pale watercolor wash. All blond. His eyebrows and hair were white blond, as was his skin, with blue veins showing through its transparency and pale freckles splattered his arms.

She asked him in and offered him coffee, but he declined politely. Every move he made and word he spoke was gently polite. As she showed him through the cabin, he walked up to the wall to examine the square-cut logs. "It's beautifully built, isn't it?"

"Yes, it is, isn't it? I wouldn't dream of harming any of the original work. It would be a crime," she said almost reverently. "But," her tone became brisker, businesslike, "I want to add a deck in the back, I don't think that would hurt, and I'd like to put double French doors into the south wall of the kitchen, since that's not part of the original structure anyway. I want to open it up to the light and the view—you know, let the mountains in, and some sky too." Maggie led David through the cabin, explaining all of her ideas. "So, what do you think? I'm not asking the impossible, am I? I'm not going to do anything I'll regret, do you think?"

"No, no. It sounds good to me. Your ideas sound fine. They seem sound enough. I think it's going to be fine. A pleasure, really. It's a beautiful old cabin. You can see a real craftsman built it. I'll have to tread lightly in his footsteps, won't I?" He took a pad from the back pocket of his jeans and a pencil from his shirt. Lifting the brim of his baseball cap exposed his pale eyes to too much sun, causing him to squint. "I'll need to make up a list of materials, then I can get a bid to you."

Maggie was much pleased with this carpenter, Heerman. "I'm glad you're going to do it for me. I can tell you've got the right spirit for the place."

He finished scribbling and looked up. "I'm working on one of the big houses up on Old Baldy, but I'm nearly finished, so I could start here in about three weeks, if that will be all right."

"That would be great," she said, excited. "That's sooner than I'd hoped for." She walked him to his battered truck and camper rig, repressing an urge to skip a step or two.

"I hear you're from back east," she said as he slid onto the seat, wanting to make casual conversation now that their business was concluded.

"Oh," he raised invisible eyebrows, "then I guess you heard that I'm Amish."

101

She laughed. "It's an awfully small town."

"Well, I like to make a little disclaimer before I do the work. Contrary to popular belief, not all Amish men are carpenters."

Maggie smiled. "And I want you to know that I didn't call you because of that rusty stereotype. I called you because I got the word that you do quality work."

David's smile was wider than his narrow mouth should have allowed. He started the truck. "Well, I just happen to be an Amish man who is a carpenter."

Crimson snapdragons trembled and tall cerise cosmos waved slightly. A brilliant green and black grasshopper clasped a dahlia stem with clawed feet, ejecting and swallowing brown bubbles of tobacco juice through the pincers of its mouth. It stopped chewing and drew a leg along the length of one antenna, bending it forward, then froze into stillness. The dahlia stem swayed, then emptied just as Gus leaped, the two creatures dancing the point and counterpoint of the deadly tango of predator and prey on the stage of Maggie's garden.

Lush growth sprawled across the soil, straining at the sun, as if magic had awakened the refuse pile from a wicked spell, bringing it alive to sprout, enchanted, bursting forth with latent energy stored through long dormancy into a beauty that had always lain hidden beneath twisted rusting metal skins.

A circular table saw stood between the garden and annex beside a neat stack of lumber. David moved between them, preparing to cut lengths of two-by-sixes for the deck. He labored silently and steadily, comfortable in his work. As the saw whirred alive, he slid a board into the blade. The wood squealed a scream that sent Gus, goosed and wild-eyed, sprinting from the ferny cosmos to the back door. As

Maggie opened the door, a blur of Gus leapt across the sill and disappeared into the house.

David flipped the switch on the saw, and the blade spun to a halt. "Did you see that?" she laughed.

"Nope, it was too fast. You can't blame him. It's a terrible racket."

"I came out to see if you'd like some coffee," she said. She stood with one hand on her hip and the other shading her eyes. Her short dark hair fell across the hand on her forehead in ragged lengths, shining in the sun.

"That's good of you, Ms. Everhardt, but if I take a cup, I'll just set it down while I work and it'll get cold and go to waste."

"Okay, then. I just wanted to offer. But I wish you'd call me Maggie."

David appeared ever so politely not to have heard her suggestion. "I've got a thermos in the truck anyway, you know. I like to be pretty self-sufficient."

"I can see that. You're a one-man industry, fully equipped." She admired the impressive array of equipment; impressive to her, at any rate. It all looked very large, heavy, shiny, silver, and tremendously efficient to her. But she was a Luddite and readily acknowledged it, reveled in it, in fact. So she couldn't resist saying to him, "But I have to give you a hard time, you know."

"How's that?"

"I thought the Amish didn't use electricity."

"Ah, well . . . now you've touched onto one of the reasons I'm not living in the Amish community anymore." He worked steadily as he talked to her, carrying the cut lumber to the deck frame he had constructed the day before.

"What, then? It was too hard living without modern conveniences?"

"No, that's not exactly what I meant. No, it wasn't hardship. It was more that the reason for not living modern becomes blurred the older you become. You don't question it as a child, like you don't question the Bible. But I worked in our dairy. All the haying was done with horses rather than machines. Yet we used modern machinery to pasteurize the milk, otherwise we couldn't have sold it. 'So why not use the machinery for haying?' I began to question. 'What's the point of compromising?' We all sold goods to the outside community. It just began to seem too much compromise to me. How much compromise was acceptable? If you start questioning and doubting, if your thinking starts to diverge from the others too much, one day you'll decide to try life outside the Old Order, with the English."

"So, how many of us 'English' have told you they dream of a simpler life, a life like the Amish?" She was thinking of her own situation as she asked.

He chuckled wryly. "I hear that from time to time. But I think there are plenty more of us coming out than there are English giving up their modern lives and coming into the Old Order. I sometimes wonder if the Amish will still be a separate community in a hundred years." He began attaching the planks to the frame with a power screwdriver, then paused to look up at her. "Then again, maybe they'll outlast everyone else. You know, I still feel the Amish community tugging at me. I feel it all the time."

He stood up for a moment, stretching, looking around himself. "Your garden is truly thriving out here all alone in this wilderness, isn't it?" he observed, then resumed his work. Maggie walked back to the house and opened the door. A beautiful strain of Chopin came from the cabin. He raised his head and listened raptly.

"Besides," he called to her, "I couldn't stand the hymn singing."

Maggie rode Limbo every other day. Every day would have made a chore of something she loved. Every day might have caused resentment in what Limbo offered so freely. So she rode every other day. In the beginning, she broke from the trot to the walk every five minutes, gasping and stretching cramps from her legs. Five minutes was the limit her body could stand. She walked Limbo until she recovered her breath, then tried again. Limbo was building muscle too, so their endurance and abilities developed together. Backaches from one ride lasted into the next. Limbo's leaning against the unaccustomed bridle contact, his search for a new balance, made her arms too sore at times to pull a shirt on over her head. Maggie the Masochist.

She carried some discarded fence posts out to the periphery of the hay meadow to use as *cavaletti*, to teach him to heighten his stride, to make Limbo float. Then she stacked the posts into low clumsy jumps. One morning when she rode out to the field her clumsy jumps had been replaced by two pairs of painted white jump standards, complete with cross poles set into low exes, and some big peeled logs. As if by magic, the meadow was a jumping course fit for a real rider and a horse with possibilities. Delighted, she walked Limbo up, with many reassuring pets, to look at each new obstacle. "These are the real thing," she told him. Limbo, being a wise horse, was suspicious of anything new, anything that might jump out and bite, that might have tooth or claw hidden beneath an ordinary exterior. Anything could be a guise, a decoy for something quite malign. Horse wisdom couldn't be faulted there. So he must snort and shy around the new jumps. She understood horse wisdom, so was patient with him, walking him over each frightening thing time and again until he saw that they were indeed the ordinary things they pretended to be. He lost faith and didn't trust them again when she tried them at the trot, a trot making all things different than the walk. If you go faster, everything is changed, after all. So Limbo looked bad. If anyone had been watching, they'd have shook their head. "He's bad," they'd have thought. "Stubborn, spoiled, maybe not too bright." But they weren't seeing things from his viewpoint and Maggie was. *Keep both legs on and funnel him straight ahead through your legs and hands,* she thought. "Be brave," she told him.

For her part, Maggie concentrated on looking up and ahead rather than down at the jumps, looking into the distance beyond the fence to convince him that they were indeed going there, beyond the fence, and Limbo, mustering all his considerable courage, if things could just be brought into perspective, responded by hopping awkwardly and crookedly over the cross pole, but over-jumping by a mile. "Whooeee," she yelped and slapped a big pat against his neck for his boldness. He began to feel some pride then. He knew he could negotiate the jumps easily and confidently. They rode the circuit back and forth in a big open canter and the jumps were nothing but another stride, nothing but a porpoise leap for fun, a little height gained to see higher, to make the horizon lower, to see it all from a different point of view. They joyfully hand galloped around the meadow to celebrate, and the metronome of his hooves matched the bellows of his breathing and the thumping of her heart, all keeping time in unison.

"He's as slick as a seal," Hale said, afterwards, full of admiration, strolling into the barn where she was rinsing the sweat and foam from Limbo.

"He is looking wonderful, isn't he?"

"The best. It's the best by far that he's ever looked. Who'd have thought a rank old desert snake like Limbo could look like a centaur. But just look at the muscles he's started putting on, especially over the top of his back." He ran his hand over Limbo's top line. "And look at the expression in his eye." He turned to Maggie and smiled. "It's good for you, too, in my opinion."

Maggie was abashed and let the compliment slide. "I don't know how I can thank you enough, Hale, for letting me ride him. And the jumps you made for me! I couldn't believe it when I saw them out there so new and shiny, gleaming in that field. It was so fine that you did that for me. No one can know how much it's added to my life to ride like this again. It's made it sterling again. And he's a wonderful horse!" she said, and pat Limbo's neck to tell him too. "I'll tell you what. If he's the horse I think he is, if he's *half* the horse *he* thinks he is," she laughed, "especially with the dressage, I may try to take him up to the three-day event in Worland next summer. There's a special, grand, new cross-country course up there that's a work of art. I mean, literally. I read about it in a magazine. A young horsewoman who's also an art teacher up there built a cross-country course that's an earth-site art collaborative. It involved the whole community. They all chipped in with money, time, materials, or talent. Isn't that a dynamite story? It sounds too good to be true, but it happened all because of this person's vision. And someone with that kind of vision . . . can't you just imagine how a community must feel about a young person like that? What she must have brought to that community? Especially a small town like Worland, way up north where it's such a test of your resolve just to live there, you know, just to even make it, through those winters. If Limbo thinks he's ready, I'm going to try entering him up there next summer at training level. Maybe Jill would want to come along and groom for me. Or maybe Jenny, the girl who braided him . . ." Maggie rambled on excitedly while she scraped the excess water from a grateful Limbo. When she finished, she gave him three extra carrots before turning him out.

"Speaking of Jill," Hale said, stowing the saddle, "she phoned to ask if she could bring her roommate with her for the weekend. So they'll be up late tonight after she gets off work. She called wanting to know if there'd be an extra room available for him."

"Hmmm. I wonder if our Jilly is becoming involved with Ryan the Lion?" *Meow.*

"Sounded to me more like he was bored and wanted to tag along."

"You'll like him, Hale . . . I think."

"Well, it's going to be an interesting couple of days. Come up to the lodge with me, and you'll see what I mean. Here," he said, gently taking her arm and turning her around to dust off her shoulders and back, "knock some of that skanky horse smell off yourself. I mean, try to make yourself a little more presentable, Maggie," he mocked. He knocked the dust from her backside while she laughed and slapped her hands against the front of her body.

"But, tell me, really, who's here? Have you got some VIP up here for a float trip?"

"You'll see," he said evasively. He dipped his hand into a bucket of water and laid his broad palm atop her head to smooth down her wild hair. Running his hand gently down her hair, he tucked a stray strand behind her ear. She reached up and slowly combed it back with her fingers. "How's that?"

"You look fine now. Fine." And there was elegance now in a step of their dance.

Approaching the lodge, she saw a small group of people sitting on bench seats lining the deck. Eventually she could make out a man and woman and two teenage boys lavishing attention on Sheila and Zeke.

"Hey, Ken!" Hale called. "You won't believe who I found out in the barn!"

Dear Jane, How are you? I'm so excited that you're really going to come see me. You're in for such a surprise, but I think you'll love the place. Ready for THE BIG SHOCK? I just saw KEN. I knew that it would happen one day up here, but I was so unprepared! He is here with his wife and sons, stopping on their way to visit her parents up north. They dropped in without notice. I think he was hoping to miss Hale altogether, that Hale would be on the river, or at least that there would be no room for them to stay. But they're here for two nights. It's been twenty years, but I swear he's hardly changed, at least physically. I don't know how I'll get through this, but I've made it this far. This is what I came for, isn't it? Keep reminding me, my friend. Mag

The boys went fishing with Hale early the next morning while the others went separate ways, agreeing to rendezvous for dinner.

Maggie worked in her garden and played gofer for David, but she could not avoid the countdown to the dinner hour. "So, David," she asked idly, picking up scrap lumber, "how many children in your family?"

"I have two younger brothers."

"Do you miss them? Are you close?"

"Oh, absolutely. We were as close as you can be. You can't help being close the way we grew up. We shared everything. We worked together, we wondered about the outside together, especially things like jet planes and computers and movies. We depended on each other to get into and out of trouble. Everything. We did nothing alone, really."

"Will they stay on your father's farm?"

"That's a problem in our community, you know. The farms have been divided until they've become too small to support families. So only one of us can stay."

"I guess that won't be you, though."

"Who knows? I'm the oldest, so it's my choice."

"So if you went back, you could step right back into your proper place?"

"I guess I'd be the prodigal son. But, yes, my father loves me and is a forgiving man."

"And what would your brothers do? I know in Victorian England the military was full of sons who weren't first born. But your brothers won't really have that choice, will they? I mean, the military as a career."

"No," he shook his head slowly. "No, they won't. And they won't be teaching at a university or becoming stockbrokers or even waiting tables. Not just because it would be against our ways, but because like all the Amish, they were only educated through the eighth grade. Their choices would be working in machine shops or in dairies or becoming ministers. I don't know. And that makes it harder to go back, you understand?"

"So, what you're saying is, what might be good for you could hurt your brothers?"

"That's right."

"Will they forgive you, then, like your father?"

"I think they'd accept it as the way things have always been done."

"That's not the same, though, is it?"

"No. It's not."

She walked through the ranch that afternoon to say hello to Limbo. David had left for the day, so Gus felt safe to venture out. He followed Maggie for a quarter mile or so, occasionally sprinting ahead with tail erect, then waiting to ambush her as she caught up, leaping out at her with back arched and claws extended. "Don't be ridiculous, Gus," she said scornfully. "Go home!" She finally had to run away from him for several hundred strides to discourage him from following the whole distance.

The sun was hot. *They must be broiling out on the river!* The pines smelled cool, though, in spite of the heat. Aspen leaves drooped limply and the air was filled with a wavy shimmer that distorted the distant view. There were giant soft white breasts of clouds pushing over the tops of the ridges to the west. *A thunderstorm is brewing. I hope it doesn't spill its guts until they're off the river.*

The meadow smelled rich and ripe as she walked through it. *Ready for second cutting.* A large hawk watched her from his high perch as she passed beneath him. She watched him watching her. *I'm incidental to him, just as he is to me,* she thought. *Extraneous, parenthetical to his life. It's all in your point of view, isn't it?* He lifted his wings, shaking loose their feathers as if to fly while she walked beneath him, but folded them gently onto his back again as she left the tree behind. *Good hunting then.*

She pulled Limbo off the pasture into the barn to groom

him. With a pair of scissors from the grooming supplies, she trimmed the bridle path between his ears and banged his tail. "You'll be the envy of every horse in Saratoga valley," she whispered in his ear. She ran a brush quickly over his coat, gave him too many carrots, then set him free again to return to his pals.

She could see several couples on the deck of the lodge and two young children running along the edge of the beaver pond. Glen was working in the corral with the dude string horses, so she walked over and slipped through the rails. "Hey, Glen."

"Hi, Maggie. How's Limbo this hot afternoon?"

"Oh, you know Limbo. He's a champ, as always."

"It's true he doesn't suffer from lack of confidence, does he?"

"No. But, you know, he tempers that with a sense of humor, so, all in all, I find him pretty charming."

"I guess I need to learn his secret," Glen mumbled.

"As if you didn't already know it," she teased. "You getting everybody ready for an evening trail ride?"

"Yup. Plus I've got to get Tonto and Ranger hitched up. It's Saturday night; chuck wagon supper night, you know."

"It looks like a thunderstorm's brewing," she said, looking at the big clouds that had changed from white puffs into a band of gray smudge swiped across the sky above the Granite Mountains to the northwest.

"Yeah, I noticed, and so have the horses," he said as the horse he was saddling sidestepped nervously when a low rumble of thunder sounded in the distance. "But we've got a large party booked for tonight from the Saratoga Inn, plus most of the people staying at the lodge, bad weather or no. So I guess that means you'll have things pretty much to yourselves tonight up there for your family get together."

112

He cinched the girth loosely around the horse's belly. "Rob's been whipping himself into a lather getting ready for it all afternoon. He's going to send José and Alfredo out on the chuck wagon so he can personally take care of all you Adamsons tonight." He finished with the horse and looked at Maggie. "Personally, I think he just wants to listen in," he said, grinning.

"Why? It'll be utterly boring. A typical family dinner."

"You don't know Rob. There's nothing he likes better than gossip." He shifted to the next in the row of tied horses, lifted a saddle off the fence, and lowered it onto the paint's back. "Besides, Maggie, in my opinion, there's nothing typical or boring about families. They're always a hotbed of intrigue. That's where all our troubles begin. Why do you think I prefer to hang around horses so much?" The paint pinned his ears at the leopard App next to him, who had stepped in his direction. "Even with their pecking order, they're a whole lot easier on each other than people are. And at least horses are honest about their differences."

"You're a regular Schopenhauer today, Glen."

"Yeah. Right. Lord it over me, Maggie."

"A philosopher. And not an optimistic one at that."

"Wouldn't an optimistic philosopher be an oxymoron?"

"Touché, Glen."

"Well, all I can say is you ought to feel sorry for me. I'll be there tonight listening to José and Alfredo make lewd remarks in Spanish about the good-looking women in the party while they're serving steaks to them. And I'll be praying none of the dudes are fluent in Spanish."

"Hang tough, Glen. You're the only real cowboy on the place."

"Don't I know it," he answered ruefully.

★ ★ ★ ★ ★

Maggie found Rob at work in the kitchen, smeared with flour, bent over the counter in front of him. "Hey there, Rob."

"Maggie, my beauty, how are you?"

"I'm hot, that's how I am, Rob. So I can't imagine how you're tolerating this hot kitchen."

"No denying it's hot, but it'll be worth it to see all of your faces tonight when you sit down to the meal I'm preparing. Besides, Maggie, you know I'd suffer the fires of Hades for Hale," he said grinning.

"You're an angel, Rob, no doubt about it. Anyway, good news, I think it's going to start cooling off soon for you. It looks like there's a rainstorm headed our way." She started to walk away, then turned back. "I was wondering if you knew where Ken and Diana are?"

"I think they went over to the Saratoga Inn for a round of golf."

"Oh, okay. Well, thanks. Do you need some help?"

"Nah, you go on. I've got everything under control, and I want you to think it all happened magically, so I can't have you watching me sweat and cuss at myself all afternoon. But thanks for the offer, Maggie."

She walked home through the afternoon heat. By the time she could see her cabin, a breeze stirred the limp aspen leaves and tossed tall stalks of blue columbine. The edge of the darkening cloud drifted toward the sun. As she passed a large shrub, Gus met her with a flying leap from where she had left him and fell in beside her as if no time at all had passed. "You're the best, Gus," she said, sweeping him into her arms and carrying him the rest of the way to the cabin.

Once inside, she undressed, then drew a hot bath and slid into it, staring dreamily through the high window at the encroaching clouds. Gus sat on the windowsill, quiet and white against the tossing blotches of trees beyond the glass.

"There's going to be a helluva storm tonight, Gus. Mark my words."

Conversation buzzed quietly around the large table decorated with a bouquet of peonies that Rob had cut from Hale's yard for the occasion. Maggie had planted those peonies herself, sixteen years before, so they sent a sad twinge through her, like remorse, but that wasn't really quite it. Rob glided quietly on crepe soles with plates of food illuminated by candle glow. The faces of the fishermen were scrubbed clean, gleaming red in the candlelight. Ken's sons, Scott and Eric, couldn't wait to tell the others about their day on the river, so the young set took center stage for act one.

"You should have seen Uncle Hale casting across the river, Dad. He could land a fly exactly where he wanted, let it drift a few seconds, and pop!" Scott imitated the quick jerk of setting a hook, "A little lift of the tip of his rod, and there was a trout on. I don't see how he saw it rise. I couldn't see a thing, and pow! There was this big trout. And it was so awesome! It ran three times. He'd bring it in and you'd think he was about to net it and it would take off. You could hear his line just screaming when it took off. Then when he landed it, he practically *seduced* that fish, sweet talking it while he made sure it was okay so he could release it. This big ole trout—he just nearly kissed it. Then he lowered it into the water and rocked it like a little baby. Then he sort of stroked it while he opened his hands, and Bam! No more trout—just a ripple in our imagination."

"You never told me your son was a poet, Diana," Jill said wonderingly.

Diana seemed amazed herself. "It's news to me, Jill. The sun must have got to him today."

"Or maybe the fishing?" Jill suggested.

"No, actually, he's always tended toward embellishment, haven't you Scott? Or even an occasional outright fabrication," she reached toward him to rub her knuckle on his head but he ducked it.

"Aw, Mom. Ask Ryan, if you don't believe me. Isn't that just how it happened, Ryan?"

Ryan seemed reluctant to abandon the beef tenderloin he was tackling for even a moment, but paused and looked at Hale admiringly. "That's the truth. Hale is a regular old man and the sea."

Eric, the thirteen-year-old, piped in, "Yea, but we weren't slackers either. We all hooked our limits today, didn't we?"

"Yeah, sure," Ryan agreed, "but we were using spinners and bait."

Maggie cut to the chase. "The main thing is that you all caught fish, fried in the sun, got dirty and smelly, played Huck Finn, and lived to tell about it. Isn't that the whole point of fishing?"

"You should know, Maggie. I have this hazy recollection of you being awfully handy with a fly rod yourself," Hale said.

"That's about right," said Ken, brushing a flake of bread from his shirtfront. "She made the rest of us look like hacks."

"Oh, go on, you two," Maggie laughed and denied it, but was all the lovelier for the praise.

The thunderhead that had been sneaking in all day had decided to keep itself secret no longer. Its low rumbling rolled across the landscape, shaking the floor beneath their feet. "Hope this storm doesn't ruin the chuck wagon party's dinner," Hale worried—the boss's job description. Low strains of jazz merged with the storm's background music.

"So, Ryan, I hear you're going with Glen on a ride up into the BLM land tomorrow," Diana said.

"Yeah. I've got to try some of everything here at the ranch, you know."

"I can vouch for that," Jill stated emphatically. "He covers all bases, our Ryan. He'll attend a concert of South African township singers at the theatre hall on a Friday night and go to a rave the next night. He goes golfing at the country club with one of his yuppie friends, but plans to ride in another friend's sidecar up to Sturgis next month."

"Oh man! You mean that huge motorcycle rally up in South Dakota?" Eric squawked excitedly, his voice subject to erratic hormones.

"That's right," Ryan nodded. "I'm going up with a friend who has a Harley."

"Is he a Hell's Angel or something?" Scott asked.

"No. He's a lawyer."

Everyone laughed. "Hey! It takes money to own a Harley these days, you know," Ryan explained defensively, which just added to the laughter.

The table calmed down and was silent as everyone focused on their food. Rob came in to check on the group. The thunder, echoing ominously in the distance, was accompanied by Paul Desmond's mellow, lonely saxophone.

"Wow, Rob. This is fabulous," Jill raved. "Isn't he the most amazing?" she asked the group. Rob waved them away with his hands as they all sang his praises. "Enough, enough." He fairly skipped back into the kitchen.

"So how'd you like the Saratoga Inn golf course?" Maggie asked Diana and Ken.

Ken spoke up, "Well, if you're asking whether the course was beautiful, the answer is a thousand times yes. If you're asking if we enjoyed playing, well, Diana had a good round." He took a sip of wine, then stayed innocently mute.

"So what about your round, Uncle Ken?" Jill prompted.

"I don't know, did you guys notice the level of the river rising at about three o'clock?" Ken answered.

"I shouldn't tell on him," Diana chuckled, "but he put three balls into the river on the ninth hole because he insisted on trying to drive from the pro tee." She smiled behind her raised napkin.

Ken acknowledged this fact with a grimace, then dodged the bullet. "Not to change the subject or anything, but the town hasn't changed much, has it Hale?" Maggie noticed that the music had shifted from Desmond to Les McCann, the soulful sax supplanted by subtly modulated piano chords.

"Nope. Not really. We sure haven't seen anything like the changes in your neck of the woods," answered Hale.

"Oh my God. You should see how Tucson has grown! And the prices are becoming astronomical," complained Diana. "We keep saying that one of these days we're going to pack it in and find somewhere that hasn't become a retirement mecca. Ken's been feeling like he might be ready for a career shift anyway." She took a swallow of wine. "But Saratoga is still so laid-back and down home. It's as if there's a time warp here. The raciest thing you see around here is a 'Save a Cowboy for Me' sticker on some teenage girl's pickup."

"I saw a racing bumper sticker today," Eric interjected. "It said 'I'd Rather Be,' and showed a picture of a barrel racer."

"Well," Diana said, ignoring her son's non sequitur,

"though it seems like a western version of Mayberry, knowing human nature I suppose Saratoga has its share of problems and scandals. Enough to shock us all, no doubt, if we were just privy to them. I imagine trouble just happens on a small, private scale here," she said blithely. Maggie took a long sip of wine and glanced in spite of herself at Hale and Ken alternately. "But, I will say," Diana continued, "it's definitely nice to drive down the street here without the concussion of some kid's rap music, or should I say hip-hop, or whatever they're calling it these days, blasting you off the pavement."

"Aw, Mom, don't be so uncool," Scott whined.

"I like hip-hop," Ryan said defensively. "It tells society that we see through its facade. Tells it what it needs to work on to improve itself. Tells it, 'up yours.' I like it." He turned an angelic smile on the others.

"Right, tells women that men feel fine stomping on them," Maggie said with some feeling.

"Oh, nobody takes that shit seriously," Ryan stated flatly.

Through the window, the reflection of a lightening flash set the surface of the pond ablaze. A vacuum of quiet hovered expectantly, then the loud clap of thunder cracked and boomed. The floor continued to tremble as deep reverberations rolled eastward.

"Wow! That's getting close!" Scott exclaimed, as they all turned to look.

"Well, at any rate," Ken said placidly as if to soothe the table's occupants, "you're right about feeling like it's back in time here. It's so quiet and unchanging, so reasonable and rational, unlike every other place along the length of the eastern slope."

The wind convulsed in a sudden violent burst and a few

large raindrops splatted against the windows. The dogs scurried under the deck.

With disintegrating candor, Ryan resumed the conversation. "So, Hale, Jill tells me you have an engineering degree. I'm curious, how is it you ended up with the ranch, while Ken ended up . . . what is it you do? . . . fund raising for some organization in Tucson, isn't it?" he asked. He thought he felt a quick kick on his shin from Jill's direction, but he left the question on the table, intent on knowing details of the lives of these other men who appeared so securely ensconced in their mature worlds.

A clatter and crash came from the kitchen, followed by what sounded like Russian swearing. "Are you all right in there, Rob?" Hale called. "Do you need any help?"

"No, boss," Rob answered in a harried voice. "You just relax," he called loudly. "I've got it under control." Then in a voice like a stage aside that could be heard all the way to the table he muttered, "It's just this *fucking* storm, that's all."

Hale had started from his seat, but sank back into the chair. He delayed answering Ryan's question, laying his fork down and taking a long drink of tonic water.

"It's kind of a long story, Ryan, that everyone else here already knows."

Ryan just looked at Hale expectedly.

The music score that had been playing ended and shifted into the first bars of McCann's "Doin' That Thing." Maggie glanced quickly at Hale, then lowered her eyes to the table, twisting in her seat uncomfortably, as if her legs had both gone to sleep. "Doin' That Thing" was not just any melody to her. Nor should it be to him. It was a song she and Hale had played over and over in the first years of their marriage while making love. With the sound of the first bars she remembered intimately the room and the bed and the feel of their sheets; she could feel the weight of a body sinking into the mattress beside her. *No boundaries!* And so should he. The song was so suggestive, so sexy, not only for its insistent, pulsing rhythm, not only for that throbbing rhythm and blood-stirring tempo, but because its very theme was the emotional escalation of sex itself. There was a crescendo in intensity and volume through the long melody that climaxed with a violent brushing of the drummer's cymbals, and that musical, tympanic climax was accompanied by a female voice softly, then not so softly, clearly and so, so convincingly simulating a moaning orgasm. That erotic ending was obvious only if you were really listening or knew it was coming.

But what if, she thought, *what if any of the others happened to hear it over the other sounds in the room? What about the kids? And did Hale realize what was playing? If he did, would he remember the way she did? He should. He certainly should be remembering.* She looked again at Hale, but he seemed innocently oblivious of the tune. And it struck her as interesting, in retrospect, that things began to be really stirred up just as that particular song started playing.

Hale not only seemed unaware of the music, he seemed extraordinarily placid considering the machinations of fate already in evidence that evening. He began to answer Ryan's question about the entire family's fate ever so didactically. "Okay, well. The ranch has been in the family for multiple generations, though Adamsons hadn't really lived on it since my great-great-grandfather. My dad's dad had become a banker in Cheyenne, and my dad was a geologist who settled in Denver. Because they lived and worked elsewhere, those two generations had both leased the ranch out to neighbors who grazed cattle and cut hay on it. But, even though my grandfather never lived here, he loved the place and enjoyed showing it off to others, so he did invest some money and time in the ranch. He had the lodge built to entertain business clients and family. It wasn't as big then as it is now, but he's the one who built the main building. A caretaker lived in what's now my house and took care of the lodge so the family could use it throughout the year, during holidays and in the summers, mostly. And that situation remained pretty much the same once my father took things over."

Rob came in and fussed around the table refilling water glasses and serving wine. He cleared dinner plates and took orders for pie and coffee. Once Rob had gone, Hale rested one hand on the cleared table and went on with his long—too lengthy,—explanation. "I got an engineering degree at CSU in Fort Collins, and ended up staying on there after graduation when I was offered a job at Hewlett Packard. Believe me, I thought I was there for the long term, and I certainly expected the arrangement at the ranch to stay just as it was for a very long time—forever, really, until our dad was gone, anyway. I had never thought of living there full time myself; I had never thought of anything other than a career in engineering.

"Meanwhile, Maggie had moved from Lincoln, Nebraska to attend CSU a few years after I started with H.P., and we met through a mutual friend. We married when she graduated." Maggie noticed that he skipped right over that part, glossed right over it, like he'd glazed a beautiful oil painting with a coat of tar. "When Dad decided to turn the ranch over to me three years later, I surprised myself by deciding to move up here and try to make the place work as a fishing lodge."

"You surprised us all," Maggie cut in aggressively. *That*

was putting it lightly, she thought, *feather-fucking-light.*

A crash from the storm wracked the air again, while a microburst of wind whipped the willow shrubs as if they were being shaken ferociously by invisible hands. But Hale didn't skip a beat, and neither did Les McCann. Maggie could have sworn his head was moving ever so slightly with the rhythm.

"Ken was just getting ready to graduate from UNC in Greeley as a business major when we moved up here . . ." Hale allowed his discourse to trail off as he saw through the window that the dogs had come up onto the deck, scared by the last clap of thunder. They stood staring into the room with gaping doggy smiles and wagging bodies, looking to Hale for succor.

"Doin' That Thing" picked up steam inexorably in the background. *There's no stopping it!* she thought, as the conversation lulled. Ken shifted in his seat, drumming his fingers on the table restlessly. *He looks uncomfortable, too,* Maggie thought. He asked Hale if he could let the dogs in now that the steaks were eaten, and Hale assented, though she knew he had reservations about allowing the dogs to join the party. Ken, seeming to grab the excuse to leave the table, walked to the door and stepped out onto the deck to watch the storm while the dogs came wagging into the dining room. She could see Ken outside, staring east as the wind blew his hair forward and flattened his clothes on his back. The dogs made their way through the rounds of people, greeting all, as the conversation eased its way back to life.

"We used to see a lot of each other at that time, didn't we?" Diana chipped in. "We were over at your place every chance we could get. I was dating Ken steadily and you two seemed so settled to us then, the perfect couple, trying to start a family. Believe me, Jill, you were a reluctant addition to the world's population. Your mom and dad wanted children right away, but it was over four years before Maggie finally surprised us all by announcing she was expecting. I think they had nearly given up on having kids of their own."

Ken had wandered back in out of the weather and eased himself into his chair just as Rob came in with pie for everyone. Diana reached over and put her hand on Ken's forearm, saying, "Yeah, we loved coming up here to see Hale and Maggie and spend time on the ranch. Ken came up to spend the whole summer after he graduated, working and trying to figure out what he was going to do with himself, and I was up here as often as I could get away from my summer job to be with him and to see Hale and Maggie."

The family members were actually musing about their own lives at this point, swept along by the story's current, drifting through the past, rather than responding to Ryan's question. Indeed, Ryan need not have been present as they continued. The narrative, having attained its own momentum, like the song in the not-so-background, was building on its own, and continued for the family's benefit alone.

"Yeah, that was a pivotal summer for all of us, I guess." Ken said, picking up the story, as if he realized he hadn't contributed much up to this point, and couldn't control its destination either unless he took it over. "When the summer came to an end, I realized I was still undecided about a career. I didn't really have a single clue. I was thinking along the lines of big business or politics or just striking it rich by doing nothing but playing the stock market, as if I had any startup money. In other words, the summer was over and I was sitting high and dry, living on nothing but a bunch of air-headed nonsense and B.S. So I joined the Peace Corps on a wild, no doubt desperate impulse . . ." The thunder moaned in chronic pain, but seemed to have lost power.

Maggie, looking around intentionally, saw several feet, including Hale's, tapping to the beat of the music.

Diana interrupted Ken. "Yes, and I wasn't too pleased about that, as you might imagine. I still had a few years remaining at UNC and was seriously in love with Ken, and he just disappeared off the face of the earth to South America."

"Bolivia, to be exact," Ken elaborated.

"Wow! Bolivia," Ryan cheered, slicing into the family's narration. "That's so awesome. I'm dying to get down there to all those Incan countries and explore some ruins and bum around."

Ken neutralized the intrusion through assimilation. "Well, as a matter of fact, that's just what I did when my stint with the Peace Corps ended. I slowly made my way back home, but couldn't quite leave it all behind as abruptly as most volunteers. My reentry was gradual, I guess you might say. When I finally managed to wander back to the states, I hung out along the border from California to Texas. Eventually, and certainly not in a straight line, I made my way to Tucson where my life from before the Peace Corps began to seem real again to me. So I called Diana and asked her to come down there and meet me." When Diana leaned her head against him as he said that, he acknowledged her absentmindedly with a shrug of body language like a typical happily married man. "I had always imagined going into politics eventually somehow, but I guess I never was really able to totally leave the Peace Corps behind, not really. So, as the closest thing to politics I felt I could manage, I joined a non-profit organization in

Tucson as a volunteer and worked my way into fund-raising."

"It was all that natural charm and blarney that landed you in fundraising," Diana said affectionately, still leaning against Ken's shoulder.

Sheila had walked up on Ken's opposite side, begging shyly at first, but becoming bolder, she laid her head in his lap and lifted beseeching eyes to him.

"Look at this, Hale," Ken said, pointing to the shameless dog.

Hale peered over the edge of the table at the dog. "That's amazing, Ken. She's usually so shy with everyone." Then he added with a sarcasm that stabbed a little deeper than an innocent gibe, "But you always did have a way with women."

The diners laughed on cue, *sure! just a good-natured brotherly crack,* but Maggie noticed Ken draw back ever so slightly and become quiet, and she concealed the chill that went through her. At that instant, the air around them exploded with the greatest of the exhalations from the lungs of black clouds that now covered the entire dome of the sky. And then, just at that same moment, as if choreographed, "Doin' That Thing" reached its climax amidst the clamor of the laughter and the thunder, its sounds submerged in the din, the possibility of detection by others that Maggie had feared erased by those more overt resonances. But Maggie had been involuntarily listening for it, and felt herself flush, her body leaping from cold to hot, straining for the gasping, panting moans to seep through the louder din. She tried to discipline her will to avoid Hale's eyes, but couldn't quell the compelling urge. She had to, she *had* to glance just for an instant in his direction, where she saw his eyes boring, just boring into hers, boring through her own eyes and right into her soul. The burn of his look scorched her quailing courage, and she looked away as fast as she could, to pretend she never *had* looked at all. How would he know if she'd looked? It was just for that instant, he couldn't be sure, not all that sure. She turned toward Zeke to conceal her emotions, leaning down to fuss over him, cajoling him with hugs and pats. "Don't be scared now, Zeke," she crooned into the lab's ear.

The others were oblivious to her sensations. The conversation resumed its flow unimpeded, the music shifting smoothly to an innocent upbeat tune. But Maggie didn't hear the conversation for the next minutes. She couldn't have recalled who spoke or what was said.

"Eric and Scott told me you all don't get up here much anymore," Ryan said to Ken. "Don't you miss the ranch?" As he asked the question he felt another knock against his shins from Jill's direction.

Ken answered evasively with an explanation that sounded rehearsed, "Well, it's a long drive and Denver's the closest airport, unless you own your own jet like the Old Baldy set. And I'm awfully busy. And then, too, I'm living in a beautiful place myself."

Diana gave Ken a scolding look. "I try to get him up here more often to see his brother and get out of the desert, beautiful as it is, but he's something of a workaholic, like so many men. He always has one excuse or another." It struck Ryan that Diana was the only one who seemed to have normal reactions. She seemed to hear and say the right stuff, most of the time, anyway.

Zeke, feeling very left out when Maggie stopped fussing over him, chose this moment to stand on his hind legs and place both front paws on the table. When his big paws slipped apart on the smooth tabletop, he knocked what was left of Ryan's chokecherry pie into his lap.

"Oh shit!" Ryan yelled, trying to snatch gooey pieces from his lap like they were red-hot.

"Zeke! That's it! You two—out!" Hale commanded in the meanest voice he could muster, dragging Zeke by the scruff of his neck out the door. Sensitive Sheila slunk out rapidly behind him.

"Oh, Hale. Are you sure they'll be okay out in this thunderstorm?" Maggie asked softheartedly.

"Yeah, they'll be okay. They'll be fine," he sounded as if he was trying to convince himself as much as the others. "It looks like the worst of it has blown over, anyway." He returned to the table. "You okay there, Ryan? Rob can bring some soda water for you."

"Naw. It's okay. They'll be all right," he replied, still wiping at the stains on his khaki pants.

"I'm really sorry. I apologize about the dogs. You see now why they're banished to the deck, Ken." Maggie couldn't believe he was blaming Ken. So unlike him to be that unfair. "Believe me, they know how to manipulate me, but it's for their own good that I make them stay out, though . . . look at them . . . the little buggers can break my heart looking at me like that through the window." The dogs pressed against the glass, staring penitently into the interior, drooling onto the glass.

"Yeah, I'm sorry too, Ryan," Ken apologized. "I never should have butted in."

Everyone's apologizing now, she thought. *Maybe I should be next. All aboard! Next!*

"No, no, everyone! It's no biggie, trust me," Ryan assured them in an exasperated tone. "These are just work pants, and the kind of work I'm doing these days doesn't exactly have demanding dress codes anyway."

"I thought you were in school," Maggie asked innocently.

"He dropped out," Jill blurted loudly. "His dad is ready to kill him." She was almost yelling, like it was something she really cared about. "Ryan's already the black sheep of the family. He's got this brother who's a math genius and a sister who's in pre-med. And now Ryan's driving a cement truck, *I'm not kidding, a cement truck,* and his parents are having conniptions." She felt a foot step on her own under the table, and, glancing over at Ryan, shut her mouth abruptly.

"Aw, I'm just taking a break for a while," he said, downplaying the whole thing. "Life's too short to waste my entire youth on school," Ryan explained lamely. "I've got some wild oats to sow. Tell me you all didn't do the same." He looked at Hale. "Well, okay, maybe you didn't."

"Well, I don't know about that," Maggie said, an edge in her voice. "He *did* decide to give up engineering and move up here to run a fishing lodge, after all."

"Maybe not *quite* as radical as quitting school to drive a cement truck, though," Hale stared at Maggie, his face flushing.

"Well, *you* sure as hell sowed some wild oats from the sound of it," Ryan directed pointedly at Ken, seeming to believe the adage "a good defense is a strong offense" applied.

"Whoa, keep me out of this," Ken shied away from Ryan's gaze. The thunder could still be heard far away east, receding post facto, leaving the mountains for the flat stretches where it would metamorphose into tornado havoc.

Maggie, looking flustered, tried a quantum jump in subject matter. "What do you think of our Jilly, all grown up and living in Boulder, working as a research scientist, Diana?"

"Right! I'm so amazed at you, Jill," Diana gushed, rallying, also relieved to turn the conversation away from Ryan's direct questions. "Young women are so independent these days! And I think you've grown up to be as gorgeous as your mother, I must say!"

"She is a beauty, isn't she?" Hale agreed proudly. This was something he could endorse.

"Except for her lighter coloring, she looks just like Maggie did at her age, don't you think, Ken?" Diana asked.

Ken shifted uncomfortably in his seat.

"Oh, please, everyone . . ." Jill laughed, turning red. "Let's talk about something else."

"I think she looks a lot like her dad," Ken stated flatly.

"She really looks more like you," Ryan asserted.

"Oh, hell!" Maggie nearly shrieked. "She looks like herself. She doesn't look a damned bit like any of us. She's an original." She had raised herself from her seat, nearly standing, as she tossed her napkin disgustedly into her plate.

"Mom. Dad." Eric interrupted. He had finished a second helping of pie with whipped cream. "Can I go to my room? I've got a stomachache."

Diana excused herself and ushered both boys to their cabin. Maggie overheard Eric telling Scott as they walked away, "Wow! Riding a Harley to Sturgis, dropping out of school, and driving a cement truck! That Ryan's awesome . . ."

"Oh, look, Ryan! There's the chuck wagon! C'mon . . ." Jill nearly dragged Ryan out of the door where she could be seen in earnest conversation using a lot of body language with him as they walked out to meet the returning chuck wagon.

Ken and Maggie and Hale sat alone at the table as Rob

cleared away everything but their coffee cups. The room seemed enormously silent; the candles guttered. The thunder and lightning had reduced to a sound and light show reflected on the giant screen of clouds above the eastern horizon. The storm had only succeeded in stirring things up without benefit of a quenching rain.

"Those people at the chuck wagon supper were lucky it never really rained," Ken ventured weakly.

"Yeah, let's hope no one was struck by lightning," Hale said, peering into the queer light of dusk after a storm.

No one spoke. Maggie tried to speak, but could only croak and had to clear her throat, then said, drily, "It couldn't have been any worse out there than it was in here," staring down at her cup.

There was a pause, a long, long pause that seemed to hold all eternity. Then the three burst out laughing.

"I'm going to tell Glen to put a burr under his saddle blanket tomorrow, I swear to God," Hale muttered menacingly.

No one had to ask whose saddle.

When Jill walked around the house to Maggie's garden the next day, there was no one visible, but Gus came trotting toward her from behind a clump of zinnias, and as Jill lifted him into her arms, she caught sight of Maggie behind some tomato plants. She was on her knees, gloved hands pressed against the earth, feet tucked beneath her body, resting on a thin cushion. She could almost have been making ablutions.

Maggie looked up when she became aware of Jill beyond the perimeter of the garden, but remained kneeling, as if she too had rooted into the Wyoming ground. A small gate allowed entrance to the garden, now enclosed by a low fence David had built, a railing around the miracle she had created. A row of tomatoes stretched heavenward, tied to tall narrow stakes, all foliage removed but the very top of their heads, where green fruits hung nodding amid the stalks trained onto horizontal cross stakes. Red chard and leaf lettuce splashed bright scarlet at the foot of the stakes, leading to a luxurious flowing purple robe of an eggplant and the lush leaves of a clump of rhubarb with wine red stems. Long oriental beans dangled from a latticed trellis, and upright stalks of celery-like bok choy stood guard at the garden's entrance. The garden fence was ringed by mixed flowers glowing against the dark soil. Yellow marigolds stretched like a row of candles along the inside of the front railing. The layout of the paths through the plantings was two intersecting rectangles with a curving line at one end of the longer rectangle where a compost pile encroached, oddly forming the rough shape of a medieval church's apse.

"I'm here to help, Mom. I'm at your command, atoning for bringing Ryan to the 'last supper' last night."

Maggie looked up at Jill, patting the ground beside her. "On your knees, then, my lamb."

Jill dropped down beside her mother and they kneeled together, pulling weeds.

"Did Ken and Diana and the boys get away all right?" Maggie inquired.

"Yeah. They pulled out early this morning. They'll probably never be back after last night," Jill laughed ruefully. She stood erect from her knees and looked at Maggie, still bent over. "I really am sorry about Ryan, Mom. I kept kicking him beneath the table, but he just blundered on and on so innocently. I mean, I learned the answers to things last night that I never had the nerve to ask in all these years.

But, my God, he managed to pick at every old wound, didn't he?"

"He did," she chuckled, "yes, he did indeed."

"You always told me that Ken joined the Peace Corps mainly because he was so upset that Grandpa gave the ranch to Dad and not to both of them."

"That's right."

"So Ken must have really enjoyed that little morsel of old baggage with his meal, I guess. And, then, bringing up that whole brouhaha between you and dad about him becoming a dude rancher instead of a distinguished engineer . . ."

"Oh, forget that, Jilly. That was just something I was going through, you know, anxiety about attaining some kind of social status. After all, how could I not have felt that way, having been raised by your grandmother?"

Maggie's mother had been an ambitious woman much concerned about her social standing in Lincoln. She never stopped pushing her husband, against his will, into the forefront of that city's social and political life, though his success in business and investments had provided her an elegant and indulgent, indolent life. She had strongly approved of Maggie's husband until Hale gave up his engineering job and settled Maggie onto the ranch permanently. When Maggie left Hale for Palo Alto, Mrs. Everhardt had thrown her considerable weight squarely in support of that decision. When Maggie's father died of a stroke soon after, Mrs. Everhardt lost no time selling her posh house in Lincoln, moving herself and all her fine things to California to reinforce Maggie's resolve, and to exert what she considered her beneficial influence on her only granddaughter. Never a warm woman, she had become stiffer and ever more unapproachable after her husband's death, attached to nothing but her beautiful trinkets and her elegant but outdated wardrobe. She wrapped herself in them as if they could warm the iciness within. Maggie's most vivid memory of her mother was a white-haired woman dressed in a severe ivory suit seated stiffly in her favorite tall dark chair at the end of a long table covered with silver candelabras. Mrs. Haversham in an Armani suit. That's how she remembered her. That's how she would always remember her. She half-believed that her fears of Wyoming's cold winters came from that mental picture.

Though Maggie seemed to need none, Jill continued her apologies. "Well, I'm still sorry he brought it up, Mom. Anyway, I read Ryan the riot act. I think he'll be on his best behavior from now on . . . although, when I think about it, his best behavior may not be all that reassuring. The worst part is that he really likes both you and Dad. It was all so innocent on his part, you know."

"Don't worry so, Jilly. I like Ryan, I really do. He's a breath of fresh air, in a way." Maggie stopped weeding to stroke Gus with her gloved hand. "I'm glad he's not my problem, though." She bent back to her weeding then stopped and looked directly at Jill. "He's not my problem, is he, Jilly? I mean, you're not seriously involved with Ryan, are you?"

"Oh, Mom. Really. Now you're starting to sound like Grandma."

When they had finished weeding they stood admiring their handiwork. "What on earth is that?" Jill exclaimed, pointing to a shape barely visible between the rows of vegetables.

"Oh, that," Maggie laughed lightly. "That's just Mephistopheles, my fake snake. He's here to ward off any rodents that Gus doesn't get."

134

"Sometimes I think you could be downright quirky, Mom, if you'd let yourself."

Maggie walked Jill through the cabin to show her David's work. "He's nearly done. I think tomorrow will be the last day for phase one."

"Phase one? It looks fabulous, Mom. What more can you possibly do?"

"Oh you might be surprised, Jill," Maggie said slyly. "As a matter of fact, you'll have to be surprised, because I'm not talking about it."

"Mom, you and your mysteries. I swear, you can be the most closed-mouth woman!"

They had coffee and leftover pie Rob had sent home with Maggie last night.

"Poor Ryan!" They both laughed at the sight of the pie. "What a fiasco!"

Jill watched Maggie as she laughed. "You know, Mom, I'll tell you again, this life is really agreeing with you. I swear you've never looked so good, and look at all you've taken on! Look how full of energy you are now that you're here . . . And your energy spills over into everything you're touching here. Just look at the cabin. Look at your garden. And even Limbo! I've never seen Limbo look so grand." She gave her mother a sly sideways look and added, "I hope there's no cheesy kind of symbolism in your riding a horse called Limbo, Mom."

"God forbid, Jill," Maggie replied, not cracking a smile.

"Anyway, I have to tell you, with you thriving here so wonderfully and all, I just don't understand why you ever left. All that bull about you hating ranch life and your disappointment with Dad for settling for a lowly career in the Wyoming outback . . . I just don't buy it, Mom."

"Oh, Jill. I can't exactly explain it myself. All I can say is

I just didn't really like or even know myself when I left. There usually isn't a logic to the things we do for emotional reasons, don't you agree?"

"I guess so, Mom. I'll never understand it all, will I?"

"I wouldn't count on it, Jillus, my poor confused lamb. I never have myself."

"Well, come walk me to my car, Mysterious Mom. I've got a surprise for you."

They walked arm in arm to Jill's little hatchback. She lifted the rear window and pulled a saddle from the deck. "Here, Mom. Here's a bona fide dressage saddle for you and Limbo."

"Oh my god, Jill, where . . . ?"

"It's just on loan, Mom. But it'll be yours for at least two years. A lab tech I work with decided to get her master's degree, so she'll be gone for at least that long. She leased her dressage horse to a woman who already had her own saddle, so she offered her saddle to me. Better to use it and keep it oiled than to store it."

"Jill, I don't know what to say!"

"Well, it'll give you a chance to see if Limbo has any real talent in that direction before going out and buying one for yourself. It should fit the big galoot all right, because it's a wide tree, large enough to fit her big broad-backed warm blood. I had been telling her about you, how you started riding again after so long. She was intrigued by that and especially your trying to do dressage on a BLM horse. She told me all about a woman in Colorado who has successfully competed all the way to Grand Prix level on a big black draft type horse that was a BLM mustang. There's even a poster of him, I guess. This gorgeous big ole black mustang doing the most fabulous advanced movements. So, see! Look what a mustang can become with the right influences! Just think of what Limbo might do!"

Maggie set the saddle tilted upright against the house on the front porch as gently as if it were made of spun glass, then walked back to Jill to hug her, planting a kiss on her cheek. "You're the best, Jill."

"Haven't I heard you say that to Gus, too?" Jill smirked.

Jill stepped into her car, lowering the window as she started the engine. "Bye, Mom. I'm going to go see how Ryan survived his trail ride. I hope he suffered a lot."

"Me too." They both laughed.

"You know what the little shit had the nerve to say to me after I bawled him out last night?"

"No, what?"

"He said, 'Your family needs to lighten up.' "

Maggie introduced Limbo to the dressage saddle the next morning. Things were quiet at the ranch after the pandemonium of the weekend. She could hear nothing but a Solitaire's call as she groomed Limbo. *This is just a one-note samba,* she hummed, buckling the girth onto the billets.

The saddle felt strange beneath her. Limbo thought so too, backing off when she tried a few tentative strides of sitting trot after warming up. She posted again. "I know. Don't worry, you nervous thing. It needs some practice, but we'll take it slowly, I promise. Okay, Limbo?"

Another challenge. You start dying the instant you stop growing, though. Didn't someone say that once upon a time? Don't fuss, Limbo. You can do this. No, I don't believe it, and it feels all wrong anyway. *No, you just wait and see, you won't believe what you can do. If that other mustang can, by God you can too. All I have to do is ask well enough.* No. Nope. No way, absolutely n . . . well, maybe just a . . . yeah, I see . . . okay, I can maybe just start to . . . After a light workout she

.urned doubting Limbo out and drove home. *No worries. Rome wasn't built in a day.*

She was happy to see David's truck parked in her drive as she pulled in. *David Heerman. Her Man. My man Friday.* When she walked around the cabin to greet him, he cut her off, blocking her view with his body. He wore a "caught in the act" look on his guileless face. "Now, Ms. Eve." He had resolved to call her Ms. Eve as a compromise to her requests that he call her Maggie. "I've got something I need to finish up out here before you can see it. So, if you'd go into the house for another fifteen minutes, then you can come out."

She did as he asked, taking the time to change from her riding breeches into her blue jeans and to grab a bite of leftovers from the refrigerator. Its door was a blank sheet in her house, devoid of the detritus others stuck on theirs, no calendar, no reminder notes, no cartoons, no magnets, no photos, no children's drawings. Finding the container she wanted, she nuked its contents in her microwave, then filled a glass with ice cubes from the automatic ice maker. When a piece of ice fell to the floor, Gus heard it land and flew into the kitchen to bat it around the slick floor, indulging in one of his favorite games. Stepping cautiously around his frenzied action, Maggie maneuvered her lunch to the table. She glanced at the newspaper as she ate, flipping through the entertainment section of the *Wyoming TribuneEagle*. The faces of a rock group glared out with sinister macho expressions. When she turned the page, it struck her that the faces of the fashion models wore the very same look.

"Okay, you can come out now, Ms. Eve," David called. When she stepped out the back door he stood to her right. Moving away from the building, he revealed his prize, a cold frame constructed of redwood and Lexan, attached to the building like a window well. He had formed the flexible plastic lid into a dome over the sunken frame below, hinged at one side like the lid of a jewelry box. And it was a jewelry box, of sorts.

"Now you can start your own tomato plants, Ms. Eve. You could even grow them in here permanently, without transplanting them to the garden. With the domed lid, there's room for their height, see?" He lifted the lid up, then lowered it again. "This way you won't have to worry about the short season. Maybe you could even grow Big Boys and Fantastics next year. I'm finishing up today, so I wanted to get this done for you before I start my next job." He paused to smile at her. "It's been a pleasure working for you, Maggie."

"Oh, David. This is so beautiful! You're a marvel! And you even managed to call me Maggie!" Maggie was so sincerely delighted that David couldn't suppress a laugh.

"I don't want to offend your religious sensibilities, David, but do you think it would be a sin if I kissed you on the cheek?"

"It might be in Lancaster County in Pennsylvania, Ms. Eve, but I think it would be forgiven here in Paradise."

When he pulled out of her driveway she was still crouched beside the cold frame gently raising and lowering the lid.

She set to work cleaning her house after David had gone, though it had gathered little of the debris of living with just her and Gus residing, tidy cats that they were. *Maggie the Cat.* She put on an old LP. In truth, Maggie hadn't listened to anything new in a decade. It would've taken too much emotional energy for her to sort through all of it, to sift out the music she didn't want to be touched by. So, with Taj

Mahal singing in the background, she changed into the yellow sweatshirt that made her look bad, stripping off her bra for the freedom she'd need to bend and stretch and reach, and just because it felt better to be unfettered. She was small-breasted anyway and thought that, as long as she could pass Ann Landers' pencil test, she was entitled to follow her natural inclination to go *au naturelle* in "to bra or not to bra." According to Ann (or was it Abby? . . . details, details) if your braless breast sagged enough to hold a pencil beneath it, then you ought to wear a bra to spare the world unnecessary ugliness. She'd laughed when she'd tried the test, telling Gus when the pencil dropped without a hitch to the floor, "See, Gus, I'm still defying gravity, even if the pencil isn't." *Or I could just say screw them and their rules, but, of course, I'd never do something like that.*

She kicked off her shoes, then pulled her socks off, traveling light, feeling the world around her with the most skin possible. Gus followed along unnoticed, undoing her work, unstraightening the magazine stack, appliquéing paw prints on the table's polish, spitting a hair clump pulled from his tail onto the carpet. He pawed and chewed a fly buzzing against the window, leaving it vibrating on the sill, spinning in slower and slower circles. It didn't matter. The cabin wasn't meant to be perfect any more than the life she was living in it or the forest it sat in or the wide world that held them all.

"I'm a goin' fishin', yas I'm goin' fishin' and my baby's goin' fishin' too . . ." she sang along.

There was a knock on the door, so unexpected that her heart pounded strongly for a beat or two and Gus scrambled under the couch. As she walked toward the door she looked with despair in the mirror at her messed hair, flushed face, and braless yellow shirt. The knock was just sounding again, and muffled voices arguing outside as she pulled the door open.

"Well, hello! Look who's here!" she said with forced pleasure, running her fingers through her rumpled hair to sweep it into some order.

"Hello, Maggie!" Two women, standing shoulder-to-shoulder, spoke in near unison. The younger extended a covered plate holding a cake, her face beaming, then pushed it closer.

"Ave! Rosalie! What on earth? Did you come all the way up here to bring me a cake?"

She ushered them in, relieving Ave of the plate. "You'll have to excuse things," she apologized, "I was just cleaning house. I know I look a mess . . ." She straightened her clothes and hair nervously.

"I wish I looked a mess like you," Ave said, eyeing her enviously.

"Oh, don't fuss, Maggie," Rosalie, the elder woman, said kindly. "I know it's terrible just dropping in on you like this. I always hate people coming to visit without notice, but Ave wanted to surprise you." As Maggie ushered them in she looked around, adding, "And besides, you look just fine. And this looks wonderful, really. The old place looks just wonderful."

Ave nodded, but said with some hesitation, "I guess you're still unpacking things, huh? No doubt you've got more to unpack to fill it up?"

"No," Maggie said. "No, this is it, Ave. I know it's kind of sparse, but I like it this way, and it's such a small space, you know, I wouldn't feel comfortable if I couldn't leave room to spread out." Ave looked unconvinced.

"Come on, you angels of mercy," Maggie encouraged, smiling, "and have a piece of this with me." She looked under the sofa. "Come on out and say 'hi,' Gus," she coaxed. His dark pointed snout peeked out from the sofa's edge.

She had to pull him out forcibly, but once exposed, Gus acted as if they'd come to see him alone, making himself the center of attention while Maggie led them into the kitchen. She set the table with plates and cups.

"This looks delicious!" she praised, cutting the cake.

"Rosalie made it." Ave readily credited her friend. "She's known for her rum cake, you know. It's nearly a legend around here."

Maggie sucked some sweet goo from her finger after she'd carefully laid the pieces on their plates. "Mmmm."

The ladies sat by the window where the afternoon light cruelly revealed every line in their faces. Ave fiddled and squirmed nervously as Rosalie settled sighing into a relieved and unmoving heap in her chair. She was a pillow of a woman, soft and rounded, with a pale creased face surrounded by undulating waves of nearly white hair. The dark blouse she wore caused her skin and hair to fade into the window's light. "We really should have called first," she apologized a second time.

"I'm totally to blame," Ave chirped. "I insisted we spring it on you. We've meant to get up here sooner, but . . . you know how spring is around here, what with calving and airing things out after winter, and gardening . . . it just flew by before we knew it. And then the kids out of school, and Rosalie and I so busy with church . . ." Ave wore a striped blouse that strongly resembled a referee's. Her face was perpetually screwed into an expression of slight worry. Atop her pinched brow, her hair sat helmet-like, unnaturally dark, short, rigid, shellacked into permanent place.

"No, no," Maggie said, "it's all right. Don't apologize,

please. It's lovely that you thought to do this for me. Really, I appreciate it . . . And the cake is fabulous—you'll have to give me the recipe, Rosalie."

"I will, I will. I should've thought to write it down and bring it with me . . . You know why it's so good, don't you? There's a half cup of rum in the batter and another half cup in the glaze." They all chuckled and made predictable jokes about getting drunk on the cake.

"We think it's wonderful, if a bit mysterious, that you've come back, Maggie," Ave said, trying unsuccessfully to hide her curiosity.

"Yes," Rosalie agreed, "we were awfully glad to see you come back. You were missed when you left, you know. And none of us ever heard from you, not once in all this time!"

Maggie didn't answer. She just looked down at her plate while Ave went on. "That's right. You just left without a word to anybody, and didn't stay in touch at all." She was nearly scolding now, then she backed off. "We'd have never heard a thing about you but for Jill's summer visits, and even then, we only heard what little she told our kids when they all got together."

Maggie seized an opening to change the subject. "How *are* your kids, Ave?"

This subject served to completely deflect attention from her, as Ave poured forth a cornucopia of information about her nearly-grown daughter and son, their academic achievements, their successes in 4-H and at the stock show that January, their sports highlights, and even their dating histories.

"Lorraine has been dating the Nelson boy, Steve, steadily for two years now. I think they're considering marriage. Her dad and I are just kind of waiting for them to spring it on us any day now." She had finished the cake and asked for a second cup of coffee, if Maggie didn't mind. Maggie obliged as Ave continued, "I think one reason it's taken them so long, I'll tell you quite frankly . . . ," she was rather proud of speaking frankly whenever she could actually bring herself to do it, "was that Steve was always about half gone on Jill every summer. I think Jill kept him awfully confused for all his teenaged years. You know how hard it can be for young people to know who they're really in love with. So, don't be mad at me, Maggie, if I'm glad he finally decided on my Lorraine . . ."

"Oh, Ave . . . no . . . not at all. Of course not. I think it's wonderful for you since you like Steve so well. I only remember him as a freckle-faced little kid, you know. Did he turn out to be a nice young man?"

Rosalie broke in, "He's a good boy—a bit timid about the world, though. You know how it can be, growing up so sheltered here. I don't think he ever gave one thought to anything but staying on the ranch. He could barely force himself to try UW for a semester before he hightailed it back here. But he's a good worker and a good son to his folks, and he'll be a good steady husband, no doubt."

"And what about your own boy, Rosalie? Dennis, isn't it?" Maggie asked, surprising herself for dredging up his name from her murky memory.

Ave laughed almost unkindly. "You have to let me tell her what Denny got into, Rosalie," she said, taking over by laying her hand on Rosalie's arm, pinning it to the table. "He went off to Oregon, went to school in Portland, and now, get this . . . for a boy from Saratoga . . . he's a marine biologist living in Monterey, California."

"Oh my gosh, Rosalie!" Maggie said, wide-eyed. "I didn't know he was living that near to me. I could've gone to see him. I went down to Monterey a lot."

144

Rosalie nodded. "Dan and I go out there to see him every year and we think that's the prettiest place we've ever been. We think he's darned lucky to have landed there. And he seems happy—he seems to feel pretty lucky about it too."

"But Maggie," Ave asked in a wheedling voice, looking around her, "seriously, wouldn't you like another painting or something for your living room? I paint as a hobby, you know, and I'd be happy to give you one of my paintings as a housewarming present. I wish I'd thought to bring one with me . . . if I'd just known . . ."

"Gee, Ave," Maggie floundered, trying to be polite yet discourage her offer forcefully enough that she wouldn't press it, "that's so kind of you, but I just couldn't take a gift like that; it'd be too much . . ."

"No, no. Really, I've got stacks of them. Gary gets mad at me for keeping on, buying canvases and paints, when they're just going to waste. Now that I've seen your place, I know one that might fit right in . . ." She looked at Rosalie, "You know, Rosalie, the one I did of the river all in greens and blues . . ."

Maggie was relieved to hear it wasn't of a clown or a chipmunk, or little children with big eyes, since it seemed unavoidable. *Oh well, I can always put it away and just hang it when I know she's coming.*

"Well, that sort of brings up the other purpose of our visit, anyway," Ave said. "I belong to a china painting class too. Just a small group of ladies, really a nice bunch of gals. We'd certainly welcome you to join us, Maggie. We always need new blood," she joked. *Fresh blood,* Maggie thought.

"Oh, Ave," Rosalie stopped her, "you remember Maggie never was much for getting together with a bunch of us hens indoors. She was a kind of wild and woolly outdoors type, don't you remember?"

145

She looked at Maggie. "But, seriously, Maggie, maybe you *would* like to join the lady's garden club. Just look at your flowers out there!" The sun shown through the transparent pastels like jewels. "Or come join our church choir," Rosalie continued. "I remember you had such a nice voice—a beautiful clear bell of a soprano, strong on the high notes—and our soprano section is so weak . . . just Lil who sings flat and Janet who screeches out the high notes like a rooster's squawking. I don't mean to be so mean about it, but it's true. And it's such a nice church, you know." Ave nodded, but didn't speak. "The pastor is new. He's a bright young man who was called from up in the Northeast—from New Hampshire, if you can believe it— and he seems a bit lost out here, but he's trying so hard, and he has the nicest family." Her eyes sparkled as she spoke of her church and the new pastor.

"And his sermons don't put you to sleep, either," Ave sang out in the middle of Rosalie's oration. "I'm not kidding. I used to be so embarrassed to wake up at the 'Amen' every Sunday when Pastor Wilson was there. I nearly fell off the pew one Sunday when I jerked awake. It was embarrassing. Rosalie used to have to dig me in the ribs—we sit next to each other, you know, in the alto section of the choir."

"She's right about the quality of the sermons," Rosalie vouched. "Just come try *one*, Maggie. What could it hurt? Everyone could use his message. He's not one of those fire-and-brimstone types at all, and he doesn't preach the same-old-same-old either. He puts a fresh face on the old stories you've always loved. He makes them stick. He makes them into something you can really use in your life. He's a positive force; he preaches love and forgiveness, none of that Old Testament eye for an eye. You know, like last week, it was the lilies of the field. 'Let the day's own trouble be sufficient for the day,' that's a great thing to keep in mind, don't you think? And 'Judge not, that you be not judged . . . the measure you give will be the measure you get.' "

"Rosalie, I don't know how you can remember word for word like that!" Ave marveled, genuinely impressed.

". . . 'Do not cast your pearls before swine' . . . Isn't that poetry? 'Seek and you will find; knock and it will be opened to you' . . . I love that whole passage. 'If you, then, who are evil, know how to give good gifts to your children, how much more will your Father who is in heaven give good things to those who ask him?' That keeps me hopeful. 'Enter by the narrow gate . . . for the gate is narrow and the way is hard that leads to life, and those who find it are few.' Isn't that an inspiration to keep trying, no matter how hard things look?" Rosalie had truly warmed to her subject and broke off her recitation reluctantly. "Who couldn't be helped in life by being reminded of words like those?" she asked as openly as the faces of the flowers in Maggie's July garden.

And, so sincerely and well-spoken were her words, so uncannily chosen, that Maggie was touched in the same way her flowers touched her. Rosalie's words seemed a message sent just for her.

"Well, anyway, Maggie, I didn't mean to run on so. I do get carried away. I'm sorry. But think about it, will you? We wanted to reach out to you. It's no good living up here if you don't join in the community. It's too lonely and big and far from everything otherwise. So think about it, okay?"

"I'll have to think about it, Rosalie," Maggie answered. "I don't know . . . A heathen like me . . ." She was wishing at this point that she had a bra on under her yellow shirt.

Ave chuckled as Rosalie touched Maggie's arm lightly.

"Oh, come on now . . . a heathen, really, Maggie . . ."
Rosalie crooned, as Ave eyed Maggie's unkempt appearance closely.

When they had left, with kind words pouring from all like syrup, Maggie picked up her dust rag to finish her chores. The dryer sounded and she folded clothes on the bed while Gus wound himself in one of the warm towels.

God does work in mysterious ways, she laughed to herself. She could see her reflection in the bureau mirror and pushed her hair back. There was a smudge of cleanser on her cheek they'd been too polite to mention, and a bit of rum glaze on her top lip. She really did look like a pagan. *And just when you're least ready for it, too.*

Seven

Jill's words came back to Maggie as she lay on her bed, stroking Gus gently. "I don't know why you left." Phrases of the dinner conversation rose to the surface, sank, and re-surfaced, merged with Jill's, gaining momentum like the rif-fles of a stream, like the deep growls of thunder that fueled the fires that night. Gus stretched his long tubular torso into a sinuous arch, catching his front claws in the blanket. He rotated his head in a gesture of complete trust, allowing Maggie to stroke his throat. She looked through the window at the edgeless sky, a seamless white screen for the movie that she had tried so hard to suppress through all these years, the scenes of which flickered now slowly into focus.

She was working in the loft of the barn, the hottest pos-sible place on that scorching day in late August. An oven. Sweat ran down the valley between her breasts, and she was covered in hay chaff. It clung to the fine hair on her arms and thighs and stuck to the salty rivulets drawn down her cheeks. She could see Diana below her in the truck bed, grappling with the hook, trying to slide it under the baling twine so the bales could be hoisted by pulley to the window of the loft. Diana was the weak link of the chain, so to speak. They had given her the job requiring the least strength because Diana was tiny, barely over five feet, and she hadn't done manual labor through the summer as Maggie and Ken had. She was determined to do her share that day, though. She worked without pause, watching the bales rise over her head where she could see Maggie's long brown arms pulling them through the window into the loft. Maggie released the hook and shoved or carried bales to Ken who bucked them up onto the stack. The wrangler in that year of 1982 was a redheaded kid named Keith Lansing. He was the final body in their assembly line, muscling the bales into place in the tight stack with arms strong from hammering steel.

They'd been at it all day, loading bales from the hay meadow into the three-quarter-ton pickup, driving to the barn, and stowing twelve tons of hay. The late August temperature rose steadily through the day so that by ten thirty in the morning the men were stripped to their waists, and Maggie and Diana to halter tops, disregarding scratches to their arms in order to survive the heat. Diana and Maggie worked well together. Maggie's feelings for Ken's girlfriend were genuine, warm. Cheerful, energetic, with an infectious gravelly laugh and a quirky sense of humor, Diana was working a summer job between semesters in Greeley, but came to the ranch nearly every weekend to be with Ken, who was spending the summer there after graduating. Ken and Diana were serious about each other and, like all lovers, inseparable, and like all young couples, interchangeably loving and fighting, laughing one day and morose the next. With her upturned nose and wide blue eyes, Diana was an irresistible stunner. And because of the magnetism of physical beauty, she and Ken were an enviable couple, drawing lingering looks from all of Saratoga. Ken was smaller than Hale, a compact athletic easy boy who had charmed his way through life with his fair hair and dark eyes and dazzling smile.

Hale and Maggie included them in every aspect of their life on the ranch. They ate meals together, worked and partied hard, shared clothes, housing, beer, fishing tackle, and toiletries. They had developed a ferocious poker rivalry, playing every possible evening. Sometimes, as they played late into the night, empty beer bottles overflowed the trash bins, covering the kitchen counter, while the game degenerated into a burlesque with pat hands abandoned in the distraction of a rambling anecdote whose ending might also be left dangling, forgotten in the telling. There was an occasional strip poker night with no one reaching full nudity, naughty but nice, almost incest, but not really.

Another bale came swinging toward the loft. Keith wiped the sweat from his eyes while Maggie and Ken bantered away at each other as they worked. "Leave it to your old man to have a cushy overnighter on the river the day we bring in the hay," Ken grumbled.

"Whine, whine, whine," Maggie chided. "You've been complaining all day, Ken. Hell! all week." She shoved the bale toward the stack and looked up at Ken as she released her fingers from beneath the twine. Her haltertop rode up the curve of her breasts with each drag or lift of the bales, so that every time she stood up, she had to tug it downward.

"What's between you and Di, anyway? You two have been at each other ever since she showed up."

"Oh, Diana's just on the rag."

"Don't be a jerk. You know I hate that misogynist crap."

"It's the truth, Maggie. Besides, you asked," Ken grinned disarmingly.

"So, you mean figuratively or literally?"

"Both. She's pissed at me because I'll be leaving soon for L.A. where she's afraid I'll (A) forget her, and (B) be seduced by some beach babe or something, I don't know. And she's also suffering from raging hormones with her period."

151

"Well, try to jolly her. Tonight's your last night, after all."

"Yeah, that's another pisser. I tried to talk her into staying a couple of extra nights before heading back to UNC, even if it meant she'd miss her first few days of classes, but she said no. I mean, we haven't had sex the whole week, and she's going to leave it that way."

Maggie laughed as *blue balls* flashed through her mind. She jerked another bale into the loft, yelling down at Diana, "You okay, Di? Need a break or anything?"

"I'm okay Mags. Let's get it done. This is the last load and I'm dying for a bath."

"Ten-four. I second that."

She watched Ken jerk the bale onto his thighs, forearms flexing, then boost it up to Keith. Sometimes he threw one with a sideways toss directly from the ground to the top of the stack. She could see the muscles tighten in his back as he twisted through his waist, stretched his arms above his head and tossed a bale overhand. His shoulders were red from sun and from the strain of the work, his face flushed with effort. Dust, grime, and hay particles covered all horizontal surfaces like powdered sugar; the top of his shoulders, his forearms, his thighs, his eyelashes.

"You're a mess!" she said, dusting the gooey film from one shoulder. "Look, even your navel is full." She pointed and laughed as he pushed his flat stomach out to look. "You're the proverbial hayseed, Kennie. You'd think this was Green Acres, not Paradise Ranch."

"Hey, you two, quit horsing around and let's get this finished!" Keith called down to them. "I'm gonna die of dehydration up here!"

They all whooped with joy as the last bale came up the pulley, and fainted onto the pile of loose hay when it had been maneuvered into place.

As they drove back to the lodge, Maggie and Diana huddled in the truck bed in the shade of the cab while the men rode together inside.

Maggie brushed the hay particles out of Diana's hair, then laughed, pinching Diana's arm. "You'd better give him some tonight, Diana. You can't part company for God knows how long without making love one last time."

"I know, Maggie. Believe me, I know. I'm dying for it myself. But I'm having the period from hell, I've taken a double dose of meds for cramps, and he's being a prick about absolutely everything. I've got to leave by nine at the latest tonight to get into my dorm by midnight. I mean, I've got to be in class at eight tomorrow morning." She had a miserable expression on her pretty face. "It's as if there's a conspiracy against us or something."

As Maggie walked to the house from the lodge where Keith had parked the truck, grasshoppers buzzed through the dry grass. The beaver pond looked like a hot spring in the mid-afternoon heat, though she knew the water was cold. Even the trout looked torpid. Hale's horses stood in the shade, ignoring grass to doze in relative relief, barely bothering to swish their tails at lazy flies. The dogs had long since given up following their masters at work. They lay under the deck in cool nests they had dug in the soil. The arched limbs of the spruce trees sagged under the sun's weight as Maggie stood on the back stoop to dust herself off. Stepping into the mud porch, she removed all her outer clothes before going into the house.

She drew a hot bath despite the hot day and soaked luxuriously, moaning out loud as she sank in to her chin. Sipping a glass of Chardonnay, she listened to the sounds coming from the living room of an old LP of Carley Simon singing torch songs. "Fair weather father; wants his wife to be a truck driver; wants his wife to be a gardener, and still look like a Hollywood starlet, and still look like a Hollywood starlet." She sang the words aloud with the intensity of a personal grudge.

Fatigue, the sedating effect of hot water and the hot day, and the wine she sipped, all blurred her focus on the task she assigned herself during the bath: sorting out the complexities of the current situation.

She could understand the difficulties between Ken and Diana because she and Hale had been at odds all summer. She knew he was walking a tightrope between herself and Ken, trying to appease them both in different ways for opposite viewpoints of basically the same dispute. Things were so tangled that even trying to phrase it created a confusing mess. She was angry that Hale had decided to live full-time on the ranch his father had given him, her opinion be damned; and both she and Hale could see that Ken was sizzling a slow burn because, now that the ranch was Hale's, Ken *wouldn't* have the option of living here full-time any longer. It was hard to understand where he was coming from. Why should he care about the ranch when he had always claimed to have grandiose plans for making the kind of big splash in the world that had nothing to do with ranch life in a remote part of Wyoming? Hale was trying to lavish her with submissive kindness, a placating attention that made her feel like an utter bitch. With Ken, he tried to keep a low profile, playing down his role as owner, operator, and even big brother, because he didn't want to rub salt in Ken's wounds. Kennie was accustomed to having his own way in everything, although, again, in the matter of the ranch, it was hard to tell what exactly he wanted.

Maybe he hadn't cared about the ranch at all until it was

given to Hale. That was one way of explaining it. There was a fierce one-sided rivalry between the two that had its origins before Ken's birth. The story Maggie had been told was that Mrs. Adamson had lost a child, a little girl named June born five years after Hale, who had died of spinal meningitis contracted when she entered school at age five. Within a year of June's death, Mrs. Adamson became pregnant for the exact purpose of relieving her own suffering from the loss. Born to replace her little girl, Ken became her obsession. Mrs. Adamson poured herself into her lastborn. She was terrified when the time came for Kennie to start school, demanding that he be held back. As a compromise, Mr. Adamson agreed to home schooling until Ken turned eight, when his mother's anxieties had subsided enough to send him to public school. By then the boy had learned well to have his own way through charm or temper or divisiveness or all three. Though self-centered and spoiled, his personal beauty, intelligence, and a core of genuine goodness had allowed him to coast through life basically unimpeded.

When Mr. Adamson gave the ranch to Hale, Mrs. Adamson vehemently objected. Hale himself urged his father to leave it to both sons, but his father was set in his decision. The ranch was his family's contribution to his marriage, and he felt justified in deciding its future in spite of his wife's objection. "You've had your way in certain things, and I've not objected, Christine, and now I'll have mine in this matter," he told her. Hale had told Maggie he believed his father was trying to compensate him for having not had the kind of motherly love that Ken had. Or then again, maybe his father intended to punish her because he himself had been stung by her neglect, neglect that resulted from her obsession with Kennie. The center of this storm remained seemingly calm. Ken had shrugged off the gift to Hale with the remark, "It's never been anything to me anyway."

Maggie poured wine into her empty glass from the bottle she'd set beside the tub. As the bath cooled, she allowed some water to flow through the plug, then began refilling it with a trickle from the hot tap. "Riverboat gambler," she sang too loudly with Carley, her voice cracking on the high note. *I'm getting snockered and the fun hasn't even begun,* she thought. She and Ken and Diana were going to a bash tonight before Di left. It was a celebration for Jo Nelson, who had not only just turned twenty-one, but would also be announcing her engagement to Paul Sifford. *But it's a dirge for us, (or is it 'we'?), three Musketeers,* she thought. *Mouseketeers, whatever. No more wine for me until the party.* Diana and Ken would be leaving and who knew when they would all be back together. Ken was taking off on some fool's errand. His mother had finagled an introduction for him to some politician out in L.A.—some old school chum or extremely distant relative of hers, or something. Frankly, Maggie thought Ken was hoping to be discovered by a movie mogul. *Yeah. Yeah, right.* But who could tell? Maybe with those boyish good looks of his . . . *Oh my God, sometimes I think I married the wrong brother.* She poured herself another half glass of wine in spite of her previous resolve. *Get real, Maggie! You're just mad at Hale, that's all.*

She had confronted him angrily when he stood by his decision to move to the ranch. "It's what I want to do, Maggie."

"You're just escaping," she had yelled. "It's an evasion, a waste of all your training, of all your potential."

"But I'm just punching the time clock now, Maggie. If

I'm going to spend my life at something, I want to love what I'm doing."

"What about what I want?"

"I thought you loved the place too."

"The ranch is wonderful, Hale, but not as a permanent lifestyle."

"There's no such thing as lifestyle, Mags. What the hell is 'lifestyle' anyway? There's only living. Everything that counts in life could flourish up here. It could be a wonderful place to raise a family." Though she disagreed because she believed a city had incomparably more to contribute to a child's development, this argument did sway her somewhat. They both wanted children so badly. She wanted to be the kind of mother she hadn't had herself. The paltry affection of her own childhood left a void she filled with dreams of a perfect relationship with a child of her own, a relationship full of unconditional love freely and joyfully offered. She could only speculate on Hale's reason for wanting to start a family right away. He had hardly talked to her about the little sister he'd called Junie Bug, a toddler with a belly laugh, the game five-year-old, full of silliness and adventure. And love. Junie, whose fierce love of him had outweighed his mother's neglect.

Hale had his voids to fill too, greater than hers. She knew that. They'd been trying to conceive a child ever since their marriage three years ago, but her cautious joy at late periods inevitably crashed when hope proved false. She had finally quit keeping track of her monthly cycles in utter frustration, and the frequency and spontaneity of their sex life had steadily waned as she became morbidly fatalistic in her certainty that one or the other of them was sterile. She began pressuring Hale to have a checkup to determine if the problem was his, but Hale dragged his feet. He was so busy trying to convert the ranch to a fishing lodge those first few months. But there was more to it than that. He also had a real antipathy for all things medical, which Maggie believed came from the family's suffering—from losing Junie so suddenly and so young. That wound had never healed. Its pain still gnawed at the Adamsons; they had lived their lives in concentric circles around it.

Sympathetic with his reasons, Maggie tried to be patient with Hale's inaction, but when tests proved she was fertile, she was increasingly, even irrationally, frustrated with Hale, blaming him for a range of unrelated complaints which, in reality, he had nothing to do with.

She downed the last of her wine. *Maybe I did make the wrong choice,* playing cat and mouse with herself. *Pffffft! Don't be ridiculous!* She made an effort to be serious and logical, but couldn't stop her train of thought. *Ken is aggressive, while Hale is downright passive (Ha! Passive-aggressive, is what he is!); Ken dares when Hale holds back; he's brash and outgoing, while Hale is quiet and inscrutable; he grins when Hale grimaces.* Her admiration of Ken's aggression and confidence irritated Hale, who labeled it cockiness, hubris. She saw Hale as Gregory Peck's Atticus Finch—tall and dark-browed, safe, and strong, and just; while Ken was James Dean in *East of Eden* or *Giant* or *Rebel Without a Cause*—he fit all three roles—dangerous but good underneath. *I mean, they're SO different. Do you think Christine could possibly have played around?* She laughed aloud at the audacity of the idea. *Don't be daft,* she told herself, *you're just pissed at Hale and pissed on wine.*

She sobered up somewhat once out of the tub, applying makeup carefully, then looked through her closet for an outfit. *I'm going to knock 'em all dead tonight,* she thought belligerently. *I'll set Saratoga on its ears.* At twenty-five she didn't want to be outshone by a bunch of younger girls barely out of braces. She chose a short red silk shift with spaghetti straps, then slid into a slip and stepped into the dress. *Nothing like red on a brunette.* She applied the reddest lipstick she owned. When she stood in front of the full-length mirror she smiled slyly.

Diana gave her an inscrutable look as she stepped up to their car and leaned her elbows against Ken's open window. "I'll follow you over in my car, then," she said.

"Wow! You look ready to party tonight, Maggie," Ken admired. "Every woman in the room will hate you. Everyone but Diana, of course. Give me a kiss, baby," he whispered to Diana and leaned over to her. He kissed her long and hard. "Mmmm." He tasted his lips as he put the car into gear. "Jo won't stand a chance as center of attention tonight against you two. Let's go raise some hell. To hell with what they think of us in Saratoga, anyway." And that proved prophetic.

The air had cooled with the sun's setting. A nearly full moon glowed gold and laid low against the black horizon. All was silver-edged in the moonlight, and the mixed smells of sage and grass hay meadows, and the sounds of insects filled the night air. They drove to the outskirts of town where Jo's father had rented the Grange Hall for the party. An ugly stone block box of a building stood alone on bare ground with nothing but a single straggling apple tree for company, a lonesome scene but for the raucous sounds coming from inside the building. Rocking reverberations from the live Western band pulled them in. Inside, a big empty wooden floor in the darkened room was ringed by people helping themselves to heaps of food and drink at tables along two walls.

"Where's Hale?" Maggie was asked fifty times before she

had reached the end of the food table. She had to tilt her head into their ears and yell her response as the band laid into another song. It was foot-stomping, shit-kicking kind of music, but everyone was too busy congratulating Jo and Paul and filling their stomachs with barbecued ribs to dance. Ken was involved with handshaking and back-slapping while Maggie and Diana stood sizing up the situation and being sized up. The floor was scuffed by herds of cowboy boots, and big belt buckles flashed through the length of the room. White foreheads topped red faces on those men who had removed their hats. There were tight jeans and tight shirts and loose tongues and roving eyes and flashing smiles and one red dress in the center of the motion and commotion, all rotating crazily like a slow motion kaleidoscope.

Jo's father made a toast that ended in a group yell. On that cue, the band struck up a gut-wrenching throb that sent Paul and Jo out onto the dance floor. The crowd whooped and clapped their enthusiasm and began to spill out around the couple. Ken nearly pulled Diana off her feet into the center of the floor, then swung her in an arc around him and clamped her against his chest.

"Wanna dance, baby?"

"Oh, it's going to be *that* kind of night, eh?" she laughed. "I can see already I'm going to hate to leave early."

Maggie never sat out a number. Single men outnumbered women and no one looked quite as fine as Maggie that night. She was emanating something volatile and knew it. She danced and laughed with abandon, half-reveling, half-rebelling. She couldn't identify what she was feeling and didn't really care.

The dark room grew hot and humid, though the door was opened to the cool night air. Men breathed against

Maggie's naked neck and shoulders through the slow dances, their damp hands trembling against the small of her back as they guided her gently around other couples. She caught fragmentary glimpses of Ken and Diana wrapped in each other's arms, twirling with elan as slow songs trailed off and switched suddenly to pulsing beats. Maggie's dark hair lay wetly against the back of her neck as she fanned herself between dances. She stepped toward the cool air of the open door, but was pulled back into the dizzying heat with a "C'mon Maggie, you can't miss this one."

At nine o'clock, Diana and Ken approached her so Diana could say good-bye. When she gave Diana a parting hug and kiss, they laughed as their dresses stuck together.

"When will I see you again, Di?" Maggie yelled.

"I don't know, Maggie. I hate to think. I'll call you once I'm settled into my classes, okay?"

"Good luck, Di!" Maggie felt suddenly overwhelmed with emotion as Diana and Ken passed through the door. She could feel tears rising. She walked to the beverage table and quickly downed another glass of wine.

It was fifteen minutes before Ken returned to the room, disheveled and a little crazy-eyed. He walked up to Maggie to say something when the band returned from their break with a honky tonk kind of number that blasted through all conversation. Ken grinned and dragged Maggie onto the floor where he snapped her into his body and danced with an energy that emptied a space around them. They danced through the room like the whole floor belonged to them, and the night too. Girls peered over their partner's shoulders as Maggie and Ken drew near. Singles standing along the wall watched their movements through the dusky atmosphere. There was a gravity in both their faces though their bodies moved wildly, a mocking dare in the looks they gave each other. Maggie tossed her damp hair out of her eyes when the music shifted without pause to a slow dance. Ken twirled her toward him as he had Diana and held her in a swaying embrace. She lowered her head and laid it against his shoulder. Jo and Paul bumped into them obliviously. Jo's eyes were fuzzy, her mascara running in dark rivulets, and her vowels indistinct as she croaked to Maggie and Ken hoarsely, "Watch out you two. You're playing with fire." They laughed and shook their heads at her.

"Boy, is she going to feel like shit in the morning," Ken said, his cheek touching Maggie's ear. He tucked his lips into the crook of her neck as they danced, singing the words of the music quietly into the damp skin of her shoulder. The stubble of his beard left a red print on her neck. They swayed together long after the music had stopped.

Taking a break, they moved outside to cool off, drifting toward the old apple tree so she could lean against its trunk, fanning her face with her hand and pulling the bodice of her red dress away from under her breasts where it stuck to her body. They said little for a time, feeling awkward, then slipped gradually with feigned lightheartedness into chatter about the band and the dancers inside.

Maggie reached up idly and pulled a few leaves off the tree. "It's funny someone planted an apple tree here. I mean, they're not the hardiest things at this altitude, you know." Spotting an apple, she said, "Look, Ken," and pointed at the fruit. "I don't think I've ever noticed fruit on this tree before. It's a miracle to actually get fruit, considering our winters. God only knows what variety it is. Most likely it's just some pippin. Some poor little bastardized nameless thing. It looks ripe, though, so it must be an early variety." Breaking the apple from its branch, she examined its ripeness. She bit into the fruit cautiously, chewing once,

162

then twice. "Mmmm. It's ripe and sweet." She ate away one side and offered him the other. "Go ahead," she urged, "it helps quench your thirst. Here, go on." She pushed it into his mouth, laughing derisively. He raised his hand to it and ate the rest, then threw the core into the dark with a sidearm toss. He licked the juice from his hand and wrist, then reaching for her hand, raised her fingers to his mouth and sucked the juice from each finger. She should have stopped him, but it was as if she were hypnotized, watching him do such an outlandish, unpardonable thing. He tried to gauge her reaction, but she was blank, sending no message.

Slipping his arm behind her back, they returned slowly to the hall as the music dissolved into the still night around them. A coyote cried a wailing song from outside the ring of light cast by the building, but the sound was absorbed by the music.

No one dared cut in on them as they danced away the last hour. "Ladies and gents," the leader bellowed into the microphone, "this will be the last song of the evening, so give it all you've got!" A boogie beat thumped forth. The crowd screeched and roared as if ready for battle. Dancers became dervishes, spinning dizzily flank to flank in a maze of circles, a seething, heaving throng of rapt communion, worshipping in a mist of heat. Ken and Maggie were bumped and jostled, and swung crashing into another couple. She laughed joyfully, panting from the violence of the increasing swiftness. A glitter sparkled through her lashes from beneath the velvet shade of her eyes. A lustrous fleck shone on her lips as a warm current of color flowed up her slim throat and across the whiteness above the black curve of her brow. Ken's eyes shone with audacity and re-bellious passion. The dancers ground the floor and gouged the air until the crowd merged into one writhing creature with a pulsating red heart at its center. The music crescendoed into the home stretch. When it reached its final peak, Ken dipped Maggie to the floor and planted a fierce wet kiss on her lips while the room reverberated with echoes. They said their good-byes, but could not find Jo and Paul anywhere, then ran to the car, gasping for air.

As Ken drove Maggie's car home, no words were exchanged. Maggie laid her head back against the seat and closed her eyes. Her breathing slowed. She could see the outline of Ken's face through her lashes, but couldn't determine his expression. He leaned forward toward the wheel, gripping it tightly with both hands. Her knees had swung toward the center of the car and her arms were crossed across her stomach. She saw him glance at her, but pretended to doze. The moonlight ran its fingers along the smooth curves of her face, down one shaded eye and around the tapered end of her heart-shaped chin. The red silk dress twisted across her hips. As they turned into the ranch's drive, Ken placed his hand on her left knee. He reached up to pull her arm away from her body and followed its length from her elbow to her hand, then drew the hand up to his mouth, kissing it wordlessly as they pulled up to his cabin. He killed the engine and lights.

She opened her eyes and slid closer to him, groggy, moony. "Maggie," he whispered, "look what you've done to me, Maggie." He put her hand against his chest where she could feel his heart pounding. Then he moved her hand down into his lap and pressed it there. "You can't leave me like this, Maggie," he whispered hoarsely, eyes pleading.

He let go of her hand and stepped out of the car. It was so late there were no lights or movement anywhere in the entire compound, not even from the horses in the corral. He walked around and opened her door. She sat staring at the floor for a few seconds so that he began to waver against the doorframe. Then she stepped out of the car and followed him into the cabin.

When the fever had broken, their illness was cured, its victims retaining virulent antibodies. She left before daybreak, returning her car to her house where she showered and fell into her own bed but could not sleep. There was no grasping what had happened, no reason, no excuse, no explanation compelling enough to explain what they'd done. Surrendering to a tide, they had casually, recklessly, almost blithely allowed something cataclysmic into their lives. They avoided each other that day, but after Hale returned from the float trip, Ken managed to talk to Maggie alone beyond the yard of the house.

"Christ, Maggie!" he hissed, "I'm so sorry. I must've been crazy last night. I don't know what to say."

"Shhh. I'm just as much as fault as you, Ken."

"I'm such a fucking idiot! I mean, I'd give my life for Hale. What the fuck could I have been thinking? And what about Diana? Look, Maggie, I don't expect you to understand how a fifteen-year-old kid could feel about his brother's twenty-year-old wife. I mean, I've been in love with you from day one, but who knows if it was because you belonged to Hale or because you are the way you are. I've been so screwed up about things. Sometimes I feel like I've been a surrogate all my life. I've been a pushy ass just trying to make some space for whoever the hell I really am. I know I'm not making any sense. What I mean is, I've been so fucked up about myself and Hale and you and Mom and Dad and the ranch. Then along came Diana. I love you, Maggie, but I'm dead ass in love with Diana. I'd give anything to take back last night. And, then again, I wouldn't take it back for anything. Christ, Maggie! What are we gonna do?"

He ripped the grass up with his foot, then looked up to search her eyes. She could hardly bear the anguish in his face. "We're going to get over it, Ken." Her voice was determined. "I don't know how I could betray Hale like this either. I'm sick about it, completely physically and mentally sick." *Spiritually too.* She dropped her head into her hands and moaned. But the demon was herself. No escaping what they'd done. If only time could be rewound and life replayed. Her shoulders hunched into a sag that slid toward collapse. Ken almost reached out to support her, but checked himself, standing awkwardly, hands pulsing at his sides, forced to keep the misery inside, until she raised her head, squared her shoulders, and looked fiercely into his eyes. "But I'll tell you one thing. He'll never find out. We can't undo it, but I'm not dragging him into the mess we've made. You and I are just going to have to live with it and move on, you hear?"

Ken clutched that command like a lifeline. "I hear you, Maggie. I can't see that it would help things by telling Hale or Diana. I agree with you there." Finally, his voice full of anguish, he choked out, "Christ! I'm so sorry, Maggie." He turned and sprinted away. The next day Ken left the ranch.

She made wild love to Hale every night for two weeks, as if she could even the score somehow that way. Six weeks later, Ken called to tell Hale that he had joined the Peace Corps right after he'd left the ranch and would be leaving the country within a few days. Two weeks after his phone call, Maggie's gynecologist informed her that she was about nine weeks pregnant.

Eight

The North Platte River originates in north central Colorado, where it is called the "Illinois." It flows north through a narrow valley between the Medicine Bow Mountains to the east and the Park Range to the west, crossing the Colorado-Wyoming border, where it becomes the "North Platte." The North Platte is forced to continue northward by the Laramie Mountains on its right, whose north end the river must bend around in order to assume the southeasterly heading that leads it eventually to the Gulf of Mexico.

The North Platte runs free until it flows against the Seminoe dam fifty miles north of Saratoga where it forms the Seminoe and Pathfinder reservoirs. Thirty miles beyond the north end of those lakes, the North Platte makes its wide right hand turn at Casper, rolling from there down to the Missouri, and on to the Gulf.

The 141 miles of the North Platte from its origins in the Colorado mountains to the Seminoe Reservoir are a fisherman's Eden. The river is in a natural freestone state, and is not stocked from hatcheries. It is also Eden for the fish. The naturalness of the river and the enforcement of slot limits which force fishermen to release the smallest and the largest fish caught, have led to numbers of healthy rainbow, brown, and cutthroat trout that are counted in the low thousands per mile.

For a distance far downstream of Saratoga, the land is open sagebrush high desert prairie. The fishing there is some of the best, so incredible that a stretch of the tail waters below Kortes Dam is named the Miracle Mile, known by those who know and love it as simply "The Mile."

Far upstream of Saratoga, the river runs through alpine forest and steep canyons. Those waters are shallow and white from splashing down the mountainside. Some stretches are nothing but riffles. The river there is prime wading water, too shallow for floating.

The stretch of river surrounding Saratoga includes twenty-six miles designated as Blue Ribbon fishing. These waters are bordered by the expansive ranches of the Saratoga Valley. Much of the river here is inaccessible by road, and most of this section runs through private land. The banks and the streambed within private areas belong to the landowners, but the water itself is public. The easiest access, therefore, is by boat. These are the waters that Hale Adamson fished.

Hale pulled against his right oar, then feathered the broad edge into the current. He watched the flies drifting along parallel to the dory in that sensuous, intimate dance that is the particular magic of float-fishing. They were mere specks of light against the purling jade water, jigging, dipping and skating among the silver jewelry of the river turbulence.

"I've got one!" Brian crowed. "Eh, Vance! Eat your heart out, Bud. The first strike belongs to me!"

"Bite my dorsal fin, Bri—I mean, Bloated Sucker." Brian and Vance had a repertoire of convoluted "Indian names" for each other—a sort of Boy Scout parlance turned nasty.

" 'Leaping Rainbow,' Vance. It's 'Leaping Rainbow' to you," Brian called, even as he played the feisty trout. When his trout leaped clear of the water, they all brayed wildly. "Look at the size of him!" "Yeah, he's purty too. A purty 'bow."

"Not a bad job, for a fisherboy wanna-be, He Who Breaks Wind," Vance almost, but not quite, congratulated Brian as he worked the trout into the net. Hale grabbed the camera to snap a photo as Brian tenderly removed the hook from the gristly lip, then stretched the fish out in both hands to maximize its length, holding it as gently as a baby and giving it the same loving look he might have given his own infant son. He struck a heroic pose with the fish for the camera and for Vance's eyes, then carefully lowered it facing upstream into the water, cupping his hands around it while the water flowed through its gills. When the big trout began to oscillate slowly, Brian withdrew both hands and watched the glint of the trout flipping into the depths.

"Good-bye, my beauty. Ah, it's like watching the green flash when the sun sets on a tropical ocean, eh Vance? An instant of unearthly color, and, poof! it's gone and you missed it if you blinked."

"Very poetic crap," Vance groused. "Say, what pattern are you using there, Bri?"

"Oh, it's 'Bri My Buddy' now, is it? Now that you want to tap into my vast store of fish lore."

"Hey, you made a rhyme."

Hale shook his head as he pulled the oars a few times to bring the dory into the main current. There was a riffle downstream at the end of an island he wanted to drift. He loved bringing these two out. They were his kind of fishermen. They were skilled and dedicated fly fishermen who only got together once a year. Brian managed a sign products firm in Fort Collins and Vance a large rental car agency in Wisconsin. But they had a common history that went way back. In their teens they had formed a rock band while in school together in Colorado. Every once in awhile they still broke into spontaneous jamming around the campfire, instrumentless, singing duets while strumming air across their thighs: *Chain Lightning, Baby You Can Drive My Car, Spanish Moon,* and a song Brian wrote to his wife, *Jalapeno Woman* ("She gives me the green chile blues"), and much of Vance's campfire "wisdom" came directly from Frank Zappa. They had good voices, funny jokes, efficient camping skills, and best of all they considered fishing life's ultimate sublimity. They'd come to Paradise Ranch for a week every late August for ten years, on their way to and from other Wyoming streams like the Tongue, Laramie, Medicine Bow, Little Snake, Green, Salt and Wind Rivers, sometimes going up into Montana to fish the Madison and Yellowstone, then backtracking to the San Miguel, Gunnison, White, Yampa, Frying Pan, Eagle, Roaring Fork, and South Platte in Colorado on their way home. They camped for most of the two to three week pilgrimage, never shaving or bathing until the last night before returning home. Brian set up his tent far from Vance's roaring snores, inflating a thick air mattress with a small portable compressor because he had a bad back. Their favorite fishing water was shallow streams that could be waded, but few fishermen could resist the large size of the browns, rainbows, and cutthroats of bigger, deeper rivers like the North Platte.

Brian was camp cook. He spent weeks planning a dozen suppers and stashing a gamut of rot gut snacks to fortify them between meals, should they ever take a break from the river. They rarely ate trout. If they did, they preferred small Brookies for breakfast, but neither of them could bear killing a fish. Each tried to foist that job onto the other, going so far as cheating when drawing for short straw. Vance built the fires, stowed their beer supply in the river and watched Brian cook. Throughout their vacation he

170

chain-smoked whenever his hands were free because his wife didn't allow him to smoke at home. They were the angler's odd couple.

They never tired of fish stories and discussions of technique. Vance in particular had analyzed every insect that lived along Rocky Mountain streams. He knew intimate details of the breeding habits of midges, caddis flies, mayflies, stoneflies, salmonflies, green drakes and yellow sallies. Occasionally he fabricated a species, inventing a volume of excruciating minutia around it. The "Hellgremite" was his favorite faux fly. Brian's store of knowledge included the effect of different types of water and river bottoms on trout activities. Both had elaborate theories of atmospheric influences on fish behavior and hatch patterns.

Vance had sent Brian a screen saver of garishly colored trout approaching and receding through the blue waters of the computer screen. Brian responded in kind by sending Vance a mouse pad emblazoned with a photo of himself holding a huge cutthroat trout. They sent each other leering and frivolous e-mails throughout the year:

Dear Brian: CHAPTER 23 EVEN MORE OBSERVATIONS

OK, I'll buy another landing net. This time, I'll get a larger one as it seems that many of my fish are just too darned big to fit into a little Orvis teardrop model. I think you should go for the smaller model, because it would make the smallish fish you catch appear larger in photographs . . . I think about that big brown you had on up on the Miracle Mile, a big Colorado River trout lost under a rock, and that darned fish that wrapped around your legs on the White, and I realize that it's OK to lose these fish. It goes with the territory. No big deal . . . You caught some cutthroat on dry flies on the White River. Big deal. Everyone knows about the cutthroats "dumb gene" that they keep handing down through their generations. They'll keep coming up for a dry fly no matter how poorly it's presented . . .

THINGS I LEARNED ON THIS FISHING TRIP:

16/ Water, flies, trout, the stars, fire, rocks, rods, willows, clouds, rain, sun, mountains, cats, and Irish Creme make a wonderful combination—which I enjoy almost more than anything in life.

22/ There are WAY too many fishermen out there.

Fishing Summary, 1999 Things I Learned.

17/ . . . The stars on the North Platte can seem to make time stand still, but it doesn't. And here's a profound thought: Mother Nature dictated that we are very fortunate, and we should thank God every time we're in church for this: We are not ants, or mayflies, or deer, or even trout. We are humans, and that gives us a big advantage right away. Then, just to make it more interesting, we don't live in Kosovo, or China, or Nigeria. We are Americans! Then, on top of that, we don't live in Newark, or Lubbock, or Omaha. We live nice little lives in Wisconsin and Colorado. We don't handle baggage or drive taxis or work in a mill. Instead, we run businesses that we control and understand. Are we fortunate beings or what? I think we fly fish as our meek little way of communicating back to Mother Nature that we know all this, and we appreciate it. That's what I keep learning every time we do this. Is this profound, or what?

Mid-winter (well, almost) update:

I went over to my brother-in-law's house last night, and with both wives gone skiing, we drank some beer and

172

tied a couple of flies. His was a beautiful #16 adams-
thing, with lovely matching wings and a fluffy hackle.
Mine, of course, was a tiny #22 hook, embellished with a
few wraps of black thread, and a tiny pinch of dubbing to
form a thorax. His took the better part of an hour, while
mine took about 45 seconds and one slug of a Miller Gen-
uine Draft. Brilliant.

I should do that more often. Tie up little nymphs, that
is. Vance

And Vance, reminiscing of the waters of Rocky Mountain streams barely dried on his waders, wrote wistful sum-
maries every year of their trips from his home in Wisconsin,
copies of which he sent to Brian:

Dear Bloated Sucker, Fly fishing 1996 Newsletter
Personal Highlights:
　　Losing a ton of nymphs on S. Platte Rainbows
　　Switching to dry flies (finally) on Northgate Canyon
　　Trying NOT to catch a whitefish on the White River
　　Catching two nice 'bows on the Little Snake River
　　Realizing that the best fish we hooked were never
landed
　　The Battle Creek hole at sunset
Personal Lowlights:
　　Losing a ton of nymphs on S. Platte Rainbows
　　Having to switch to dry flies (finally) on Northgate
Canyon
　　Catching a whitefish on almost every cast on the
White River
　　Realizing that the best fish we hooked were never
landed
　　Having to leave the Battle Creek hole at sunset

One year a microburst shredded their tents and destroyed their camp while they were out on the Laramie River. Though it was only the third day of their trip, they had to lay up in cabins for the duration. They sought out the seediest, cheapest spots available to save funds. They were not into frilly fishing. They considered their stay at Paradise Ranch "The Big Splurge." Hale had begun offering them a cut rate because they were regulars and because he enjoyed them so much. They fished from dawn until dark without a break, ate a hearty dinner, and drank beer for a few hours each evening, rehashing the day with worshipful awe in their glazed eyes, then turned in so they could be up at daybreak to start it all over again. Trout fishing was their Nirvana.

Hale never fished when he contracted as fishing guide. He wanted to focus all his attention on finding fish for his clients. Besides, he felt as much thrill in their success as if he'd set the hook himself. He also didn't want to catch a fish that could potentially hit a client's fly, and he certainly didn't want to land the largest, the first, the most, or the last fish of the day. Better to just row the boat.

His hands were padded with thick calluses, and long blue ropes of veins stood out along the length of his arms, even at rest. He stayed fit through winter by working out and from the normal routine of ranch chores, so May rowing came as no shock to his body.

The river unfurled toward them. The dory dragged a lace train of eddies alongside which eventually broke away into independent strands of foamy chains floating tangential to the green sluice of the main current. Roiling circles heaved to the surface and were pushed outward by the next series. Small swirling whirlpools sang sucking sounds until swept apart to resurface on the same mark for an encore.

174

They shared the river with other fishers: herons, Mergansers, belted Kingfishers, Eagles, Osprey, and of course
the fish themselves. Big fish eat little fish. "Just leave
enough for us," Vance called to a heron poised to dart in
the shallows. They hauled out to wade the shallows where
the land was public, keeping their posture low, thinking like
trout, reading the feeding lanes so they could cast to the top
of a likely run in the center of the lane, casting deftly,
landing rippleless their invisible fluorocarbon tippets and
not the more visible line onto the water's surface. They
fished with nymphs just below the surface, sadly acknowl-
edging that the days of catching limits on dry flies seemed a
thing of the past. They looked for spots natural food would
float into, beneath overhanging willows, below riffles, where
tributaries entered the main stream, behind boulders, in
deep pools, along the overhanging banks of oxbows. They
were serious stalkers of trout, seeking out the wiliest and
the wildest.

But on that particular day, Brian was catching all the
fish. "Did you switch patterns again?" Vance asked. "How
deep are you floating that nymph?" They were using essen-
tially identical equipment: four-piece five-weight Trident
Power Matrix #10 graphite rods, with Orvis 'Battenkill'
reels, loaded with floating line and 5x or 6x leader and
tippets. They were both outfitted in breathable Gortex
waders, but Brian's were Hodgmans while Vance preferred
Simms, and both wore identical Orvis vests with epaulets of
flies clustered at the top of the pockets. Brian dragged a
clip-on landing net in the water behind him, but here they
parted ways. Vance believed in *beaching* the trout, es-
chewing nets, the reasons for which he explained in an e-
mail to Brian entitled "Landing nets are for babies!" ("I
particularly enjoy it when you're carrying one, but not

catching any fish"). Neither carried a creel because they never kept the fish they caught. Brian's wife JoAnn particularly detested eating any and all fish. They also parted ways in hat styles. Vance wore the kind of floppy hat one might see on a lady golfer, while Brian covered his thinning hair with a more masculine baseball cap. People insisted on giving them hats that read "Fish fear me, Women want me," but those hats remained in drawers at home. The only real difference between them was the ever-present fag dangling from Vance's lower lip.

Hale informed them of the hole they were fast approaching beneath a large willow copse. The water entered and exited swiftly, but lingered in a deep slow hole beneath a small jam of debris. A dead snag raised its arm as if drowning at the far end of the hole. As they neared, Hale warned that the moderate headwind would make it difficult to advance a fly. "Listen, I've seen four or five fellows lose a huge brown in this hole this year." He tried to position the dory for a clean cast. Both men floated a nymph shallowly through the dark water. A flash of skin and a movement of the water behind Brian's fly that couldn't be accounted for by the patterns of the current were the only evidence of a missed strike. "Damn!" he muttered. And then, as Vance's fly floated through the identical run, his rod tip bent nearly double. The line stripped squealing from his reel as the fish dove for cover. "Don't let him run under that snag or you'll lose him and all your tackle," Hale called to Vance. Vance panicked as the fish ran toward the snag. "Shit! I'm getting outta this boat and play him on foot." Vance handed his rod to Brian while he stepped into the shallow water at the boat's off side. He retrieved his rod from Brian, who had to grit his teeth to give it back.

"Oh, man! That's gotta be the biggest fish of the day! Of

the week!" Brian cried enviously. To persuade the trout to stay away from the deadwood, Vance began walking upstream and out into the deeper water, keeping the tip of the rod high and upstream from his body. He worked the trout toward the surface, but when it spotted Vance, it ran for the deep water beneath the overhanging bank, forcing Vance to give up the gains he'd made reeling in the line. He was working his way closer to the hole when the ground dropped out from under him without warning. Finding the current too strong to return to shallower water or find firm footing, Vance could not attempt swimming. For one thing, he could barely swim, but, more importantly, he'd have had to allow slack in his line to attempt it. He took in his situation in an instant, and, raising his legs in front of him, surrendered himself to the mercy of the current, bobbing swiftly along, rod tip upward, reeling for all he was worth to draw the trout away from the clutches of the snag. Floating now in the center of the rapids of the mainstream, he disappeared from view around the far side of a willow-covered island.

Brian and Hale threw fearful looks at each other, as Hale gave a mighty pull on both oars to propel the dory back into deep water. By the time Hale could maneuver the boat into the main current to drift around the near end of the island and catch up with Vance, Vance had managed to edge himself closer to the shore at the distal end of the island and had dropped his legs, bumping and skidding for thirty yards over submerged boulders, bruising his shins and cracking his knees, but finally managing to skid to a halt in a vertical position with his rod tip still raised and the fish still on. Brian leaped from the boat and rose dripping wet from a head plant, but dragged himself up behind Vance, positioned himself slightly downstream, and lowered his net

177

into the river so Vance could finally angle the tiring fish into its tilted rim.

"Look at the size of this dude!" Brian called out. "I got 'im, Vance. C'mon baby, come to poppa. Awright!" Brian netted the giant rainbow, and lifted him over his head like a boxer's championship belt, as Vance stood grinning from ear to ear with his cigarette still hanging from the corner of his mouth. "Not bad for a guy who can't swim, eh?" he asked, the cigarette bobbing with each word.

Brian, looking in wonder at the monster in the net, said, "Okay, okay, Leaping Rainbow. I admit defeat. *You!* You are the master." He saluted, then dipped his body in an extravagant salaam, never loosening his grip on the net or tilting the rim from its perfectly horizontal position.

Hale sat slouched over the oars in his dory, beaming broadly. "God damn! Is this the greatest job in the world, or what?"

Nine

The horses nipped at each other across the barrier that sep-
arated them in the three horse slant trailer. The larger dark
brown gelding scrambled wildly, leaning against the brown
and white paint beside him as they rounded a curve.

"There goes Limbo again," Hale said, wincing. He de-
creased his speed and cut the corner to reduce sway.

"I hate it when they do that," Maggie said tensely, gripping her seat as if that could somehow stabilize the horse. "I
thought he might be better about his scrambling if we
hauled in your slant load."

"Oh, he'll be all right, Maggie. I'll just take it easy."

The hills flushed rose in the rising sun, shading the blue
and white pickup to lavender and mauve as it traveled the
coils of Highway 130 east into the Snowy Range. Pungent
sage embraced the roadway in twisted arms. The blue
mountains slumbered atop the golden plains, giant quiet
bodies heaving slow as eternity, their breath exhaling eons,
oblivious to the machinations of the strange guinea pigs
crossing and recrossing their surfaces in random patterns;
recognizing neither dawn, nor stories, nor status, nor mo-
rality, nor any strength but their own; traveling through a
separate dimension; superior cells in the cosmic organism.
We are here. We will always be, they sang with each rotation
of the earth. The tires skimmed across their skin, an illusive
progression, mere spidery legs of water striders skating on a
gently flexing reflection of the indifferent heavens. Dark
bodies of subalpine firs shrank in the heights of their
brooding summits, victims of cruel altitude, stunted,

crooked, tortured by montane winters, grown feeble from breathing an empty, arid atmosphere.

The road to the Snowy Range Mountains wound toward the sun, the thread of asphalt drawing a gray ampersand across the elbow of land curled to the north, overshadowed by moraines, ridged edges of glacial gouges. Open earthen maws exposed gleaming teeth of the distant Mummy Range, the Rahwahs, the Never Summer, jaws covered by green stubble, gulping in the blue water of the sky. Below the peaks, the surface of a glacial pond shone opaque from the sun, a cataract over its Cyclopean eye, blinded by light bouncing off quartz cliffs; the range a three humped golden serpent gilded with glaciers, its skin a surface of lithic scales, frozen in motion, thrashing its tail at Polaris; stretched along hills falling away to the east, legs drawn up to its belly, huddled against a heat source at its center while the sun warmed its back. A shimmering chimera. A yellow sphinx crouched, paws extended.

"I've never seen stone like this anywhere else in the world," Maggie sighed in awe as she watched the lustrous ridge crawl past her window. "A whole mountain range of quartz crystal."

"And look at the color of the lake, Maggie. Like a peacock feather in sunlight."

"Think the horses will appreciate any of this?" Maggie asked airily.

"I think the two things horses appreciate are other horses and grass," Hale answered. "But, fortunately for us, they'll do what we ask whether they appreciate it or not."

"Strange how easily they're coerced into our hairbrained schemes, though they're so much stronger than us," she puzzled.

"Hey, it's a fair tossup. We recognize their superior

physical strength, they recognize us as their mental superiors. Besides, nothing's hair-brained about this little jaunt today, Maggie."

"Of course, you're right, but, if you think about it, just hauling in a trailer is hair-brained from their point of view, I would guess."

"You and your points of view. You're a shape-shifter, Maggie. A chameleon."

"Let's see, then. You, you're the opposite of me. I'd say . . . you're the lichen that grips the rocks. Stays put, toughs out a harsh living, is what it is, has Spartan requirements. How's that?"

"That's good. Yeah. I like that."

"That's you. It really is." She looked at the side of his face. "It's funny. A lot of the things that used to bother me about you are what I admire now. For example, what I thought passive then, I see as patience now. Or maybe it's actually more stubbornness."

"Hey, now, hey."

"No," she laughed. "I don't mean that negatively. I mean stubbornness as in, insisting on what's right for yourself . . . what's right in general too. I guess a nicer word for it would be integrity." She thought for a moment. "Or resolve, maybe."

"So you're telling me you've changed your mind about me, huh?"

"I guess you seem more valuable to me now. Yeah, I took a lot for granted in the old days."

"I must've improved with age."

"Or the rest of the world is just looking worse by comparison to you these days."

"Well, thanks . . . I think." He glanced over at her in the seat beside him as he eased from a curve into a straight stretch of road.

The stiffness of their dance persisted. Steps grew less cautious but more intricate. There were still so many maneuvers to be avoided and so many nuances of subtlety to be heeded to recapture the beauty.

"You're a different person too, Maggie. You've learned a lot, I think. You're calmer; you seem like you can wait now."

Her laugh rang silvery. "Are you referring to the fact that I used to pass every other car on the highway when I was young. God! I was so terrible! In those days I felt like everyone else was in my way, impeding my progress." She shook her head, remembering. "I used to fantasize about driving a bulldozer down the highway to get rid of the other cars."

They laughed together at how callow she'd been. "Don't get into putting yourself down, now, Maggie," he said. "You're a better person than you ever give yourself credit for. Stronger than you think you are, too." A tease came into his expression. "Well, you look stronger, anyway. You've kind of stouted up there a bit."

"Stouted up? *Stouted?"*

"Don't get mad about it. You look a lot better. You couldn't have been taking care of yourself properly all those years in Palo Alto. You weren't eating enough spuds and gravy or something before you came back here."

" 'Spuds and gravy!' Where on earth did you get *that?* For heaven's sake, if we *have* to talk about it, it's just that I'm doing more physical stuff now. I mean *real* physical work, not just aerobic workouts or something. It's felt good using my muscles, my body, I guess my brain too, to do something productive beyond just keeping myself in shape. Now I keep fit, but I have a lot to show for it . . . a salvaged piece of property, my beautiful garden, and even a horse in training who'd been going to waste. I guess that's what feels good about the work I'm doing right now. I'm salvaging things that were going to waste. It's not just doing in the abstract. I like that I'm doing something that gets concrete results. 'Spuds and gravy!' "

"Okay, forget the spuds and gravy. But you hit the nail on the head. That's exactly why I decided to run the ranch, Maggie. It's not abstract work. It's absolutely real. I feel an immediate, a direct sense of accomplishment in the work I do. And I believe it's beneficial too. At the least, what I offer here gives people some respite, so they can go on with the daily grind of their lives. At best, it's the stuff dreams are made of. I remember when I was a kid, I couldn't sleep at night for dreaming of the next day's adventures. Exploring, building something, fishing. When my dad and Ken and I fished up here then, I could hardly wait to see what was beyond the next bend in the river."

"Huck Finn stuff."

"Don't be smug, now. Don't give me that 'must be a guy thing' crap. I'm serious, I've seen river floats change men's lives. Successful, even powerful, men. Young men, too. They've made major career decisions from their stay at Paradise Ranch. I know because they've written me or come back and told me personally about it years later. Men in mid-career have reversed themselves—switched boats in mid river, if you will. One thirty year old guy left an engineering job . . . yes, engineering . . . in Denver to start up a small business in Steamboat Springs after a float trip. He just couldn't face the prospect of sitting at a desk his whole life. Think of living your life in a cubicle, Maggie, when you could have . . . this!" He gestured at the entire vista of the Snowy Range. "The stuff that dreams are made of, Maggie."

"You stole that from Shakespeare."

"Yeah? Me and everybody else."

Maggie pulled a roll of Life Savers from her supplies and peeled away the circle of foil at the top of the roll. "You and I both know that people in cubicles are reaching beyond those narrow walls with their minds."

"Yeah. I admit that. It's true, of course. But I want to actually be out there accomplishing things, not just dreaming them up." He paused. "But that's just me. If everyone had my attitude, the world would be in bad shape. So it's a good thing we don't all think alike."

Maggie popped a Life Saver into her mouth and sucked noisily for a moment. "Actually, I understand what you're saying about loving what you're doing. I do understand . . . now. It took me a long time, but it's one of the things I finally figured out. If I hadn't gone through a long period of barely hanging on by my fingernails, I'd have never learned it. For awhile, you know, after I left you, I could barely face life, barely crawl out of bed in the morning. After a long time, after I'd recovered, when I could finally look back on that period, it made me realize that a passion for life isn't a luxury. It's a necessity. You've got to have a reason to get out of bed in the morning, it's as simple as that. Otherwise, we're just all doing hard time for the duration. Just wasting our lives killing time." She looked out the side window silently for a moment. "I think a lot of women don't understand that about men. Women who are jealous of a man's passion for his work don't realize that without it he'd be nothing. It's what keeps him vital. Alive, even. I think women need to find their own passions too, and I don't mean passion for a man. Everyone needs to find their golden thread and stick to it like hell."

Hale stared at her for a moment. "You really have changed, Maggie."

"Well, just so I don't shock you too much, let me play the devil's advocate for a moment. Okay, you chose to simplify your life to do what you love. But what about the need to accomplish something really big in your life? You know, make your mark in the world?"

"Yeah, there's that," Hale nodded slowly. He was silent for a moment. Then he spoke earnestly. "I'll be honest with you, Maggie. I can understand why you had a hard time accepting my career switch. I've wondered myself if I did it out of fear. Did I choose a simpler, smaller life because I thought I couldn't compete? Because I was frightened of the larger world? Or afraid that I couldn't take the pressure? Was settling on the ranch just an easy way out for me? Anonymity is such a sanctuary."

"It took some guts to go against the flow, though," Maggie countered, the devil's advocate's devil's advocate now. *No boundaries.* "It certainly wasn't the trendy route you chose to take, after all, and you had to stand up to a lot of flack from me, and from Ken, and from your mother, and probably others that I don't even know about, no doubt. Plus, you took a financial risk."

There was another long pause, then Hale said, "But no one wants to feel they've made no mark on the world, Maggie, believe me. And I'm no exception. Of course I hope what I'm doing matters somehow to someone. And I try like hell to be a good steward of the land." They drove on in silence awhile, comfortable enough to not talk, assimilating the words each had spoken, trying to integrate them into their own established thinking. "Speaking of which," Hale eventually resumed, "what do you plan to do with yourself once you've settled in and finished renovating your place? I take it you're not in a position to live off the fat of the land forever."

"That's a good question," she answered, not flippantly. She offered him a Life Saver which he declined. "I've been thinking of trying my hand at less technical writing. *Way* less technical. But I'm also thinking of maybe teaching part-time somewhere. Trying to give to the community somehow. Or, if all else fails, I've also thought of trying to get on with a newspaper, or, if I stay here, of starting up one of my own, you know, something really small that could be a forum for the community. That's what I've been thinking, anyway. You know, something *productive*. I didn't say *practical*." She smiled.

They were silent again, Hale focused on his driving and Maggie watching the blur of the passing trees. The green tundra laid like a subtly floraled cushion atop the rolling land. She sighed softly and shifted in her seat, then spoke quietly. "I should've stayed, Hale," she said almost to herself. "I should have tried harder. I should have supported you in what you thought was right for yourself. I just couldn't see things from your view point at all back then."

There was no response from Hale. "But don't think I'm back here to pick up where we left off," she added briskly. "I'm not so arrogant as to think you'd want that or that I have the right, and besides, it's not what I would want either in my life right now. So don't worry."

"I'm not worried, Maggie."

"Well good. Don't worry. I swear I'm not after you."

"It never crossed my mind, Maggie." She couldn't precisely determine his tone.

Dust swirled around them as the trailer rolled to a halt in the graveled parking lot. Hale eased forward into the shade of some fir trees. They unloaded Limbo and Grumby (short for "Grumbacher") from the trailer. Limbo came out first in an explosion of energy, staring around, his neck raised to its limit and ears rigidly erect, and blew a loud whistling snort. Grumby stepped out calmly, looked casually left and right, then tried to pull Hale towards the nearest clump of grass. They tied them both to the trailer and, opening the door to the tack compartment, removed their gear, and began brushing the horses.

The August sun was tempered by a cool breeze that flowed across the summit. Tiny brown birds flitted in dwarfed gnarled conifers ringing the parking area. A gray jay dropped down to the picnic table nearest them, eyeing their possessions hopefully. The air was fragrant with piney aroma of summer sap. Closing her eyes, Maggie inhaled deeply. "This was a great idea, Hale. I've always loved it up here. What a magical place this is!" She lowered her English saddle onto Limbo's back as Hale tightened the cinch around Grumby's girth. The paint pinned his ears against his head as it tightened around his belly, then flipped them happily forward again once it was done. Hale slid the curb bit over Grumby's obliging tongue while Maggie struggled to bring Limbo's head down so she could slip the snaffle into his mouth. "C'mon, Limbo. Make it easy for me. Oh, to be tall like you or Jill."

"You need a leg up?" *again,* Hale asked, when she was ready to mount. He lifted her easily onto Limbo's back, holding onto her ankle for a few seconds as she adjusted her reins. His large hand spanned her entire foot. She could feel through her paddock boots the warmth of his palm across the arch of her ankle.

When Hale settled into the saddle his long legs extended below Grumby's girth. *He's all arms and legs,* she thought. *A lanky torso and a set of snake hips on stilts. No wonder he can stick a horse.* "You could wrap your legs twice around his body," she told him.

The midmorning sun warmed the right side of their faces as they headed north where the lumpy ridges taughtened into long plateaus. They lined out single file, Limbo's larger strides propelling him into the lead. "He hates having another horse ahead of him, doesn't he?" Maggie said, twisting in her saddle to grin at Hale behind her as he urged Grumby to keep up. "Yeah, Limbo's got to be out front. He's the alpha horse in the herd, you know."

"Good!" she answered. "That means he'll be brave over fences."

They climbed gradually for an hour through the flower specked tundra along a narrow wavering trail, stopping frequently to let the puffing horses catch their breath in the thin atmosphere, until they finally topped out on a green ridge where the sky met the land. They dismounted to ease their horses' backs and surveyed the long open vistas encircling them. The hills rose and fell in lazy undulations away from them, jade swells of a tossing ocean. The distant ranges were oscillating mirages on the horizon, indigo islands floating on the valley floor. The Granite Mountains, Laramie Mountains, Park Range, Uintas, and the Sawatch Range.

"It's like flying over the Marquesas, in a way," Maggie said aloud, but half to herself.

"Or looking out at Andean peaks from cloud level," Hale added.

Another view opened to Maggie. She saw clearly for the first time a Hale she'd never known. The impact of this sad discovery had snuck up on her, blindsided her. "We missed out on each other's lives, didn't we?"

"Yeah."

There was a bottomless emptiness as big as the sky in his answer.

Maggie refused to have their day mired in what had been lost. "We've been far and wide between the two of us, haven't we? We need to sit down one night and compare notes."

The horses munched short grass clumps on the hilltop. There were no other sounds but the chiming of the tiny brown birds and the low sigh of the wind in the firs.

Maggie sat down on a flat rock, holding Limbo's reins. "Okay," she challenged Hale. "Your favorite travel experience of all time."

Hale responded without hesitation, "I stroked the tail of a genet cat at the Masai Mara dining lodge in Kenya one night."

"A what?"

"A genet. It's not really a cat. It's related to civets and meercats, but it looks like a gorgeous spotted jungle cat. I was the last one out of the dining room that night. The cooks waved me over to watch them lay a piece of food on top of the open beam near the exterior wall. They'd been taming it, see. They'd been enticing it closer and closer each night until they could stroke him as he snatched his prize. They gave me the honors that night." He paused, then added, "Or maybe watching in the moonlight while some teenaged elephants rough housed in the watering hole at Treetops, like big playful porpoises. When all of them had drunk their fills, they glided away as silently as swans, not elephants. It was amazing how quietly they left." He picked up a pebble and threw it out over the slope. "That was five or six winters ago. So, how about you?"

"Hmm. I don't think I can top those. Let me think a minute." She moved her legs to one side to turn away from the sun's intensity. "A sea tortoise swam round and round me as I snorkeled in Hanauma Bay on Oahu like he was studying me, instead of the other way around. No, wait, wait. Maybe it's as simple as walking along the dirt road at night at Tamarindo Bay on the west coast of Costa Rica. There were horses set free to graze along the road. I could hear their soft footfalls in the dirt. The air was warm and moist, and I had never seen so many stars. I loved everything about Costa Rica, though. A man carrying a long iguana dangling from his bicycle. Driving from the hot windy beaches of the west coast into the volcano mists within an hour. Toucans in the glossy trees along the canal at Limon on the Caribbean side. It's hard to choose."

She waited, then added an afterthought, "There was another memorable experience too, a rather strange one, not what you'd expect to consider a travel highlight, but still . . . I was traveling with mother about five years ago through San Paulo on the way to Iguacu Falls. We were stranded at the airport because our Varig flight had been cancelled, when a Chinese man standing in line behind me responded to some caustic remark I'd made about the lack of information we were getting about our flight's status. He offered to buy us a soft drink in the airport cafe while we were waiting. Something about him connected so strongly with me! I don't think I've ever felt such a connection before or since. He felt it too, I'm sure. He directed his conversation exclusively at me, and shortly into it, looked straight at me and said, "I will tell you frankly that I'm a smuggler." He was smuggling black market goods, and possibly money, I can't recall, in from Paraguay while they were building that huge dam in Brazil, you remember the one? Anyway, my mother, who was in her mid-fifties then, was quite miffed at having been ignored, and made snide insinuations afterwards implying we'd been sexually attracted to each other or something. But I swear that wasn't it. It was just this mental connection . . . maybe a spiritual connection, I don't know. Maybe we were attracted by our differences. But, isn't it funny? I've never forgotten the strength of the feeling, and that strange little episode is definitely one of my most memorable travel experiences to this day."

She turned and looked out across the ridges toward the Snowy Range peaks to the south. "This could be right up there, you know. If we were from Europe, say, we'd be totally blown away by this."

"Familiarity breeds contempt, eh? Who'd I steal that one from?"

"Damned if I know."

They remounted and rode further north a short distance, then curved to the east and eventually headed back south. The horses picked up the pace voluntarily. "They always know, don't they?" she laughed.

"Yeah, the laggards," he answered.

From the top of the ridge at their ride's end they could see the length of the sheer east faces of the Snowy Range peaks, pearly; gleaming white wet Mobys breaching the dark waves under them, through icy wakes that foamed across their foreheads, spouting snowy glaciers.

The Medicine Bow Range. Like all the ranges of the eastern division of the Rocky Mountains, an uplifted mass of a Paleozoic seabed from a half trillion years ago. Three hundred million years later, during the Jurassic period, a blister like injection of magma from the upper mantle of the Earth's molten interior forced a massive uplift 100 miles long and ten thousand feet high, dissecting the surrounding upland. The highest portion of the uplift, formed of a Precambrian core of quartzite, covered a length of five miles and rose to

12,000 feet. This peak became known as Medicine Bow Peak.

Awed by its beauty, they stood motionless, awash in a glare intensified by the shining quartz as if a magnifying glass had concentrated a beam of light directly on its surface. The horses grew restless at the long delay, breaking the spell and bringing the voyeurs back to earth. Hale finally broke the silence.

"Here's a question for you, Maggie. A trivia question. Where did the name 'Medicine Bow' come from?"

"Aha!" she cried. "For once, even my sieve of a brain remembers the answer to that one." She recited her answer. "It's called 'Medicine Bow' because the Indians came here for 'making medicine,' you know, their sorcery. And they collected branches of mountain mahogany here for making bows. See, it's all around us, there's thickets of it all over. So this was the land of 'medicine' and 'bows' to them . . . 'Medicine Bow.' " She smiled impishly. "Do I get an A plus for that answer, or what?"

"I'm impressed beyond description. Hey! Don't look at me like that! I mean it, I really am impressed. But, here, just wait a minute before you get too smug. I'll bet I know something else about it you *don't* know."

"What?"

"The Medicine Bow Mountains were the setting for *The Virginian* . . . you know, by Owen Wister."

"I knew that," she asserted.

"Sure you did."

Hale pointed out a spot near the summit of Medicine Bow Peak. "Look, Maggie. See if you can find the site where that plane crashed into the mountain. See up there where I'm pointing. Isn't there a black spot? Don't you think it looks all scraped up?"

192

"Where?" she said, stepping behind him to follow the trajectory of his extended arm.

"See, right *there*." He grabbed her and positioned her in front of him again, facing as he was facing, holding her with one of his arms wrapped around her chest while he sighted past the side of her cheek with his other arm. He held his face near hers, just brushing his cheek against hers to see from her viewpoint.

"Oh," she said softly, "yes, I see where you mean, now." He dropped his arms from around her. "But refresh my memory," she stayed where she was, standing directly in front of him. He could smell her damp hair as she swayed slightly backward, almost touching his chest with her back. "I vaguely recall the story, but it's been so long."

He stepped forward alongside her. "Well, if I can remember it myself . . ." he said slowly. His composure seemed rattled. It took longer for him to recall the details than it should have. "I just saw an exhibit at the art museum in Laramie a couple of years ago about it," he said, delaying, trying to recover himself and the memory. "Let's see, okay. Yeah. I got it. It happened in 1955, I remember. I think in September, no, wait, in October, yeah, it was October, 1955. It was a DC-4, I remember that for certain, headed for Salt Lake from Denver. There were over sixty people on the flight, and it smashed straight into the mountain there, killing everyone on board." He paused and added, "There were some people on board from Palo Alto, I remember that, too."

"Really? I never knew that. Palo Alto . . . Just imagine, I may know someone whose relatives were killed here, then."

"It's possible. Maybe you should check out the list of victims sometime."

"I ought to." She stared again at the spot on the side of

the mountain, trying to picture it and trying *not* to picture it. "Don't you hate to think of such a terrible tragedy happening in this beautiful place?" She winced with her whole body. "But, why did it crash? Was there a storm or something?"

"No, it's even more tragic than that. It crashed because the pilot was taking a short cut."

"What! What do you mean?"

"Yeah. It's true. I guess it was something that was routinely done on that particular route. They were supposed to fly due north until they cleared the north end of the range and *then* make a left turn, but pilots took a short cut over the top. They did it a lot, all the time. I guess this time he just miscalculated."

"But, why would his altitude have been so low at this point in his flight, so far from Denver?"

"Because in those days, flying was completely different than today. Remember it was 1955, and he was flying a DC-4. They flew at a much lower altitude."

"Obviously he didn't see the mountain because it was night." She thought a moment. "Or maybe there was bad weather. I guess it could've been really bad in October up here."

"Yeah, I don't remember that part."

"But what about radar? Why wasn't he warned?"

"Commercial flights weren't tracked by ground radar in those days. Only military flights were tracked back then."

"You're kidding?"

"No. As a matter of fact, that crash was considered the worst air disaster in U.S. history at the time, and it made the powers that be aware of the need for radar coverage for all flights. So I guess some good came out of it."

"My God," Maggie said quietly. "All those lives lost to

save a few miles or a few minutes! What a waste! Just for the lack of better judgment." She shook her head gently. "Imagine all of them, Hale, flying blithely straight into a mountain; everything over instantly without warning, without time to prepare yourself for even one second. The pilot must not have seen the wall at all to fly headlong into it, so he probably died not even realizing he had caused a terrible disaster."

"You're probably right. I'd never thought about it, but I guess so," Hale agreed.

"Maybe he was better off," Maggie said firmly, after thinking a moment. "Better not to have to know when you've made a fatal mistake. Better not to have to live with the consequences." She spoke these last words with an excess of conviction.

Hale looked at her profile closely while she continued to search the cliff wall as if it held some answer to a puzzle. "And yet, Maggie," he said gently, "no one hates the pilot after a plane crash. Think about it. For some reason, it's not like a shipwreck where people think the captain should go down with his ship. No one ever blames the pilot. Even when the reason for the crash is found to be pilot error. People don't despise the pilot for it, do they? . . . Why do you think that is?"

She thought about it, staring across the radiating expanses of rock. It took time to answer. "Maybe . . . maybe it's because in a plane it all happens so suddenly. There's no time to think. You're in such a dangerous environment. There's so much room for error. And the results of an error are so irrevocable, aren't they? I mean, you could float in the ocean. You'd last long enough to be rescued. But in the air . . ." She hesitated. "Yes, you're right. It's strange, but no one hates the pilot afterwards, do they? He's always considered a victim too, whether he lives or dies. He's always forgiven, isn't he?" she asked in an almost dreamy voice, not really expecting an answer. "It's just a horrible defining moment, unforeseen, beyond his control once it's gone past the point of no return, a fatal mistake of time and place at that point. He is a victim, in that sense, don't you think?" she asked, not waiting for a reply. "He's swept along by forces larger than himself. And every time he steps into the cockpit, a pilot puts himself in that position, the possibility of that precarious loss of control over things. I think we all recognize that. Maybe that's why he's forgiven."

Hale silently digested what she had said. "Maybe you're right, Maggie. Maybe you've figured it out." She turned her head toward him. His chiseled profile was outlined by the jagged edges of the cliffs. *Tawny heads of lions. That's what they're like,* she realized, having tried to crystallize in her mind what the crouching shapes reminded her of.

They stripped the horses of their tack when they reached the trailer and offered them water. The horses drank their fills greedily then picked hay from the hay nets Hale had hung from the side of the trailer. "Time for our grub, too. Come on, Maggie. Let's eat over by the lake."

He pulled a small cooler from the truck cab and led the way along a westerly trail.

The ground felt soft and sounded hollow underfoot. "Look, it's pure mountain peat up here," she commented. They hop scotched on rocks across the shallow inlet and searched the ground for a dry spot before laying out the picnic. Before sitting down to eat, Maggie walked the short distance to the west side of the lake and climbed onto the glittering gray boulders, the largest as big as a small car. The scree between them clanked underfoot. *Like ground glass,* she thought. She chose a small rose tinted piece of quartz to take home.

Yellow marsh flowers stood above the mossy groundcover, sprouting from fleshy leaves like water hyacinths. "What are these, Hale? Do you know?"

"No, but we can look them up when we get back. I've got a field guide to native wildflowers at the lodge for guests." She walked back to the inlet they had crossed to feel the temperature of the water. "Brrr. It's pure ice water," she told Hale when she returned. "Remember that time we floated the Yampa the second year we were married? I just had to wash my hair the third day out, so I went a little way up a clear creek, soaped up my hair all over, then couldn't bear to go completely under to rinse it out."

"I remember. You finally went under for about three seconds. I could see you under the water frantically shaking the soap out of your hair. Then you sprang up like you'd been launched, gasping and grabbing your heart and shaking off like a dog." They both laughed at the memory.

"My heart felt like it was going to burst when I went under. I had no idea it was going to be that painful, or I'd have never opened that shampoo bottle."

"You and your hair." He rumpled her short mop with his hand. "You must've been pretty vain about it then, to have pulled that stunt," he teased.

"Who, *moi?*"

"Well, you were justified," he said, squinting in the glare reflecting off the lake and the rocks and the stream nearby. "I always did think your hair was a nice color, Maggie. Let's see . . . it reminds me of . . . of . . ." He screwed up his eyes in mock concentration.

"Oh, go on . . ."

"No, wait. I've got it. Of a mink stole. Or a dark, dark fox, maybe."

"Okay. Yeah, I like that. And yours . . . yours is like lichen."

"Back to lichen, are we? I can't win."

She laid back and stretched out full-length on the ground, looking into the sky.

"Hey, Hale," she murmured.

"Yeah?"

"Do you still dream in Technicolor?"

"Every night."

"Can you still dictate what you want to dream and then really dream it?"

"Yep."

"I wish I could do that," she said, closing her eyes.

Rob had packed the lunch. "Oh, look what he did, Hale! He's made us a paniolo picnic. A cowboy luau!" There was lau lau pork wrapped in spinach leaves in lieu of ti leaves, which no force in heaven or earth could have provided in Saratoga. Papaya strips and sticky rice came from containers tied with corny plastic leis. "Where *did* he get these? Goodwill maybe?" The dessert was coconut cake. "Mmm. As good as Haupia," Maggie raved. And at the bottom of the cooler, tucked into a corner for safekeeping, were two white dendrobium flowers. "He must've picked these up at a florist in Laramie," she marveled. "He made big plans for this, that sneaky devil."

"Can't you just hear him now," laughed Hale. " '*Aloha Oe,*' he'd be singing in that nasal voice of his, strumming his ukulele like he was Alfred Apaka or something. Doing a hula around the table."

"Thank God we're out here and he's there." They

laughed at the images they'd conjured.

"Really, it was awfully sweet of him," she said, tucking one of the orchids behind her ear. "Is it supposed to go on the left side or the right?"

"Depends if you're looking for trouble or not," Hale answered.

"I'd better not take a chance," she said, reaching for the orchid to remove it.

"No, don't. Leave it there, Maggie. It suits you. I won't make any assumptions, I promise."

The horses stomped eagerly into the trailer. *Goin' home.* The pickup traveled south, then turned into the sun again. By the time they reached the ranch, the hills were glazed into mist by the warm light of August dusk. A stream sliced molten through tranquil meadows that caught the slanting golden light in their open palms, holding it while it flickered and faded, blown out by the evening breeze, guttering into cool gray. A half shadow that was neither dark nor light crept across the meadows. *Aaaaah,* they sighed. *Aaaaah.*

He drove Maggie home after the horses had been put away. As she opened the door of the truck to step out, he said, "So, Maggie. Do you really think, then, that I'm so horrified by the thought of you trying to 'interfere' in my life?"

She raised her eyebrows as she gathered her things and walked to her cabin door without replying.

Ten

"So, what do you think?"

Jane could hear Maggie's voice through the thick steam.

"Where are you?"

"Over here."

Her disembodied head floated forward through the vapor. Jane sank beneath the surface of the warm water, reemerging with head thrown back, hair sleeked flat.

"I think it feels fabulous. The perfect remedy after our hike and that torturous ride."

"C'mon, Jane, that ride was nothing."

"Maggie, Maggie. Do you think I have rubber bands for ligaments? Think my butt is cast iron? I'm dying. How could you do this to me?"

Maggie laughed, choking in some water. She swam in a lazy breaststroke around Jane. "But that wasn't what I meant anyway."

"What wasn't?"

"I didn't mean, 'what do you think of the hot spring.' I meant, what do you think of the whole thing—Saratoga, the ranch, my cabin, Hale, my life here. The whole thing."

"I think you're out of your fucking mind."

"Don't mince words to spare me, Jane."

They sat on the bank to cool off in the evening air. The steam curled around them.

"No, really, Jane. Tell me what you think."

"Okay. I'll try to be a bit more . . . detailed. Look, I know the traffic in Palo Alto is an insult to one's humanity. The pace of life there can be absolutely frantic, I'll admit.

The air quality sucks a good part of the time, but, damn! Maggie, did you have to go to such extremes? I mean, what about mental stimulation? The arts? Prosperity?"

"Jeez, Jane. It's not like I'm here in chains, you know. I am free to come and go. It's not like I'm living in a vacuum here either. Saratoga isn't totally shut off from the rest of the world, you know." She paused, thinking, then added forcefully, "And I can give you a different list as rebuttal; what about room to breathe? A challenge to your fortitude? Getting down to what's real? Being in the midst of a fabulous wilderness? What about living life to your own rhythms instead of everyone else's? You know, like waiting for the seasons to change instead of waiting for a pump at the gas station. There aren't as many stop signs here, Jane."

"Oh, I'm not denying it has its own kind of beauty. But, my god, Maggie, it's the loneliest place I've ever seen. It's too open. You're too exposed here to a big emptiness. It hovers over you—it's sort of terrifying, I think. It's like the first lines of Rilke's *Duino Elegies:* 'If I cried out, who would hear me?' I always remembered that because it's so desperately beautiful."

"You get used to it, Jane. You carve out a little niche and you hunker down."

"*You* may like 'hunkering,' Maggie, but I don't see myself in that kind of posture, not now, not ever. Sorry."

"Oh, Jane. Always over-dramatizing everything."

"Okay. Your cabin is wonderful. *Primitive,* but wonderful. Aged, authentic, good aura, I'm sure. And your garden is obviously an absolute labor of love. I can't even begin to imagine the amount of work you've done. I swear, you're a masochist, Maggie. You have a need to punish yourself. Speaking of which, the situation with Hale seems almost hopeless."

"God, Jane!"

"I'm sorry, Maggie. I just don't see how you can do this. I think you should come back to Palo Alto, that's all. I mean, what do you expect his reaction will be when you tell him? And *how* are you going to tell him? And *when* are you going to tell him? Just try to see the reality of your position."

"I'm going to tell him *soon* . . . just as soon as I figure out how."

"Yes, well, that is a toughie, isn't it?"

"Don't make fun, Jane. I've rehearsed a hundred different ways to say it, but every one is ghastly. And under what circumstances do I tell him, even if I figure out how to say it? Do I just blurt it out when he's happy and having a good day? Do I do it when he's distracted, working at something—you know, sneak it in on him? Over a meal? He'll feel like it's the last supper or something."

"Yeah, and you're Judas."

"Oh, Jane! You're not helping!"

"I'm sorry, Mag. I'm being intentionally outrageous because it seems a no-win situation for you."

"We've been over this, Jane. You of all people know how sick I've been over this for fourteen long years. I *have* to tell him." She paused, then added in a lower voice, "I need forgiveness."

"And what if he doesn't give it to you?"

"Well, at least if I tell him, I might begin to forgive myself. There's no undoing the mess I've made, I know that. I've tried and tried to think of a way, but there is no way in heaven or on earth."

"Well, you're wrong there," Jane said

"What do you mean?"

"Oh, there's a way in heaven, Maggie, and maybe there's your answer. You don't need Hale's forgiveness, my best, my truest, my dearest, most kind-hearted friend. Forget that. You're just torturing yourself. He's only human, and it was a damned unforgivable thing you did from his point of view. So forget it! But you could find some peace, Maggie, if you focused more on your own soul. You need some distance from what you did—a whole universe of distance, but certainly not what you've got here—this dreadful isolation. It's so terribly lonely, it makes you feel there's no point in praying. Plus, living right next to Hale . . . it's masochistic, I tell you. You're in the lion's den, girl."

"Okay, Jane. If you want to get religious on me . . . I *have* tried to soothe my soul, believe me. I used to drive over to the coast on the stormiest days to walk. Those walks were filled with my mind racing and racing, rehashing the tangle of my life, and with visions of how to make it right, or at least how to escape. I never saw the scenery I was walking through for the scenery of where I'd been."

She slipped back into the water, and Jane followed. Maggie swirled the water with her arm. "I searched and searched for inspiration. I was so desperate, Jane. Obsessed. I opened my bible for the first time in over a decade. It was weird. You know what it fell right open to? Like it was just for me, this passage. You know the story where a 'woman of the city who was a sinner' is forgiven because she washes Christ's feet with her tears and dries them with her hair. Who could forget that imagery? You remember?"

"Vaguely. Yeah, I do. It rings a bell."

"Well, what you probably *don't* remember is that Christ says to this self-righteous man who finds her disgusting . . . he says, 'I tell you, her sins, which are many, are forgiven, for she loved much.' I wrote those words down and I read them over and over. They're the panacea for my dilemma, Jane. I really believe that. I made them my mantra on my journey back so I'd have the courage to go on. They tell me that I won't find forgiveness in some retreat or through some kind of meditative Zen detachment or by living a repentant life in Palo Alto. I'll only find it by facing up to what I've done and loving the ones I've sinned against, even if they don't forgive me. Then maybe I can start to forgive myself. And that might open the way for what might actually make me feel forgiven . . . the hardest thing of all for me. I have to figure out how to love a God who allows us to inflict such pain."

Maggie sleeked back the hair that had curled around her face. " 'She has loved much.' That's the only chance I have, Jane. And I don't think that's masochistic. And I do think that's the reality of my predicament." She paused, then added a final thought. "I had to open a line of communication. I needed to be here now to do it."

Jane looked at Maggie compassionately. "Oh, Maggie, you break my heart. You really do. Maybe you're right and I'm a fool for trying to tell you differently. I can see how hard it's been for you to come to this point. Oh, Mags, how I miss you! I wish I could help you through this somehow. I'd give you a hug, but I'm feeling too slimy."

Maggie laughed. "You're just too wild, Jane."

Their laughter was a relief. "*Me* wild? Just look around you, speaking of wild." Jane's expression was comically aghast. "Have you ever been to this place's namesake, the hot springs in Saratoga, New York, Maggie?" Jane didn't pause, wanting no answer. "Well, I have. We vacationed at the Gideon Putnam once and went to the Lincoln Mineral Baths. My God, Maggie, they're in a building that looks like the Campidoglio! And here we are sitting in a hole filled with stinking hot sulfur water—a hole that looks like the fires of hell burnt through the middle of the sage!"

"Well," Maggie said dryly, "it feels the same either way. And look at the bright side. Here we have it all to ourselves, after all. Plus, it's free. How much did it cost you to soak in 'The Campidoglio'?"

"Sixteen dollars for twenty minutes."

"Ha!" Maggie was triumphant. "You just don't have the right spirit about this place at all, Jane. Our Wyoming hot springs is a model of egalitarianism. Hey, even the Indians who used to wage war against each other around here declared the hot springs neutral ground. It's here for all comers, just as it is, without pretension."

"Forget it, Mag," Jane said, looking around even more critically. "I can buy into a lot of things, but . . ." The words were garbled as she ducked beneath the surface.

"Notice the sinner was a woman of *the city*," Maggie muttered to the bubbles on the water's surface.

Jane's loneliness was catching. When Maggie waved good-bye to Jane the next morning, she stepped onto its elevator, going down. Jane was the only other person Maggie had ever fully confided in. It had been a relief to talk to her about her troubles, no matter how blunt Jane's opinions. Having to bear up alone again sent her spiraling into depression. She made a commitment to tell Hale as soon as possible.

She put her plan into motion the next afternoon when she stopped at Hale's on the way to ride Limbo. Espying Hale working in the yard off his back porch, she squared her shoulders, gave herself a stern pep talk, and forced her best guess at whatever was her "natural" behavior as she walked over to him. A pair of long-handled loppers extending from both arms, he stood knee-deep in chartreuse curdles of plant material beneath a large pine whose trunk sported a ladder.

"What on earth are you doing?" she asked.

"Hey, Maggie. Quite the mess, huh? It was time for this old granddad's annual exam, see? I'm playing tree doctor. I'm cutting out mistletoe before it strangles my pine tree to death."

"Oh." She examined the large bunched clumps, which she'd never seen up close. "Yeah, we had mistletoe all over some of the oaks back in California. I always thought it was sort of pretty, especially in the winter when it was the only green left in the trees. Kind of a wild color of green, too." She looked into the upper branches of the tree.

"What's the matter? Couldn't you reach those with your ladder?" She pointed to a few snarls still hanging in the pine's crown. "Or did you just miss a few?"

Leave it to a woman for instantaneous supervision. "Nah, I'm leaving those."

"What?" She laughed a little incredulously at such an idea. "How come?"

"You'll laugh at me if I tell you."

"I already laughed at you." She gave him an exasperated look, waiting for an answer.

"Okay. Well, I'm leaving those because of what you said."

"What? What did I say?"

"You said you thought mistletoe was pretty."

Maggie laughed again in spite of herself. "I told you you'd laugh," Hale accused.

"I'm sorry. It's just so unexpected from, you know, a *male,* that something related to, say, mosquitoes or ticks . . . no, let's say, to *leeches* . . . would cause such sentimental feelings, in a *man.*"

"There you go male bashing, Maggie. Women have be-

206

come downright ugly about that these days. Mistletoe bashing, too." She laughed again. "Laugh away, Maggie. Go ahead. But I take my mistletoe seriously. I even did some research on it."

"Do tell," she purred sarcastically. *Meow. Pffft.*

"Sometimes you're a real smart ass, you know that? I don't think I'll tell you now."

"You're playing me like a trout, aren't you?"

But he stayed stubbornly silent on the subject of mistletoe until she voluntarily began picking up the prunings and loading them into his pickup bed.

"Okay, since you're so obviously *contrite,*" he relented with a sneer, taking down the ladder, "I'll tell you." She hopped onto the end of the pickup's tailgate with a phony rapt expression on her face, for which he punished her by assuming a superior, academic tone. "Well, first of all, it's not a parasite, not completely. It's a *semi-parasite.* It does have some chlorophyll and makes some of its own food." He dropped the school lecture momentarily to say confidentially, "So, you see, it's not all bad." This aside aside, he shifted back into his professorial persona. "It grows verrry slowly" (he almost rolled the r's), so it's extremely long-lived, dying only because the host tree finally dies." Letting this soak in for a second, he downshifted into his own voice again. *A regular Jekyll-Hyde.* "That's a sort of touching image, don't you think? The Romeo and Juliet of the plant world. A marriage made in heaven, so to speak."

"Ouch!" Maggie said. *So that's what this lesson is really about.*

If Hale knew he'd struck a target dead center, he didn't let on, didn't miss a beat.

"Anyway, the other reason I left a little of it in the tree is because there's a bit of magic in it, you know. All that stuff that led to people hanging it at Christmas."

"Tell me about that," she said, with sincere interest now. "I've never actually known where that custom came from."

"It has this little bizarre role in our early history that intrigues me. It used to be gathered up for the midsummer bonfires that were a part of the ancient Druid priest's sacrificial ceremonies."

"Don't you just love picturing us when we were still pagan?" Maggie's imagination kicked in, and her mind drifted with the image. "I think that's part of why our church has lost some of its power in modern times. The ministers have taken all the magic out of religion. Who wants a religion without magic?"

"You're interrupting, Maggie. You're digressing."

"Oh, sorry," she squeaked, in mock contrition.

"Anyway," he drawled in mock irritation, "the Druids believed that mistletoe, especially the mistletoe that grew in their sacred oaks, had not only medicinal but also magical powers."

"Maybe they believed the mistletoe absorbed magic from the oaks," Maggie commented, risking further censor for interrupting again.

"Hmm. That's an interesting idea," he said, intrigued enough by her interpretation to tolerate this interruption. "Anyway, that's where the custom of kissing under mistletoe came from. The Druids believed if you kissed someone under a mistletoe, that its magic led the person you kissed inevitably to marry you."

Her smile was lovely, like a child's who has just heard an encore of the ending of her favorite fairy tale. "I never knew you were such a mystic, Hale."

"Go ahead, laugh at me again," he said. "But, if you

look up in the tree, you'll notice I'm mostly pragmatic. I don't want to lose my pine prematurely, after all, so I cut all of it out but a clump or two. It's just that, with all that history and with that garish, almost fluorescent color and the white berries, it really would be a shame to destroy it all."

They finished loading the pile into the pickup. "It's poisonous too, you know," he warned, closing the tailgate. "To animals and to man. But I still have this thing about it, I don't know. It's dangerous, but it's worth keeping. Who knows, maybe a little adversity is good for the old tree, keeps it vigorous or something. Stimulates it into staying on its toes, so to speak."

"You really are a Druid yourself, aren't you?" Maggie marveled, teasing.

Hale laughed. "I don't mind that label at all, I have to say." He would have the last word on mistletoe. He hemmed, then postulated, "Maybe I like it because it's a bit like a woman, wouldn't you agree?"

"I'm outta here," Maggie laughed, shunting his remark and turning to walk away.

Hale caught her arm. "Here, you don't have to go away mad," he said, amused. "Where are you off to, anyway?"

"I'm headed over to ride."

His hand still held her arm. "Maybe I'll come over and watch once I've put this load into the Dumpster."

"Okay. It'd be nice to have an audience for a change."

He pulled her toward him, stooped before she could react and kissed her on the mouth, lingering for a moment with his lips almost touching hers, like he might kiss her again, before he stood up.

Maggie staggered back a step, off-balance. "What was that for?"

Hale smiled slyly and pointed up at the mistletoe left in the tree.

"That's another good reason to keep it around," he grinned. He stepped into his truck and drove off. The last word on mistletoe.

Limbo was warmed up but still full of energy when Hale pulled up at the edge of the hay meadow. She waved briefly, but didn't stop, riding on to retain her own and the horse's concentration. She had finally begun to feel natural in the dressage saddle. Her body was adjusting to the stretch of lengthening her legs against the horse's sides, toes in, calves swept back, while opening up the torso. *He's so much happier when I get it right,* she thought, as a slight adjustment in her position lifted and loosened the swing in his trot. In a relaxed balance that relieved his forehand, she could channel him through shortened reins in elastic contact with the bit that must never, she constantly reminded herself, block the freedom of the movement. *Forward, forward,* she reminded her hands. *Supple wrists. Don't hold, and NEVER pull back.* She squeezed his barrel through the length of her legs, regulating the increase in power by consciously maintaining the tempo of his footfalls with the precision of a metronome, controlling his rhythm through her trunk. Then she ceased driving and allowed the increased impulsion to spring up under her seat. After a series of such transitions, Limbo's power floated like a cloud. She regulated their connection with a touch as sensitive as a concert pianist's, feeling for the delicate balance between drive, suppleness, and control. When she tried some lateral work she had just begun teaching him, he moved fluidly away from the pressure of her inside leg, yielding in a diagonal flow across the field in each direction. His mane swung with the two-beat rhythm of the trot. Relaxation extended clear through his ears, which had fallen sideways, flopping gently with each stride. When she gave an aid, they flicked toward her, then dropped back into complete relaxation. She tried a shoulder fore position in each direction, taking care that the gait remained pure and expressive, reminding herself that it was like driving on ice—a disaster if you tried to over-control things. She brought him to a springy round halt through the trot, then let him stretch his neck down and out like a released coil as she headed toward Hale. White foam flecked with orange carrot flakes bubbled and dripped from his muzzle, splattering the front of his fore-arms and knees—a badge of work done properly with a soft mouth, of work done well.

She patted his neck, beaming. "See what a talented guy he is, Hale? Isn't it amazing what's lurking in his big mongrel's body? Who'd have guessed!"

"Good man, Limbo," Hale praised, stepping up to rub Limbo's forehead. "I'm impressed, Maggie, I really am. He looked like a completely different horse out there."

"I think he enjoys showing off, which will be just great if and when I compete him," she said. "He struts his stuff like he's made of gold, doesn't he?"

"You bring out the best in him, Maggie, like you do with a lot of things. You always were great with animals and plants." His hands had stayed, touching Limbo's shoulder. "Remember that feral cat you tamed here at the ranch that loved you but would never let anyone else touch it? Maybe you've got some of that pagan magic yourself. Maybe that's why you like hearing about the Druids."

"Oh, so now you're saying I might be a witch?" she bluffed.

"Well, no. Don't make it into something negative, now."

He checked himself, held his breath a second, then said, "Maybe more an earth goddess." He knew it was an outrageous line, but weighed the risks and took his shot. Besides, he half-believed it.

Far be it from Maggie to shoot down even a two-left-footed step in their *pas de deux,* so she sidestepped with grace. "Sometimes you do say the right thing, Hale, you know that?" Maggie was built of strong stuff.

He followed slowly behind her in the pickup to the barn. She hustled inside to halter Limbo and give him a double helping of carrots before Hale came in, so he wouldn't see her pampering him.

Hale held Limbo's lead rope while Maggie removed the tack, then groomed the fidgety horse.

"You know, Hale," she said, red-faced, standing up from brushing under Limbo's belly, "I was thinking about exactly why I love doing this so much." She leaned against the horse's side with one arm crooked over his back. "And it came to me that my riding and your fishing have similar appeals. It's that we're both connecting into something completely wild—we both hook onto wildness for a few moments, you through the line and me through the reins. We get a brief glimpse into the will of another creature in both our sports. You see what I mean? And we've got this fragile connection to that will for those few moments, channeling it but not taming it, just on the edge of control." She brushed again like she meant to polish the horse.

"So we're both looking for something that puts us in our place and at the same time opens another world in a way, is that what you're saying? That's kind of a nice thought, Maggie. Maybe you're right, maybe we're after similar thrills . . . but I should point out, I've also got the added bonus of latching onto the unknown, you know, not knowing what's down there beneath the surface. It's a sort of treasure hunt every time I cast my fly on the water."

"Well, eat your heart out, Boris, when I'm up there on Limbo, I'm tied into a thousand pound adversary. So there!" Maggie could whinny, too.

After they'd turned Limbo out, while they strolled to their vehicles, Maggie took a deep breath and thought, *It's now or never.* She tried to muster the most casual attitude possible, but her voice squeaked in spite of herself, "By the way, if you have a chance, could you come over to my place tonight after dinner? I've got something important I need to tell you." She exhaled a long shaky breath.

Hale seemed to have not noticed her tension. "Sure Maggie," he answered, unconcerned. "I'm supposed to eat supper with a couple of fishermen who are checking in this evening, but I'll be free by 8:30 or so. Will that work?"

"That'll be fine," she managed to answer.

It was a day to finish important business, she decided. She drove into Saratoga to drop a sealed document at the office of the local lawyer she had chosen to represent her, leaving it with instructions to the receptionist that the lawyer should call her if he had any questions. When she arrived home she responded to the message on her answering machine to call the legal firm's office.

"I just wanted to be absolutely clear on this before I file it, Ms. Everhardt," the voice said. The words were precisely clipped, but had a reassuring deep resonance that reflected the competent man she'd met only once before. "So, this is a codicil to your will leaving the cabin property you just purchased this April to your daughter, Jill, and your nephews, Eric, and Scott Adamson, jointly."

"That's right. Yes," she said, then repeated, "that's exactly right."

He switched from his business voice to a more personal tone. "So you're going to hang onto the place? You don't intend to sell it?"

"That's right," she answered firmly. "Absolutely."

He became more neighborly yet. "You'll be making Saratoga your permanent home, then, Ms. Everhardt?"

"Oh, no," she corrected his misconception, "no, I mean, I'm not sure about that at all." She waited, then continued, realizing further explanation was needed. "But whatever I decide to do, I'm going to find a way to keep the cabin, to keep it in the family. That was my intention from the beginning."

She was a nervous wreck by the time 8:30 arrived. There was good coffee brewing. A large bouquet of the brightest flowers from her garden shown from her table like a ray of hope in the dim room, where she had extinguished all lights but one low-wattage lamp and a few candles. *I don't want to be seen too clearly tonight. I wish I could do this from the darkest, farthest reaches of outer space.* She played a CD that was a collection of quiet old standards. *For my nerves.*

But she jerked tensely when he knocked, and had to force a tight smile as she opened the door. *He looks so calm. How can I destroy that kind of peace?*

"Hi, Hale," she rattled casually. "Thanks for coming. I made some coffee, if you'd like some. Have a seat at the table."

Hale followed her lead and took the coffee. He seemed to have no curiosity about the reason she had asked him over, sitting relaxed and patient, wearing a smile that might have been interpreted as mildly amused.

Maggie sat down across from Hale and looked into his eyes. Anything but amused. She cleared her throat. "I have something that I've needed to tell you for a long time, Hale," she began staunchly. *Let's get this over with!* "It's the reason I returned after all this time." Her eyes were a trapped animal's.

"Okay, Maggie. Whatever it is, I'm sure I can take it," he reassured.

"Don't be so sure, Hale." He could see her hands trembling as she raised her cup to her lips. The low glow of the lamp lit her face obliquely as she glanced nervously out the window, gazing into limitless darkness, as if she could escape there. He could see a trickle of sweat barely creeping down the smooth skin beneath the curves of dark hair she tucked obsessively behind her ear.

Johnny Mathis sang in the background. *Come back to me darling, I must make you see, that things aren't always what they seem to be. The girl in my arms meant nothing to me. I was telling her about you, I was telling her about you.*

"Oh god, Hale," she wailed, "I can't bear to do this. It's something I should've told you years ago. You're going to hate me . . ." She covered her face with her hands, shaking her head slowly before heaving a sigh, then abruptly lifted her face toward him, stern now. "There is no good way to say this. The best way I can think of is to say it right out, as quickly and short as possible." The words had started out in a gush, but now slowed to a crawl. "Painless is out of the question. Please . . . please, just . . . brace yourself."

She could read nothing from his eyes. He wore a neutral expression devoid of everything—either encouragement or condemnation, or even curiosity. She floundered alone in a terrible sea. Boring her eyes into his desperately, she finally blurted, "It's possible, Hale, it's just possible," she nearly choked on the words, "that your daughter could be your niece."

She watched him with sickly eagerness. Her stomach convulsed. Her heart pounded in her ears. Tears started to her eyes involuntarily. "I can't bear to hurt you like this, but I had to tell you. You have a right to know," she added in a desperate whisper. She couldn't breathe. There was no saliva when she tried to swallow. She waited silently, expectantly.

Hale sat still as stone. He might have been under a spell. Then his lips parted as if in slow motion. Everything slowed to an impossible grinding crawl for Maggie. She felt she was floating above the table watching a tableau being played by two anonymous actors. She could not find a grip on her fear, floating higher and higher away from a situation she couldn't bear.

"I know, Maggie," the words dropped quietly between them. "I've known for years."

Her eyes blinked rapidly several times as her mind wrapped around those words, those simple sounds that stealthily shattered the years of agonizing anticipation of a cataclysmic burst that would never happen. It was as if she'd come through a gory battle unbloodied and unscathed. It was impossible! All her expectations melted away a step beyond her as she trod toward the light of the truth. She was caught without one shred of a contingency plan. Her rigid back slowly caved, slumping slackly. Her mouth crumpled; her eyes hung expressionless in her pallid face.

Hale stood up and walked to a cupboard where he found a bottle of brandy. He poured a small amount into a glass and handed it to her.

"Here, drink this. Go on. You look pale."

She did as he said.

"Let me explain, Maggie. Here, come lie down a minute." He led her to the sofa where she stretched out and turned onto her side to watch him. He sat in the easy chair opposite the sofa, pulling it closer.

"It's true. I've known since right after you left me. It's like this . . ." he sighed, looked down, talking to the floor. "You know how you had been riding me about being tested for fertility the summer after we moved up here? We were both so discouraged about trying for a child for three years with no success. Well, I had finally done it. I had stopped in at the medical center in Laramie to have my sperm analyzed at the end of the summer." He leaned forward, grasping his hands together in front of his knees. "They called me with the result a few days after you told me you were pregnant. My sperm count and motility were very low, they said. They asked me if I was taking any medication that might cause that, and when I told them I wasn't, they said it was probably a chronic condition that may have been caused by something like a childhood illness contracted as an adult. That made sense to me because I caught the measles my first year at college, but hadn't thought much of it at the time. I wasn't even all that sick from it."

Hale stopped to rub his palms on the knees of his pants and then clamped them around his knees again in a grip so tight she could see the white knobs of his knuckles. "Anyway, when you told me you were pregnant, I just thought we'd been lucky to beat poor odds, so I didn't mention the test results to you. You were so excited, and there seemed no reason to bring it up. It's not something a man wants to tell his wife anyway."

One of the candles fluttered and died out but neither of them noticed. The darkening room suited them both. Gus, who'd pestered Maggie for attention jealously when Hale had arrived, had curled up in his bed on the top of the refrigerator where he slept soundly. Maggie could hear the tick of the clock in the bedroom. The CD had finished playing and the hush of the room hummed heavily.

"Would you mind putting in that other CD on top of the player?" she asked Hale, wanting to alleviate the numbing quiet of the room. He did as she asked and sat back down as the music began softly. *You make me leave my happy home. You took my love and now you've gone, since I fell for you.*

Hale rubbed his hands over his face and left them folded over his mouth, talking through them when he continued. "I thought we'd just been lucky, like I said. I didn't suspect anything was amiss at all until I got a long letter from Ken. It was right after you left me. He had just become a father for the first time. I think he was feeling terribly guilty when you left. I think he wanted me to know what had really caused you to leave; that it wasn't something I had done. And I think for the first time in his life, he was considering just how a man might really feel about being cheated in his marriage and possibly in his paternity. Anyway, he told me in the letter about what had happened between the two of you. I think he had carried that letter around with him a long time before he mailed it, from the condition it was in. Maybe he thought about not mailing it at all." Hale removed his hands from his mouth and studied them.

"That letter is what made me drop the custody suit. You must have wondered at the time why I did that."

Maggie didn't respond.

The music shifted into another song so sad that Maggie wished she hadn't asked Hale to play the CD. *When a man loves a woman, she can do no wrong . . .*

"At the end of the letter," Hale went on, "Ken begged me not to tell you that he'd spilled the beans. He said he had promised you that he would never tell and he gave a long explanation of why you two had made that decision. I think he didn't want me to think you were covering your own asses. He made it clear that you were trying to protect me.

"The crazy part is, Maggie, that he hadn't thought about the question of Jill's paternity at all until after she was born. Mom was writing to him in Bolivia and told him about your pregnancy, but she never told him exactly how far along you were. So he didn't make a connection until after she wrote to him that Jill had been born, when he figured out the dates."

Maggie looked up at the ceiling, and her words came out clogged. "Even then, Jill was actually born two weeks late, if I conceived that night with him." She didn't look at Hale as she spoke. "So it was never obvious . . . never a certain thing . . ."

They were both silent for some minutes, he staring past his hands at the floor, she unmoving at the ceiling. *If she's wrong, he won't know it* . . . the music played.

"I guess none of us will ever really know, Hale. I was so punitively sure she was Ken's at first. That's why I finally had to leave. As she grew up, I kept looking for signs. I would look from her to you and from you to her. I had to get the two of you away from each other or I'd have gone insane.

"That's been the worst punishment of all. I'll never know, Hale," she cried. "She's tall like you, but she has his coloring. I've tortured and tortured myself over it. I think in my masochism I almost wanted it to be him. But as time passed I've come to believe that God's no Puck. He wouldn't find perverse humor in causing such misery to a good man like you." The tears dropped from the back of her head onto the sofa.

Hale stood up. "Are you going to be all right if I go, Maggie?" he asked.

"I'm okay, Hale."

He gathered himself to go, but stopped and looked down at her from behind the chair. "I could've told you that I knew, Maggie. I could've made those fourteen years easier on you. I knew you hadn't left just because you were pissed off at me about the ranch. You'd have never left me for just that. I knew that."

She could see his large hands gripping the back of the chair.

"But, the truth is, I couldn't forgive you. I didn't forgive you. I guess I haven't ever forgiven you in all these years, Maggie."

"Will you be okay?" he asked again as he headed for the door.

She nodded . . . *she can do no wrong* . . . The door closed behind him.

When he was gone, when finally the sound of his truck had gone, she melted into a puddle of sorrow. It descended on her like a bird falling from the sky. Maggie keened and keened that night for what could have been, and then she laid it to rest.

Eleven

They didn't see each other for several days, which both distressed and relieved each of them. They picked up the threads of their everyday chores like lifelines. There was no urgency in renewing contact, since there was no longer anything unsaid between them. For the first time in twenty years, they knew that they knew all about each other.

It was somehow fitting, then, that their first meeting was accidental. And it was easier than anticipated. The dreaded post-revelation scenarios that had played in Maggie's imagination for fourteen years all proved flawed rehearsals. She did not find herself shrinking or quaking. In fact, she had been cloaked in calm since that night. Regardless of having received no pardon, she was suffused with a sense of utter peace. As it flowed through her, the soothing relief of mind and body felt so unfamiliar that it struck her that she hadn't experienced a single instant of it since that night with Ken. She had been through twenty years of relentless unrest, even in her dreams. She was sleeping more deeply now than she could remember. She floated through the hours on a buffer of calm untouched by the fact that she had received no overt forgiveness. She had known that it was not really in Hale's power to free her from guilt anyway. But she had come clean with the person against whom the sin had been committed, and that seemed enough.

So when she and Hale both reached for a tube of sealant at the hardware store, she felt no trepidation; her peace wasn't shaken. There was a calm detachment that told her she was beyond further harm.

"Hey, Maggie," his tone was friendly. "Have you been okay?" he asked, concerned.

She just nodded.

"That's good. I was worried about you. I didn't know if you'd be all right the other night. I'm sorry, but I just had to get away. I had to get out of there to regroup. And I thought I should just let you work things out your own way, too. I told you I've always thought you were stronger than you believed."

He searched her face and seemed satisfied with what he saw there. "I'm glad I ran into you, though. I was going to stop by your place later today because I need to talk to you about something interesting that just came up . . . something that involves you."

They were striving to maintain a tenuous momentum, to not allow its destruction. "So . . . what's up?" She took in his face more clearly than she'd done since her return to Paradise Ranch. *He's really not scary at all,* she thought. *He looks fine. What have I been so terrified of?*

Hale forged onward. "I got a call from this guy named Duncan McMurray. He's one of the Old Baldy members, maybe the richest of them all. You know, one of those people with so much money that it's lost meaning for them." They slowly navigated the aisles together as he talked, looking at and occasionally handling items on the shelves.

"What's he do?" she asked, half-attentively, perusing the goods.

"His family had old money, but he made more than the family ever dreamt of in the communications industry."

"I'm always in the wrong line of work," she muttered vacantly, as she picked up a package of green plastic stretch ties for her garden.

222

"Anyway, he wants me to meet him for dinner Wednesday night at the Old Baldy clubhouse. Says he has an interesting proposition for me . . . and he specifically asked me to bring you along." He stopped walking and directed his full attention at Maggie. "I have no idea why he wants to involve you," he told her. "He's a regular client of mine and we've come to be fairly good friends because I've knocked myself out to accommodate him and his associates through the years, you know, dropping everything on short notice when they wanted to book a float. But the only thing he knows about you, as far as I know, is that we were divorced long ago. And since I haven't seen him or spoken to him since you moved back, I have no idea what's up, really." She could see Hale was in the dark.

"Well, we'll just have to see what it's about when he tells us, won't we?" Maggie said, smiling.

"So, you'll go?"

"Sure. I'm game. You just never know what might happen at Paradise Ranch, do you?" If Maggie meant to convey a double meaning, she seemed innocent of it.

"I'll pick you up at 7:30 Wednesday night, if that's all right, then."

"No, wait, Hale. I wanted to bring some things from my garden over to Rob, so I'll just meet you at your place after I drop them off, okay?"

"That'd be fine. I'll see you then." They meandered apart, catching partial glimpses of each other, but not simultaneously, and each of them slowly lost interest in the objects surrounding them, the shopping that had so engrossed them.

She stopped by The Silky Filly dress shop after the hardware store, to find a new blouse for the upcoming dinner, something from Saratoga rather than Palo Alto. She wanted

223

something less austere than her existing wardrobe, the majority of which was dark and rather severe. She flipped through the items along the wall until she came across a blouse that brought a smile to her face.

When she walked into Rob's kitchen Wednesday evening he was busy preparing dinner for a full house. Though rushed, he worked with the aplomb of an expert, perhaps even an artist.

"Maggie, my darling!" he called when she stepped into the kitchen with the sack of garden vegetables. "Look at you!" He laid down his knife to turn and admire her. "I heard you're headed up to Old Baldy tonight. I pity those poor old millionaires with their weak hearts tonight, when you walk in . . ."

She was loathe to slow him down, so put the sack in the cooler and waved a kiss to him as she left for Hale's house.

She could see Hale talking on the phone as she stepped onto his porch. He saw her too and waved her in. She sat down in the living room, listening to snatches of the conversation from the kitchen. Soon bored, she walked over to the bookcase and read the titles. *The Journals of Lewis and Clark*, *A River Runs Through It*, *Walden Pond*, *The Ox Bow Incident*, *Desert Solitaire*, *Powell's Exploration of the Colorado River*, *Moby Dick*, *The King Must Die*, *The Immense Journey*, *Lord Jim*, *Leaves of Grass*.

"Okay," she heard, his loudening voice signaling that the conversation was concluding. "That's great. Yeah. Say 'Hello' to Mom and Dad for me. Yeah. Bye."

"That was Ken," he told her as he stepped into the room. "You're a little early. You want something to drink?"

She shook her head. "No thanks." She sat back down in the chair. "I thought you two hardly ever talked."

"That's how it's been until recently. But Ken's been calling since they were up here."

Maggie just raised her eyebrows to ask why.

"He says his boys had a great time up here, and he wants to know if they could come up here next summer to spend some extended time with me."

"Wow! That's super! I thought those two were great kids. Funny and enthusiastic . . . nice kids," she remarked.

"He wondered if the oldest might be able to work for me next summer. I told him I could probably find work for both of them, for that matter."

"I'm awfully glad he's talking to you, Hale. And I'm glad you're going to have a chance to get closer to his boys, if not to Ken. The terrible distance I caused between you has been part of my hell."

Hale went around the room turning off some lights, preparing to leave. He stood looking at Maggie directly when he had finished. "I told him that you finally told me about it."

"Oh." If she was taken aback, she didn't show it.

"Yeah. I thought it was about time for all the cards to be on the table."

"I'm glad you told him," she said quietly, head down, eyes averted.

"Strangely enough, I think the fact that we happened to all sit down at a table together, face to face with each other, and lived to tell about it . . . and even managed to laugh about things . . . I think that's sort of turned Ken around."

She looked at Hale. "What about you, though? Do you want to be close to your brother again?"

"Don't ask me that, Maggie." He opened the door for her, and as they walked toward the car said, "I'd absolutely like to be closer to my nephews, though."

They took Maggie's car. "Do you want to drive?" she asked him. "You'll have to navigate otherwise."

"I'll drive." When he settled himself behind the wheel, he pointed to her windshield. "Look, Maggie. You've got a crack beginning to run here."

"I know. Luck can be such a bitch sometimes."

There was still daylight left in that long midsummer day. They drove straight into the lowering sun, straining against the glare.

"You know, Maggie, I offered Kennie half-ownership of the ranch right after Dad signed it over to me."

"I didn't know that."

"Yea, well I did. But he turned me down. He said he didn't want it because it hadn't come from Dad. He didn't want my charity, I guess."

"He was so competitive with you, Hale, I'm sure he thought he could never take such a generous gift from you. How could he ever have repaid it? I don't think Ken would've wanted to be in your debt back then."

"You're probably right. Ken was a tough nut to crack in those days." They rode in silence. "Actually," Hale began again, "that was one good thing to come out of what happened that summer . . . I mean, other than Jill, of course."

"What? What else could be good about it?" Maggie asked. "It would be impossible for me to imagine any other good from it."

"Kennie," Hale said. "I think it shook him up enough, what he'd done, to turn him around. You know how self-centered he was. He didn't seem to give a damn about anyone else. You know he'd never have joined the Peace Corps if he hadn't scared himself half to death with what that attitude could lead him to. And it was his stint in the

Peace Corps that led him to a career that, while not exactly Mother Teresa's, has served some good."

They turned north, out of the sun's glare.

"I used to tell you that Kennie suffered from hubris, if you remember," Hale said.

"Yes, but I never quite knew what you meant," Maggie answered.

"Hubris is when you have so much arrogance that you outrage the gods. I'd say he pretty much fulfilled that little prophecy."

"I never blamed him, Hale. I was older than him; I was the one who was married. And I've always believed that I probably should have been able to control the situation more than him."

"Maybe," Hale said. "Maybe not."

They were quiet, then Maggie spoke. "There's one thing I'd like to know," she said, looking straight ahead rather than at Hale. "Do you know if Ken ever told Diana?"

"He told me he didn't and that he never planned to. It was between you and me and him."

"And Jill," she added, quietly.

"Yeah. And Jill."

Maggie looked over at the side of his face. He was focused on the driving, with both hands on the wheel. "Look, Hale. I have to tell you, I've never felt the same pressure to tell Jill that I did to tell you."

"I never wanted to tell her either."

"She wasn't hurt by not knowing, the way I see it. Oh, I guess you could say she was hurt, if Ken should have rightfully raised her instead of you. In that case they were both being deprived of a relationship that should have been their birthright. But I took care of that possible injustice, didn't I? I took her away so neither of you was more deprived of

227

fatherhood than the other. It was the only fair thing I could think of." Maggie turned in her seat toward Hale. "You're her father by choice, though, Hale."

They turned east toward the distant bluff where the clubhouse was located.

"I never wanted to tell her," Hale explained, "because I was afraid I might lose her. As reprehensible as it is, I've wanted Jill in my life at any cost. No matter how it was done, you did bring Jill into my life. You gave me a daughter, Maggie, and I don't want anything to take that away."

The sun was just setting as they pulled into the large parking lot. When Hale killed the engine, he looked over at Maggie.

Neither made a move to open their doors. Maggie sat quietly with her hands still in her lap. "We could find out, I guess, if we really wanted to," she said.

"What? You mean DNA testing?"

"I suppose we could."

Hale sat motionless, then shook his head slowly. When he spoke he was emphatic. "No, Maggie. I don't want to know. I want to hang on to the belief that she's mine. God forgive me, but that's how I feel."

"I feel exactly the same, Hale. I want to believe that in spite of the terrible thing I did, that good comes from good, which would mean that Jill has to be yours, as she surely would be in a just world." She dropped her eyes. He could see her fingers limp and lifeless in her lap. "Maybe something will cause us to have to tell her someday. Otherwise, I say we leave it as it is."

She started to open the door, but he grabbed her arm to hold her there for one moment more.

"You know what made it so terrible, Maggie? It was that

I could still be in love with you without forgiving you. It was just a matter of how much pain I wanted to put myself through. If I kept loving you, it meant I would suffer like hell. I tried zoning out, but it was only worse. So I talked myself out of loving you, Maggie." He let go of her arm and put his hand to the door handle, but stopped, without turning back to her, and said, "It's still a matter of how much pain I want to feel."

Duncan was waiting at a table for them. He stood and shook hands genially with Hale, clasping Hale's right arm with his free hand, then turned to Maggie and took her hand carefully in his. He waved them to their chairs, pulling Maggie's out to seat her. Looking around her, Maggie saw a large understated dining room with a high beamed ceiling. Sedate waiters in white shirts and dark trousers moved efficiently through the linen and china–covered tables, catering to every need of the patrons, assiduously refilling crystal water glasses. The entire atmosphere exuded quiet dignity. There was a cocktail lounge at one end and a long glass-fronted hallway to the west, which led to the pro shop and the golfers' locker rooms and saunas. The south wall was all glass, encasing the view of the driving range and the first fairway. That fairway was bordered on the east by a lake, stocked with trout that could be fed from a bucket provided for that purpose. Antelope often wandered onto the course, as did deer, and occasionally elk. Also visible below the clubhouse were the luxurious homes of some of the members, and beyond those, the whole Platte valley, the river, and the dominating blue bulk of Elk Mountain.

When she turned her attention to Duncan, she apprised him to be a very handsome man with enormous self-assurance. Of medium height with close-cropped, graying hair, he appeared to be extraordinarily trim and fit for a man she guessed to be in his early sixties. Hale had told her that Duncan was on his third wife, each younger than the last, and that his latest was a paradigm of the gorgeous trophy wife. *No wonder he has to stay so fit,* she thought. *Meow. Maggie the cat.*

He ordered wine for himself and Maggie, and the usual for Hale, tonic water with a twist of lime. He obviously knew Hale well. "What do you think of our little clubhouse?" he asked Maggie, sweeping his arm around its perimeter.

"It's what I expected," she answered, "but not in Saratoga."

They chatted over their drinks, then Duncan offered several suggestions as they ordered dinner. He was aggressively flirtatious with Maggie.

"Don't you think brunettes look all the more beautiful in red?" he asked Hale. "Ah, sometimes I wish I hadn't remarried."

"Oh, I find that hard to believe, Duncan. I've seen your wife, after all," laughed Hale.

Maggie didn't quite know how to field Duncan's compliments for several reasons, including not being accustomed to being objectified. She felt he was speaking about her as if she weren't present. He soon turned the conversation to a more comfortable subject, however.

"I told you I had a proposition for you, Hale. It also involves Maggie, if you're both willing that it should."

Duncan reminded Maggie of someone from long ago, someone she couldn't quite identify. The conversation was interrupted by the arrival of the food. Once they began eating, Duncan resumed.

"Well," he began, wiping his mouth with his napkin and

replacing it on his lap, "I have recently bought a place on Vancouver Island."

"Oh! I love that area!" Maggie gushed spontaneously.

"Good! Then you may be happy to hear that I need your advice, both of you, but particularly you, Hale, concerning some guest cabins I'm building on the property."

"Is it a blank piece of land, then?" Hale asked.

"No. There's an existing house, and it is beautiful just as it is, but it isn't large enough for all the entertaining I do. So, rather than add on to the house and risk destroying the integrity of its design, I decided to have a series of guest cabins built." He looked from one to the other of them and said enthusiastically, "You would love the house. It's on a wooded hilltop overlooking the landing for the ferry that comes in from Victoria, not far above the village, but completely secluded by the forest around it."

He broke off to sip his wine. "Let me freshen your glass," he offered Maggie, and refilled it.

"I'm not completely satisfied with the plans for the cabins that have been presented to me, though, and I want you to give me advice, Hale, because I've admired your style at the lodge."

He took several bites of his food. "And you, Maggie, I'm including you in this project because I've heard from several people around town that you have converted the worst eyesore in the valley into a beautiful garden. And also that you are a woman with restrained decorating tastes, a trait sadly lacking in my wife. Carol, God bless her, hasn't the foggiest notion of restraint in anything."

They all chuckled as Duncan wiped his mouth again.

"My proposition is this: I'm flying up there early Friday. I want you both to come along with me. I feel the place has to be seen in person for you to tender any useful advice. I'd fly you up there on my jet, spend the afternoon showing you what I have in mind, then you would have the house to yourselves for the weekend, since both other business and my new bride have claims on me this weekend. My pilot is supposed to return me to Vancouver Island early Monday, however, for a meeting with my contractor and architect, and he would fly you back here that morning. Well, what do you say?"

Maggie laughed rather nervously, raising one questioning eyebrow as she looked at Hale. Hale also hesitated, looking from one to the other. Duncan seemed to feel more encouragement was needed. "I know it's short notice, particularly for you at this time of the year, Hale. But it would mean a lot to me if you could swing it."

Their continued reticence made him add, "I can see you need to consult with each other, so please talk it over this evening and let me know first thing tomorrow. You know how to reach me, Hale."

They finished the meal discussing the season's fishing. A fishing fanatic, though not quite in Brian and Vance's league, Duncan was concerned with the effect of whirling disease.

"We've been lucky so far in Wyoming," Hale told him. "We've seen very few fish with any obvious signs of the disease. The researchers think it's because of our water quality. It's the streams that are most disturbed by man that are suffering. Unfortunately, the parasite has been detected in a tributary of the Green River that feeds a couple of our hatcheries, but they're working on protecting the hatcheries, and they'll not stock any fish that test positive. The state's trying to be proactive, but they sure don't want to have to kill wild populations to control it. You'd be looking at wiping out the last remnant population of native cutthroats. They're hoping that if it does get into our wild waters, that levels of infection will drop over time. After all, Europe has had it since the 1890s, and they still have rainbow trout over there."

"We're lucky on the North Platte, because they don't stock it anymore from the hatcheries. But we've all got to do our part to prevent spreading the infection. I'm having to disinfect everything that goes into the water and I tell my fishermen not to dispose of fish parts in any Wyoming waters. I'm also telling them about a new wading boot that doesn't pick up the spores. The experts are doing all kinds of studies on the disease, and there's a foundation in Bozeman that's raising funds for further research, ahem, Duncan. But one thing's for sure . . . unfortunately, we're all going to have to learn to live with the threat of the disease and its parasite, because they're here."

"You know what's weird?" sighed Maggie, who'd been staring into her wine glass as Hale talked. She didn't wait for an answer from them. "It's like it's the era of these terrible chronic wasting diseases in animals, or something. I mean, there's whirling disease in our trout, and Feline Leukemia and AIDS is a terrible threat to all domestic cats (*Gus!*), then Britain had that cataclysmic mad cow disease outbreak, and now the chronic wasting disease in Wisconsin's wild deer has shown up in the deer and elk in northern Colorado, and it's spreading into Nebraska as we speak . . . I mean, can you imagine America's wild areas without deer and elk! And even the die-out of frogs around the world turned out to be not from environmental pollution, but from some virus or bacteria or something (*damned swiss cheese of a memory!*)." She frowned and looked at both men as if for an explanation. "Then, of course, there's HIV in humans. And none of these can be cured. It's just real scary, if you ask me."

"Yeah. Good point," Hale nodded and shook his head at the same time. "Whenever we start to think we have a handle on things . . . If anyone thinks humans are at the top of the heap on this planet, they just aren't paying attention to what's in the microscope."

"To say nothing of what's beyond our seeing," added Duncan, ominously, then said in a brisker voice, "Well, all I can say is, I'd sure hate for anything to hurt the great fishing of the North Platte, Hale, for the sake of us fishermen who think it's the best kept secret in Wyoming," returning to the topic of fishing with a devotee's obsession.

They drifted through the final acts of the evening's routine. As they parted, Duncan lifted Maggie's hand to his lips and kissed it. It was then that she recalled whom he resembled.

"You are a most lovely lady," Duncan told her as he continued holding her hand. "Don't doubt for a minute that that's another reason I would like to have you with us on this little project of mine."

"Somehow I don't," laughed Maggie pleasantly. "I don't think I'd be inclined to doubt much of anything you say."

"Well, what do you think, Maggie?" Hale asked once they had enclosed themselves in the Beamer.

"He's rather predatory," she laughed lightly. "I won't have to fight him off, will I?"

"Oh no. Duncan really is the perfect gentleman beneath that sharky come on of his. He just includes women as a part of his epicurism. But you notice he's not gluttonous."

"Good point."

"Actually, he's an interesting man. He owns a part of several sports franchises and has backed a variety of individuals like boxers, musicians, artists, scholars, as well as various philanthropic causes." Hale explained a theory he'd developed about Duncan. "I think Duncan enjoys playing god to a degree. Or maybe guardian angel would be more accurate. It's a power thing, but done positively. Anyway, I seem to be one of his pet projects. He seems to have taken an interest in my welfare, for some reason. He's offered to help me out financially in the past, but I never wanted to be in debt to Duncan. I make sure I do him as many favors as he does me. He has sent plenty of clientele my way, though. And they're not cheap blighters, either. He's a man who could own anything he wants, including most people. But he does try to leave a man, and a woman, for that matter, their self-respect." He summed it up. "Duncan is all right."

"So, what do you say?" he asked again, looking in her face.

Flights over the Pacific Northwest follow one snow-capped volcano to the next in a tremendous dotted line. The landscape's lushness and pure hues prove nature an exhibitionist. The traveler, seduced by voyeurism, wants to never land.

They were taken by private boat through the blue waters of the Juan de Fuca strait, paralleling the public ferry, a white wedding cake carrying its own party. The island had thrown off its gray veil to let in the summer sun. The verdure of the hills spilled unchecked down steep slopes into the sea, where quaint villages huddled along the sea's edge, their toes in the water. They glided into the fishing village of Tofino near the entrance to Clayoquot Sound.

Duncan's property was as he had described it. The house exceeded his description, however, sculpted in sinuous curves in the style of Le Corbusier, with a front entirely of glass facing the harbor below.

Because they had lunched on the jet, they set to work immediately. Duncan was not a man to waste time. The "cabins" would need much sophistication to blend with the elegant house. Duncan's employment of Hale based on his admiration of Paradise Ranch's lodge seemed more and more a guise. But Hale's engineering skills were of some use. Hours later, when they had finished their discussions and had toured the house, Duncan left them a set of keys to the Lexus in the garage and they said farewell.

It was the time of day of earth's uncertainty, those uncommitted moments between dusk and complete darkness, when a thin line of fading light hugs the horizon, waiting. When Duncan pulled away, rounding the curve behind tall conifers, his sense of urgency remained, as if left behind by him accidentally in his hurry. For, as his taillights vanished, Hale reached for Maggie like a drowning man, pulling her against his body. He kissed her full on the lips long and hard with a fierceness borne of self-denial. When they broke from the kiss he didn't let her go. He pulled her toward the bedroom, and Maggie willingly allowed herself to be led. They drew together like a deep inhalation. "Are you sure, Hale?" she breathed, her eyes a flushed fawn's.

"Shhhh," he hushed, laying his finger over her shivering mouth.

She could hear a distant buoy rocking in the gentle waves of the ocean, dinging and dinging. And now, finally, it was as if the silken glide of their dance had never been interrupted.

Duncan stepped aboard his boat in the harbor below and looked up at the house. He could just make out through the trees a light in the bedroom which came on and quickly went off again. A smile spread slowly across his face. The engine of the ferry moored next to him caught fire with a gentle rumbling purr, then began huffing louder and louder. As it began to move away from the dock, a blast from its horn sang out into the night. Standing on his bow, Duncan felt a slight breeze at his back and fancied he felt it rustling his wings.

Twelve

The approach of summer's end prodded Maggie into action. There was an urgency to complete projects before the forced idleness of winter dormancy. She formulated a larger concept for her landscape, and began implementing it, planting borders of chokecherry and native plum, of junipers, wild roses, and flowering crabapples and glossy serviceberry for windbreaks and wildlife shelter. She created islands of native plants, or at least plants that should have been native (*close enough*), rabbit brush, silver sage, yarrow, grasses, and lamb's ear. And for the assurance of life that only evergreens give in winter, she planted a garden of conifer shrubs including mugho pine, native juniper and a new dwarf globed spruce that no one had introduced to the area, but which she felt should be perfectly hardy and worth an attempt.

A branch of a small feeder creek that had once flowed beside the cabin had been cut off by Herb years before when he'd found it bothersome. Maggie dug out the entrance to its original course and watched transfixed as the water crept slowly forward with blackened fingertips through the pale gray pan of dry earth. It was the water's sound and movement she sought, its animation. She planted willow shrubs, alder, river birch, and shrub maple along its course and added blue columbines and red penstemons at their feet for hummingbirds and butterflies, and for herself. She even planted catmint for Gus, surrounding it with a subterranean border so it couldn't trespass.

Hale sent Alfredo over with the tractor to move some large boulders into place along the stream and among the other plant groupings as Maggie pleased. One stone with a shallow concavity that held water she centered on a mound outside her kitchen window. Gus explored the changes, viewing them as disruptions in his established sentry rounds. He was busy for days leaving his mark to make them his own, *mine, mine.*

As her project coalesced, she decided the property was worthy of naming, like the ranches around her whose entrances brandished fancy titles. She came up with a few half-hearted possibilities: the "Ponderous," or the "Meanwhile, Back at The" ranch. Neighboring ranches incorporated their brands into their names, using letters and symbols like slashes or bars. Why not the Full Circle Ranch, then? Or . . . no, wait . . . what had the family called the place? Oh, yes . . . the Paradise Lost Ranch. That was perfect, of course. Returning from town one evening, she was conscious for the first time of a certain feeling as the cabin came into view. *I love my place. Paradise Lost Ranch. Mine. I love it now.*

She called David the next day to ask him if he could come by to discuss an idea she'd long mulled over, but had not yet felt committed to initiating. She enticed him with a promise of cake and coffee, and they made an appointment.

David came punctually, as always. It was good to see him again. She realized how much she'd missed him when she saw that ethereally pale, solidly honest face.

"Hey, David. How have you been?"

"Hi, Ms. Eve," he answered with his too big smile while she waved him across the threshold. "I'm fine." He swiped off his hat, baring his translucent hair. "I've been busy," he added, but with a quiet, patient voice that belied the words.

They caught up on events as she served him the cake she'd used as bait. "You know, I'd have come just as soon, anyway," he said, mouth full, pointing with his fork at the half-eaten cake, scolding her for having plied him with food, while eating it with gusto. Gus rubbed against his leg, sniffing obsessively at a specific spot on the toe of one boot as David ate.

"Don't be rude, Gus," Maggie admonished.

"Oh, that's all right, Ms. Eve. I don't mind," David chuckled.

She sat down with him to have a piece of cake herself. "Would you have time," she began, finally coming to the point, "for a rather large project, if there were no time constraints involved?"

"You're talking about an addition, I take it." His answer was a question.

Maggie nodded. He'd wolfed down the cake, so she offered him a second piece, but when he shook his head, politely as ever, she took his empty dish to the sink, then returned to her chair.

"Yes, but . . . I have this idea, David. You know how I love the authenticity of the original cabin. I really need more space, but I've hated the idea of tacking on anything new. No matter how hard we'd try, it would never blend in. I mean, have you ever seen a new addition to an old cabin that looks right?"

"Oh, I don't know," he began to dissent, prepared to rebut, but stopped in his tracks and smiled. "I guess not. Not really, when I think about it."

"Exactly!" Maggie cried triumphantly. "They always look to me like a bad facelift on a lovely, aged woman. Worse than nothing, you know what I mean?" She refilled his coffee cup, but he had her stop at half a cup.

"So I take it you've come up with a solution," David prompted.

"I have," she answered, unable to conceal a tinge of pride. She was sitting across from him now, eyes widening with enthusiasm as she drew him into her scheme. "I want to find another old cabin that would be a good match and buy it so we can move it here and attach it to mine," she said rapidly. "See, come look." She led him eagerly outdoors to the end of the kitchen. "Don't you think we could attach it here? Then my kitchen would open onto a family room or a study, and I could have another bedroom and bath beyond." She looked at him expectantly. "Well? What do you think, David? Would it work? Couldn't it be wonderful?"

David rubbed his jaw a minute, visualizing and assessing the idea.

"Well, I don't know . . ." he began again, shaking his head doubtfully. *Doubting Thomas.* But when he looked at her face, he laughed at her expression. "I'm just kidding, Ms. Eve." She gave him a look that made him more serious. "Okay. No, really, I think it's an intriguing idea." He regarded the building soberly now. "Yeah. Yes, I think if we could find the right match . . . it could be a real challenge. I'd probably have to move it piece by piece . . . but . . . if there were no time constraints . . ."

"There'd be no time constraints," she promised.

"It won't be cheap, though, you know." Still skeptical.

"It's an investment," she said firmly.

"You know, it wouldn't even have to be another cabin, exactly," he said, envisioning the possibilities more clearly. "It could be any suitable old structure, or even a group of structures, as long as they weren't a mish-mash cobbled together."

"Oh, I trust that you'd never do anything like that, believe me, David."

He continued his train of thought with growing enthusiasm, a flush blooming into his pale skin. "A stone pump house could be beautiful added on. I moved one a few years ago, block by block, and it turned out perfect." That kind of project was his forte, completely suited to his personality and his philosophy.

"Or an old barn or stable if it was just the right one; one with architectural character, one that was solid and sturdy and could be insulated. And not too large. Even an old carriage house, maybe, come to think of it. Yeah." He looked at her with a spreading smile. "This could be interesting, couldn't it?"

"Aha! I've got you hooked, don't I?" she laughed. And, in truth, her enthusiasm was contagious. "I was going to tell you next that I was also thinking of moving in a small barn as a garage, so I could tear down that awful annex," she said, "but, look, you beat me to it." She leaned toward him. "Could you start looking for me, then?"

"Sure. Sure I could."

"I mean, if we don't find anything suitable, or if it turns out to be astronomically expensive, or totally impractical, I'll give up on the whole idea and just pay you for whatever time you spend looking, okay? But it's worth a shot, don't you think?"

David nodded, "Absolutely." Beguiled by her zeal, appeased by her cake, convinced by her conviction, how could he resist?

"And, while you're here, come see what I planted in the cold frame you made me." He followed her around the corner, docile now, completely capitulated. When they reached the cold frame, she waved her hand at its contents as if presenting him to royalty. "Look! It's an artichoke! Isn't it gorgeous?" She knelt down to pick up some dropped leaves from beneath it, hovering like a pediatric nurse. Some hair fell into her face, which she brushed back gently with her slender fingers, not realizing she'd left a streak of reddish dirt across her temple. "I'm not going to harvest the choke, you know. I'm going to let it open and bloom. Have you ever seen an artichoke blossom?" He shook his head, focusing on her eyes so he wouldn't alert her to the dirt on her face. "They're beautiful! So exotic, they look tropical, like a protea or something. I can hardly wait. And with any luck, you'll be here to see it, David Heerman, putting in a foundation, I hope." She stood up and smiled at David, leaning with one hand against the rough cabin wall, her fine, thin hand laid on its rough skin like a caress.

Afternoons she galloped Limbo over the makeshift cross-country course Hale had helped her build. The course included a drop into a shallow creek and a coffin-type jump improvised over a narrow ditch. She had steep hills to gallop. Downed logs had been maneuvered into strategic positions, and a battered wooden feed trough set in place across the course's path. Segments of wooden fencing were formed into a zigzag. They had even managed to design some options into a few of the obstacles. All in all, she now had a decent schooling course that gave Limbo an excuse to pull her arms out as he galloped through, energized by adrenaline and his own aggressive nature, and by the same exhilaration she felt.

Other days she rode him out to climb the hill beyond her cabin, listening to the sound of his regular footfalls in the quiet, watching his shadow slipping sinuously in seamless mutability over the lumpy terrain.

She stopped in often to see Hale, but he was gone most days, on the river. Tofino was an episode they hadn't repeated since their return, though each assured the other that it wasn't for lack of wanting to. There was something, though, some indecipherable impediment here that hadn't existed in Tofino. Maybe, she thought, we were burnt by the sun. But she also knew with certainty that it would happen again. *There are no time constraints on this, either.*

Jill came for a weekend visit, stopping by the house before the three of them were to meet for dinner at the lodge. While Maggie finished dressing, she heard Jill call to her from the living room. "What's this, Mom?" Maggie stepped in from the bedroom. "Isn't this new?" Jill said, pointing to the wall. "This is really different for you."

Maggie's laugh rippled. "Oh, that. Yeah. Yes it is. Believe it or not, that's a painting from . . . well . . . wait . . . you tell me first. Whose work does it look like?"

"Well," Jill answered, walking over to the blue and green painting to look more closely, "I can see it's amateurish, but it really has a Mattisse look to it, doesn't it? I mean, with a heavy, unsure touch, for sure, but still . . ." She looked over at Maggie who stood, arms crossed over her stomach, wearing an enigmatic smile. "C'mon, Mom, where'd you get this? Did you go to a student show at UW or something? It's certainly a stretch from the rest of your decor . . . bright and loose and crude. Primitive, but wonderfully fresh."

"Yes, I love it, don't you? Really, I do." She laughed again. "It's a gift from Ave. She paints, you know."

"Ave Ingram? You don't mean the one whose son used to be sort of sweet on me? You mean, the one with the hair?" Jill held her hands rigidly above her head. "You're kidding! Who'd have ever guessed!" She looked closely at the painting again and stepped back from it. "I like it, yeah, it's just great," Jill said incredulously.

"So do I. I think she's got a lot of talent. And you should get one for your place, Jilly. She's got a whole stack of them."

It was still uncommon for them to all be together. *We'll never be a normal family again,* Maggie thought, but with a resignation she hadn't felt before. She no longer expected absolute resolution of matters. That would be somehow greedy, she believed. Jill seemed to expand when they did manage to all come together. *All children want to hang onto that leaky raft, the idea that their parents love each other,* she thought. The three of them were comfortable together now, free of prickliness, though there was no guaranteed structure or ossified pretence to familial duty to account for the newfound ease.

The lodge's dining room ebbed and flowed as one shift of diners and drinkers gave way to another. Weary, freshly-scrubbed fishermen drifted inexorably toward the bar where snatches of their conversation floated aloft into the mainstream of the room's general babble. They replayed the day's experiences, shaking their heads over the forces of fate that sided with trout who'd won battles, disappearing forever into fabled waters of time. Fish were described with a poetry never used for the women in their lives. They embellished their feats while strategically concealing their most successful ploys, especially the best fly of the day. They were fishermen, after all.

The bulk of them wandered off to their cabins in the early hours, driven by anticipation of the proverbial early start. There remained, then, families shifting in their seats to ease body parts unaccustomed to the day's activities. Children picked at food, wishing for McDonald's happy meals, tired but still reflexively hyperactive from the day's adventures. They too broke away early, leaving a flotsam of stragglers held captive in the log jamb of tables near the bar. Late nights were not a feature of Paradise Ranch.

Rough hands slapped Hale's shoulders when he entered the dining room and pulled two chairs out from a table for Maggie and Jill.

"Hey, Professor! How'd it go today?" Hale asked heartily. Depending on the speaker's luck or temperament, the fishermen spilled a few phrases about the day's triumphs or agonies, much abbreviated from their barroom version. As the stream of greetings slowed, the family shifted attention to the events of their own lives.

"I got a call from Duncan today," Hale informed Maggie and Jill.

"Oh you did?" Maggie sounded very interested.

"He told me to give you both his love."

"Oh, that Duncan! He'd like to give his love to a lot of women, I think," Jill said, but with no real malice.

"Meow, Jill," Maggie chided, and added in Duncan's defense, "Duncan is a gentleman and a perfect angel at heart. You can't convince me differently."

"He may be part angel, after all," Hale agreed. "He's sending a group of clients my way this week for a float."

"Gee, Dad, you seem to be having your best year ever on the river," Jill commented.

"Well, Duncan's been a good part of it." Hale made room on the table as their food arrived. "He wanted to talk to me also about the bison situation; you know how he's always looking out for me. He'd read in the newspaper about the dropping prices and wanted to know what the scoop was and if there was anything he could do."

"Are the prices really so low, Hale?" Maggie asked.

"The price of the premium bull at the Denver livestock show this January was half the amount paid two years ago," he answered, hungrily swallowed a couple of bites of food, then elaborated. "Two years ago the top bull sold for $100,000, and this year it topped out just below $50,000." He took a sip of water. "I think the bloom is off the rose for bison ranching. Good thing I'm really a fishing lodge. The whole boom thing was a sort of pyramid, I think, like with all the exotics, you know, llamas, yaks, ostriches, even the European breeds of cattle like the Limousins. The bottom drops out of those markets as soon as the novelty wears off or when breeders stop paying ridiculous prices amongst themselves for breeding stock." He thought he'd better slow down his eating pace to let the others catch up, so laid down his fork and turned sideways in his chair. "In the case of buffalo meat, it turns out that the public wouldn't eat in the nineties what they had advocated in the eighties. They don't want lean buffalo meat, in truth; they still love their marbled beefsteaks. Don't tell anyone I said so, but I can't blame them," he said gesturing extravagantly with his eyes at his near empty plate.

"It won't be Custer's last stand for the buffalo again, though, will it?" Jill worried, choosing a metaphor with some bizarre quirks.

"No . . . no, they're here to stay. Safe and sound, back from the brink. And, truthfully, I don't care if I make a dime on them; it's nice to know I'm contributing to their comeback. Besides, it's like you said, Jilly, the fishing business is booming."

Maggie pushed her plate away as Jill still noodled her food around. She looked at Hale and smiled while she stretched in her seat. "Oh, and I got an e-mail from Brian," he laughed.

"Oh, I love him and Vance! They're my absolute favorites, those maniacs," Jill gushed.

"Mine too, Jilly. I always knew you had good taste. Wonder where you get that?" Hale grinned and winked at her with an exaggerated Popeye squint he had used to tease her when she was a giggly kid.

Jill had noticed a series of changes in her dad ever since Maggie's arrival, from moody distraction in the first months, to an increased animation, and lately a calm that had made him ever more gentle to her, and to Maggie, for that matter.

"Brian told me Vance has been rubbing it in mercilessly since he caught that trophy fish last month. He says Vance hasn't let up one iota and he doesn't know how he'll manage to wait until he gets the chance to even the score. He attached a copy of an E-mail he got from Vance. It's the funniest thing I've ever read in my life. Vance keeps apologizing for *kicking Brian's butt.* He tells him over and over how wrong he's been to keep rubbing it in that he caught the *biggest fish.* He must've said *biggest fish* fifty times in this so-called apology. I nearly died laughing."

The dining room radiated a wonderful warmth from the fireplace and with the kitchen sounds and smells and the buzz of mellow conversation, Jill felt buoyant, buoyed by it. She felt like stirring up a little trouble. Looking at her parents slyly, she prodded, "Mm, by the way, so how was Tofino? You two haven't said one thing about it."

Maggie feigned nonchalance but felt a flush creep into her cheeks. "We haven't? I thought we told you all about it already. No? Well, it was absolutely beautiful. It was like Glaucamora, Shangri-La, Valhalla, and fantasy island all rolled into one."

"Oh, Mom. What a description!" Jill laughed.

"Okay, okay. It was a really green island and the sea was really blue and it was really pretty. How's that?" She laughed back at Jill, who pulled an exasperated expression, and waited that way, like it was cast in plaster, until Maggie finally relented. "Watch out, or your face will stay like that. Besides, curiosity killed the kitty cat, as you well know, Jill. Okay, okay, I'm just kidding; I'll get serious. Um. No, really, Jill . . . I feel sort of lost for words about it for some reason. Let's see . . . well, okay, let's put it this way—it's no wonder people flock there. The scenery really is nonpareil. And there's everything under the sun to do. There's whale watching and world-class fishing . . ." She sounded like a travel ad.

"So, did you get to fish, Dad?" Jill asked. Hale shook his head, coughing into his hand.

". . . and there's sea kayaking, and wildlife viewing, trail hiking, rock climbing. You name it. Even surfing, if you can imagine. Surfing on Vancouver Island! Oh! and there's even a hot spring in Tofino, coincidentally. I guess there's great shopping too, isn't that right Hale?"

"I think that just about covers it, Maggie," Hale agreed too readily.

"And which of these things did *you* actually get to do?" Jill inquired. Maggie blushed and looked to Hale for a bail out. Hale floundered for an answer, finally sputtering, "We had a lot of work to do, Jill, and not much time, so we didn't actually get off the grounds of Duncan's place much."

Jill regarded them both. "But I take it you had a good time?"

"We had a great time, Jilly," Hale answered, louder than

he meant to, relieved to be telling the truth. "Take my word for it." He took a long drink from his glass. "Wouldn't you agree, Maggie?"

Maggie smiled sweetly. "Absolutely . . . The time of my life, actually."

Jill studied them carefully. "You two," she muttered.

"So, Frilly Jilly," Hale said, changing the subject, reversing the aim, "how is life with Ryan the Terrible these days?"

"Oh, Dad. You're so transparent sometimes."

"Whaat?"

"What you mean is, am I involved with Ryan, isn't that what you're dying to know but afraid to ask? You shouldn't leave yourself so open, you know. I could make your life so miserable if I wanted to. You're both so concerned about Ryan and me."

"Whoa! Whoa there, Miss Paranoia. All I want to know is what he's up to these days. It has nothing to do with you," Hale said, defending his motivations self-righteously.

"Yea." Maggie came to Hale's aid, his reinforcement. "Who has Ryan sabotaged lately, other than himself, I mean? What new destruction has every parent's nightmare wreaked on the world lately? Don't keep us in suspense, Jill."

"I wish you wouldn't outflank me like this. It's unfair of you two to gang up like this," Jill pouted artificially. "Actually, if you really want to know, Ryan is back in school, is wearing his hair natural again, has had nothing new pierced, and never made it up to Sturgis."

"No way!" Hale said, genuinely impressed.

"I'm not kidding. I swear it's all the truth, cross my heart. So, you see, he's all bark, and you two have nothing to worry about . . . He's not my type anyway. He's way too straight," She said, smiling behind her napkin as she patted her mouth.

"So, what's he majoring in?" Maggie asked.

"Law," Jill answered slyly, watching their expressions. "No, really, he's in computer science. And, just watch, he'll probably end up a mega-millionaire and leave us all in his dust with egg on our faces."

"I think that was a mixed metaphor, Jill," Hale commented dryly.

"Well," Maggie said, straight faced, pushing her chair away from the table, "I for one always did like Ryan."

Jill and Maggie hiked up to the top of the hill across from her cabin the next afternoon. They tromped slowly and steadily up the steep incline, not speaking for the effort. When they reached the top, they caught their breath, looking out over Paradise Ranch and Maggie's cabin to the mountains surrounding their valley.

"It's something else, isn't it, Mom?" Jill asked.

"It is, Jill. I come up here a lot, you know, just to look out so far. I stand up here and think of a folk song I always liked from an old movie." She sang it for Jill in a clear voice, belting it out outrageously: "When I got West, the hills were steep/T'would make a tender person weep/To hear me cuss, and crack my whip/To see my oxen pull and sweat/To the road, to the road to Wyoming-O/To the road, to the road to Wyoming-O."

They laughed at her macho rendition, but as Maggie's laugh faded, she became serious. *Cats are so unpredictable.* "Aren't those great lyrics? I like those words," Maggie smiled, looking frankly into Jill's face. "Know why? Because they show how tough people had to be to make it here. They're about how scary the mountains can be. I can understand that."

"You're not scared anymore, though, are you, Mom?"

"No. I guess I'm not anymore. I hadn't even thought about it," Maggie answered dreamily. "I just think about how beautiful they are now. Not how scary." She didn't speak then, and shaded her eyes to look at the farthest view. Then she turned to Jill, excited, having just remembered, "Oh, I keep meaning to tell you, I found an arrowhead the other day when I was digging in the yard!"

"You did?" Jill felt a tender pang looking at the joy in her mother's face.

"It was so bizarre. I was on my knees, scraping some loose rock into a shovel, and I swear it jumped right into my hand. I swear, *right* into my palm. Like it was alive. I would never have spotted it otherwise, and it would've been tossed over the fence with the rubble in the next instant. I was so excited! I've never found one before, you know. Never. I'm not usually lucky like that." Her eyes still glowed over this treasure. "I'll have to show it to you, Jill. It's just too beautiful and mysterious to have come to me by chance. It's a clear agate, transparent, but with black fossilized moss suspended in it like algae floating in water or something. It's small, you know. Only about an inch long; but perfectly shaped. I'll show you when we get back down . . ."

Dear Jane: I just wanted to tell you that you and Rilke were wrong! One can *be heard from here, if one cries out.* This is not a godless place, Janey. *All my love, Mag*

Thirteen

The river was a silver thread of filament spooling out in both directions from the ellipse of the dory. It twisted and turned, a loosed string coiled in on itself, then ran lazily in long smooth arabesques, unraveling in a release of tension from the tautness of the rapid freestone flow upstream.

The day swam by smooth and lovely. Fishing had been slow through the middle of the day. Maggie had caught virtually nothing and felt justified in her waning interest. So she felt no guilt when she reeled in her line and stuck the barbed end of the fly into the cork handle at the rod's base, then laid the rod carefully in the bottom of the dory. By turning sideways, perpendicular to the boat's progress, she could stretch out on the wooden plank that was her seat, hanging her feet beyond the boat's edge and propping her head against the opposite rail, lying across the boat. She lowered the brim of her gaucho-style hat to shade her eyes from the sun, still high and bright and warm in the sky, though it was late September. It was a steel blue day she stared up into, the air swept clean and bright by the chronic high pressures of fall. Cottonwoods and willow shrubs sent subtle flag signals across the river to each other, coded messages flashed in yellow that read "summer's over."

"I give up," she sighed, laying her head against her arm.

"Coward. Slacker. Wimp."

"Go ahead, call me names. It's fine for you. You're catching fish."

It was true. But they'd been few and far between, and he'd caught nothing over twelve inches.

"If you can call it that," he muttered. "I'm going to switch to a Woolly Bugger. They're just not going for this #16 Adams."

He used clippers attached to the front of his fishing vest to cut the fly from the tippet, hooking it onto the pad on the front of his vest pocket, among a cluster of flies from which he pulled the Woolly Bugger, every bit as ugly as its name.

Maggie watched him deftly tie the new fly onto the leader, poking the leader through the eye of the hook, pinching the top of the eye with his index finger, wrapping the leader around the finger to form a loop, then twisting the leader five times (for 5x leader) around itself; creating another loop at the top of the twists, then guiding the end of the leader through the top loop and back through the bottom loop as he removed his finger, pulling the line tight, choking it into a nonslipping blood knot.

"How do you do that so quickly and easily with those big hands of yours? It takes me four times as long with my small fingers, and I have to use my teeth besides," she carped.

Hale laughed at her. "Practice, Maggie, practice," he admonished. "Actually," he said as an afterthought, "there was a time I was rather miffed at being labeled 'handy'."

"Why?" she asked, looking up at his face from under the brim of her hat. Her hair had grown long enough now that it curled out beneath the hat several inches. The breeze stirred it now, blowing it back from her face and neck.

"I like that hat on you, Maggie. Did I tell you that?" He looked at her as if seeing her anew, his gaze lingering as he delayed casting.

Maggie just smiled at him in response. "No digressing," she said. Maggie the Fool.

"Oh, yeah. Well, all right then. I was in sixth grade and my teacher was choosing a small group of the brightest kids

254

to go on a science field trip. She chose seven or eight kids, all her pets, in front of the rest of the class, while those of us that weren't picked sat there feeling like a bunch of losers, as you can imagine. Then she said, like an afterthought, you know, 'and Hale Adamson will come along too, because he's good with his hands.' I guess they were going to need something technical done. I was so insulted that I refused to go along."

"A sixth grader with conviction. What a lousy teacher!" Maggie exclaimed. She shook her head in mild outrage, trailing her own hand in the water. "They're good strong hands, Hale. Capable. You can do almost anything with your hands. I've seen you." She pulled the hat farther down over her eyes.

Hale turned toward the river and pointed his rod straight out. "Okay," he said in a determined voice. "Now I'm going for the big boys." He played the line out with his left hand as he raised the rod tip briskly to a twelve o'clock position, paused just long enough for the line to travel its full length behind him, and cast gently forward to the nine o'clock position, his arm pointing straight down the length of the rod at his target. Lifting and recasting the line several times, he pulled out more line with his left hand as he picked the fly lightly off the water, synchronizing his hands in a counterplay, allowing the weight of the line and the centrifugal force of the forward cast to play out more length. The fly landed softly and cleanly, the tippet rolling forward onto the water without a ripple.

When several casts brought no response, he lifted his rod tip to pick the fly off the water without drag, then reeled in the fly, and reached out to grab it in mid-air. He raised his hand above his head, forefinger extended, reaching forward for the leader. The swaying line caused him to move his hand left and right, chasing the elusive, nearly invisible fly, left again, then quickly right. The motion of his arm reminded her vaguely of something, but she couldn't quite place it. When he finally caught the fly, he switched to a less repulsive big streamer, adding some split shot for more weight.

"The big fish are hanging out on the bottom, Maggie. They've got the best seat at the banquet because they're big enough to take it from the others. They hang out down there in the deepest pools, having their pick of the buffet delivered right to their table by the river. It catches the insects, drowns them, and sends them their way on the current. All they have to do is point themselves upstream and open their mouths. Besides, they're safer down there where they think nothing can get them. If they come to the surface, an eagle or an osprey might swoop down on them, or a heron might dart them, or, for all they know, a bear might take a swipe at them. They didn't live to grow so large by being stupid, you know, Maggie."

"Fish wisdom, eh?" Maggie chuckled.

"Yep. God gave them just brains enough to know that you live longer if you don't take unnecessary risks." He cast against the bank as he finished his lecture. The fly sank without a ripple below the surface and within the time it took to reach the river's depths, the rod tip suddenly bowed double. "What did I tell you?" Hale yelped, quickly lifting the rod to set the hook.

There was no sign of the fish but the line wandering frantically in erratic revolutions above the dark water and the rod tip quivering and flexing left, then right, as the fish ran. Hale waited out this initial wild raving, then began to reel in the line as the actions stabilized. Soon a golden flash was seen through the green water, close, far, deep, shallow, gone now, sometimes it seemed to be in two places at once. Then a commotion broke through the surface, a flash leapt through the air like a bucking bronco, then plunged and disappeared, so that the scurrying line was again the only evidence the fish was still on. It fought and ran while Hale patiently played it, until the trout finally tired, allowing Hale to bring it in parallel to the boat, staying at a depth of twelve inches or so, where it was angled into the landing net Maggie had dipped into the water, leaning over the side of the dory.

"Wow! Look at that. Isn't it a beauty!" she admired.

"Yea. Look at that! It's a big cutthroat. I always love hooking one of the natives."

After removing the hook with a gentleness that seemed impossible from such hands, Hale lowered the trout back into the river. She could see that it was hard for him to let it go so quickly, this evidence of his passion. Over too fast, the contact could never last long enough. It needed admiring and some committing to memory since there would be no photo or varnished trophy as testimony. So Hale lingered until the big cutthroat gave a lively flip within the cradle of his hands. Then he took away his hands and it was gone.

"Adios muchacho," Hale murmured. "Go spawn and make lots more just like yourself," he called at the river.

"Hey," he remarked after the excitement abated, "that made the whole day worthwhile."

"I think it was worthwhile with or without Woolly Buggers and big cutthroats," Maggie declared. "It's a gorgeous day and my absolute favorite time of year, and here we are drifting and drifting on a beautiful river through paradise. What could be more worthwhile, I ask you?"

The wind stirred lightly, heading into the dory from

downriver. The boat was rocked by the gentle rolling of the current, heaving slightly as if breathing. Maggie turned onto her stomach and looked through the transparent beauty of the river's skin. The depths were velvet green. She gazed dreamily into them, watching the ever-changing kaleidoscope of purling turbulence. She heard the call of a mourning dove and watched a willow shrub drag its fingers through the current.

"It's lovely to live on a raft," she murmured.

Hale had laid down his rod to row gently back into the river's center. He lifted the dripping oars out of the water and folded them backward above the tail of the boat, letting the dory float wherever the current wanted it to.

"What?" he asked absently.

"Huck Finn said that," she answered. "It's lovely to live on a raft."

Hale sat quietly, gazing into the brilliant water. "That about covers it, doesn't it?"

"So simple but so ample," she agreed.

"Short but sweet," Hale added. On the same brainwave length.

They drifted past some fishermen on the bank too focused on their own river dreams to notice the dory. The boat pressed onward in the current. A group of cattle came into view and disappeared, then they passed a stack of hay rolled into the shape of giant wheat puffs. A man could be seen moving in the distance through a grassy field.

Funny how transitory life seems along the river, she thought, *though you are the one moving.*

How wonderful it was to go with the flow. Why had she ever struggled so? Why had she fought so hard against the current that swept through her life? Swimming "against the motions of the mighty tides of all the oceans," as Goethe had written. Had she really caused all that had happened, all the ripples in the lives around her, or had it all been laid out in advance? Did she really believe she could swim her way out of her dilemma through her own efforts? She had thought she could steer her own course when all along she was really in a free fall. The things that had turned the tide in her life, the things that had shattered it and might still salvage it, had proved beyond her control. Could her life have unfolded differently? Or had she "made her own luck"? Though she had always blamed herself and knew she always would, didn't it make sense that she could no more control the big picture than she had been able to foresee it? Life was water in a sieve.

Maggie tried in vain to see the bottom of the river. It struck her that her greatest flaw was having never seen clearly. She had been malcontented without reason, had regretted failed dreams that were fabrications, she'd been driven by a false sense that she was missing out and that time was running out. And she'd been half-destroyed by a terrible doubt that might be a groundless phantom. She had never really seen the big picture at all.

An inky spot spiraled almost beyond sight in the depths of the metallic blue above them.

"Look, Hale! I think there's a bald eagle way up there," she said, pointing. She followed its lazy sky-writing until she could see it no longer. She'd always thought she'd like to have seen the world from its viewpoint. Was it all clearer from that distance? But as she gazed dreamily back down into the water she found that view just as fine.

She looked at Hale who was staring across the fields to the distant mountains. He wore a look of quiet contentment. *I never saw him clearly either,* she thought. She had read the contentment that was his strength as weakness, a passiveness, a settling for too little. But Hale recognized his golden thread and had never swerved from its path, while she had rushed headlong through escapist maneuvers without compass or goal.

Here on the river, so much seemed irrelevant. She no longer sought absolution. It was no one's to give anyway. There was nothing she could do to right the wrong. Absolution resided in a place beyond the reach of her strivings. And all the length of her journey from the west coast to Paradise Ranch, all that long wild distance she had traveled, had less to do with her recovery than the short length of the journey from the murky depths of the river to its bright surface. Her life had been a penumbra, like the water that flowed just below the surface—neither completely in shadow nor completely illuminated.

"It's going to be later than I thought before we reach the truck and trailer," Hale remarked, looking at the sun's position.

"That's fine with me," Maggie said dreamily. "I'd love to be on the river in the dark. Maybe we'll see some shooting stars. Can you imagine how they'd look from out here? Think how far we could hear out here on the water in the dark and just think how deep the sky would look if we lay looking straight up. That's from *Huck Finn*, too."

"Runaways, huh?"

"Yeah. Bound for freedom."

"Think, Hale. We might see night hawks or swifts. And you know we'll hear owls calling back and forth. Oh, I hope we *don't* reach the truck until it's good and dark."

"Just so we've got plenty of mosquito repellent and gorp with us, in that case," Hale said.

"Always the pragmatist," Maggie said scornfully.

"It's a dirty job . . ." he countered.

They turned through an oxbow to the west. The lowering sun turned the river gold. Maggie sat up and stretched her arms over her head, then behind her back. She looked downriver into the sun. "Nothing gold can stay," she recited with feeling. "Don't you love that poem, Hale? It's also short and simple, but so beautiful and deep. Like an ultra-American Haiku."

A hatch of insects danced above the river, transformed by the sun into a golden shower. "Nothing gold can stay," she repeated quietly.

"Oh, I don't know, Maggie," Hale said after thinking a moment. "It's true that nothing lasts forever, but there's always some new source of gold, always something being born just out of sight around the next bend or over the horizon. That's a way that gold can stay."

Maggie was reflectively silent, then said quietly, "There are *some* things that stay." She looked up at him. "You've stayed gold. I've been fool's gold, but you've stayed gold, Hale."

She picked up her rod and removed the fly she had tied on. Fishing around in a little plastic box she retrieved from her pocket, she selected a Royal Coachman. She didn't care if it was the right fly. She just knew it had been around forever.

"How about you, Maggie? Are you going to stay?"

She laughed. "You mean, have I made up my mind whether I'm making the cabin my permanent home? That kind of staying and not the metaphoric kind?" Holding the fly in her palm, she waited for his response.

"Yes, that's exactly what I mean."

Maggie played with the fly in her palm, rolling it back and forth as if it were alive.

"I don't know, Hale. I don't know how I'd be about the

winters here, for one thing. I just don't know . . ."

There were things he could've said to her, things that would've made the prospect of winters less lonely, less cold. But something held him back. Something that had been a part of him a long time checked the words even as they were coming out.

"Besides," she said, smirking, "I wouldn't want you to think I'm trying to horn in on your life or anything."

Hale guffawed. "Oh, Maggie. Shut up," he laughed loudly. "Shut up, Maggie, and tie that fly on."

He picked up his own rod off the floor of the boat. They both began casting to opposite banks of the river.

"It wouldn't take much to make me stay," she said toward him, as she watched her fly float along at the same speed as the drifting dory. Her voice sounded contrite, or wistful, or hopeful. He couldn't tell which.

Hale picked his fly up and laid it back down several times. A fish flipped and a leaf fell and a bird called and the earth kept turning.

He stopped fishing, letting his rod tip drop, a thing he never did. He stood still a moment, looking into the glassy water, then turned to look directly at her. "I think you should stay," he said. But the wind caught the words, and the river swallowed them, and she didn't quite hear.

About the Author

Living in northeastern Colorado since the age of seven, I grew up mostly outdoors in the distinctive landscape where the plains meet the Rocky Mountains. A loose cannon in school, I studied English, Sociology, Pre-Veterinary Medicine, and finally managed to earn a Bachelor of Fine Arts degree at age fifty. I have been a landscape designer/weed puller in a nursery business owned with my husband since 1969. In the interim, we also owned and shoveled manure in a horse boarding stable for a year, managed an antiques emporium in central California for eight months, remodeled a few derelict properties, and I groomed for a professional dressage trainer for two years. I have exhibited my art in a couple of shows since 1997. Married forever, my husband and I have seen our share of islands and continents, having traveled nearly everywhere except the Far East.